Praise for
Mingled Souls

"*Mingled Souls* immerses the reader in a remarkable love story forged in letters. In 1916, Edmund Shea and Dorothy Thigpen met only briefly before returning to the sweep of their separate lives. In this exquisite read, author Sheila Harvey Tanzer weaves a rich narrative around excerpts from her parents' letters to reveal a mingling of souls made manifest through Edmund's and Dorothy's own thoughtfully penned words, and through the invisible hand of destiny. Transporting."

> — Joni B. Cole, Author, *Good Naked: Reflections on How to Write More, Write Better, and be Happier*

"The eloquent writing of Sheila Harvey Tanzer brings to life the remarkable courtship of Edmund Shea and Dorothy Thigpen. Set in the Pre- and Post-World War I years, the memoir is told through the letters exchanged between the two, and through the perceptive observation of their daughter. Interlaced with literary references and a strong expression of faith, this accomplished book is a powerful read."

> — Mimi Baird, Author, *He Wanted the Moon: The Madness and Medical Genius of Dr. Perry Baird, and His Daughter's Quest to Know Him*

"*Mingled Souls* is a captivating love story, elegantly told. Sheila Harvey Tanzer reveals the growing maturity and generous spirit within the four-year courtship of her parents, Edmund Shea and Dorothy Thigpen. She gracefully weaves together excerpts from their lively correspondence to reveal two young people who overcame huge obstacles to fashion a life together. Filled with wit and charm, this book is a delight to read."

> — Geraldine North, Author, *Butcher Bird: Tales from Down Under*

MINGLED SOULS

A Love Story in Letters
1916-1920

Sheila Harvey Tanzer

Published by Back Channel Press
Salem, NH, USA
Printed in the United States of America

ISBN: 978-1-934582-62-6
Library of Congress Control Number: 2016960873

Edited by Kirsten Giebutowski
Designed by Deborah McKew
Text set in Book Antiqua

In memory of Dom Ambrose Wolverton, OSB

1930–2016

Acknowledgments

I wish to express my gratitude to two patient typists, Sharon Stys and James B. Murphy, who transformed my handwritten pages and crossed-out words into a polished typescript. My thanks also to several archivists: Mary Hardy at the Howe Library, and Eric Esau and Barbara Krieger at the Rauner Special Collections Library at Dartmouth College. Each one supplied archival material that deepened my understanding of the history. Geraldine North, Joe Medlicott, and Dana Grossman gave me encouragement to write at crucial junctures. Joni Beth Cole, a gifted writing coach, generated ongoing enthusiasm for the evolving structure of the book. Her insight into the architecture of the narrative was especially helpful. I am grateful to Kirsten Giebutowski for her sensitive and meticulous copyediting; to Helmut Baer for his skill in creating the cover design and for his beautiful photographs of the key, the ring, and the box; and to Deborah McKew for her thoughtful design of the book and her skillful typesetting of the manuscript. My gratitude also to Dave and Dana O'Neill at Northlight Editions for their care and expertise in giving old photographs new high resolution clarity and life. Judy Hottensen, an experienced publisher and a granddaughter of Edmund and Dorothy, shared her extensive knowledge of the publishing process, and gave her guidance and visionary support. I thank my younger sister, Wendy Randall, for discovering Dorothy's letters in two unmarked boxes in her basement, and my older sister, Elizabeth Slugg, for her generosity and unwavering support of the project. My daughter, Elizabeth Harvey, inspired me to believe that these letters could be brought to life in a book. Finally, I am grateful for my experience at St. Thomas Church in Hanover, a place where I have felt welcomed as I continue my journey as a Christian pilgrim. Faith is a verb, and my mother's insight about devotion is a continuing reminder: what one loves and believes in supplies the oil and keeps the lamp burning.

Contents

Sir, more than kisses, letters mingle souls,
For thus, friends absent speak.

—John Donne, "To Sir Henry Wotton"

Introduction
Fitting the Letters Together

Won't it be interesting someday
to fit the letters together ...
— Edmund Shea to Dorothy Thigpen, letter, 1918

T hey were there the whole time, in the rambling turn-of-the-century house where my three siblings and I grew up. But we knew nothing about them then, the hundreds of letters our parents exchanged before their wedding.

Our big house in Fox Point, Wisconsin, named White Woods for a grove of birches that surrounded it, stood on a bluff overlooking Lake Michigan. When we went to live there in 1931, they brought along the precious archives, and stashed them away inside desk drawers and in a third floor attic cubby where they stayed until after my mother's death in 1963.

A year later, when I went to Milwaukee to visit my father, he mentioned the letters for the first time. And though more than fifty years have elapsed since that August afternoon, the details of the setting and the content of our conversation are still crystal clear.

From where we were sitting near the west end of the garden my mother had created over the years, the blue expanse of the lake spread out in the distance. In late summer, the perennials stood at their luxuriant best, especially pink, white, and cranberry-red phlox, giving off their elusive fragrance with a hint of clove. Flowerbeds that curved on the left and right sides of us created an open-ended figure eight, leaving the grass within their borders to form a smaller shape resembling a green hourglass. Everything about the place looked reassuringly familiar, but without my mother there, nothing felt the same.

It was living in the house alone that led my father to search for their correspondence, he said, and to his amazement he soon discovered half of the treasure had been hiding almost in plain sight.

My mother's slant-top desk stood in one corner of the beamed-ceiling living room, near the windows that looked toward the lake. And when he knelt down and opened its bottom drawers, there they were tied in bundles, still in their envelopes, every letter she had received from him from 1916 to 1920.

After taking them out and arranging them in order, he said it was bittersweet to sit by the fireplace after dinner each evening and read one letter at a time, beginning with the first one sent in July 1916, a few days after he said goodbye to Dorothy Thigpen in Montgomery, Alabama. They had been together only briefly, and after his return to Wisconsin he wondered if he would ever see her again.

More than two years passed before they did meet again, an interval when momentous changes took place in both their outer and inner worlds. In early April 1917, the United States declared war on Germany. The next day my father enlisted in the army. By early January 1918 he was in Bordeaux, France, with an American Expeditionary Forces (AEF) field artillery unit, and it was during the next eight months that he and my mother fell in love. In the course of sharing their innermost thoughts and feelings in their letters, they came to understand that the ideals they believed in and wanted to live up to were in fundamental alignment. Their courtship was unconventional, but they believed their love was real and that destiny called them to spend their lives together.

In October 1918, soon after my father returned to the United States on a three-month army assignment, he took a train to Atlanta to visit my mother who was then a junior at nearby Agnes Scott College. In the pocket of his olive drab shirt he carried an engagement ring.

My mother accepted his proposal, but their initial joy was cut short. Both sets of parents responded to the news of their engagement with shocked outrage and genuine concern, convinced that a marriage between two people who had spent practically no time together would end in failure. In addition, their distressed parents feared there would be an unbridgeable chasm between the beliefs of a Catholic husband and a Protestant wife. My mother was raised in the Episcopal Church in a staunch Protestant setting in the Deep South. My father grew up in a large Irish Catholic family in northern Wisconsin. Yet in spite of strong parental misgivings that continued to linger during the next two years, the day finally arrived in November 1920 when Edmund Shea and Dorothy Thigpen stood together in the candlelit parlor of the Thigpen house and made lifelong promises to one another.

While my father and I were sitting in the garden in the afternoon light and he was recounting details of his story, I had already begun to imagine the faces and personalities of these two daring young correspondents, and to contrast them with the well-known mature adults I had always known as my devoted parents. Then after several moments of silence my father spoke again. He said the letters would go to me after his death. "I think you'll find they have a wonderful story to tell," he added with a trace of a smile, bringing that part of our conversation to an end in the understated way that was an intrinsic part of who he was.

Five years after our conversation in the garden, my father died instantly, stricken by a heart attack in JFK airport. The news reached me at five o'clock in the morning when the phone rang in Bellosguardo, Italy. My husband Lawrence Harvey and our four children and I were living there in 1968–69 during his Fulbright fellowship.

My aunt Elisabeth was speaking on the phone, my mother's younger sister, often called the Angelic Child in the letters. Her voice was calm despite the shock she still felt over the dire news she was about to deliver.

She and my father had visited us in Bellosguardo only two weeks before. My aunt's husband had died a few months before my mother in 1963, and my aunt and my father, connected by over forty years of family history, kept in touch by annual visits to Milwaukee and Montgomery. This was their second — and last — trip together to Europe.

After they had said goodbye to us in Florence mid-May, they travelled north to the Italian Riviera and then on to Zurich where they boarded a Swissair plane to JFK.

Even now I can remember their faces and the scene, waving goodbye to them outside the Excelsior Hotel as they were leaving Florence. The last thing I said to my father was, "I'll send my letter to White Woods so it will be waiting for you when you reach home. Goodbye, goodbye."

My aunt Elisabeth went on to describe the details of the scene in the New York airport: she and my father were standing in line at JFK waiting to go through customs, their last bit of time together before they would catch different planes — his to Milwaukee and hers to Montgomery. Instead, she heard him speak his last words: "I don't feel well." Then he fell over backward. A doctor, quickly summoned by a Swissair attendant, pronounced him dead. Two days after my aunt Elisabeth's telephone call, I flew to Milwaukee, dazed before, during, and after the funeral.

My older sister Betsy and my younger sister Wendy both lived within a few miles of our family house in Fox Point and generously took on the enormous challenge of sorting through forty years of accumulated belongings and dispersing them in appropriate directions. My brother Charlie and I had returned home to New England.

Several months later Betsy sent two large boxes labeled "correspondence." Responsibilities with my husband and four adolescent children ruled out an immediate chance to go through the precious collection of letters, but when the gift of time did arrive, I sat down and read each letter slowly, listening in as the voice of a young man in his mid-twenties spoke to his correspondent in the Deep South, a young woman with dark bobbed hair. Dorothy was eighteen years old when she received Edmund's first letter in July 1916.

It was over thirty years after the arrival of my father's letters that a telephone call from my younger sister Wendy brought astonishing news. While reorganizing her basement after a move, she had come across some unlabeled boxes from White Woods. Inside she found hundreds of Dorothy Thigpen's letters, the long-lost companions to Edmund's four-year correspondence!

We agreed that the letters should be reunited, and after Wendy sent the boxes, I discovered inside one of them the fragment of a diary my mother kept in the summer of 1916. I sensed in a flash that the chance to discover who Dorothy Thigpen was the summer she met Edmund Shea would be a gift beyond reckoning. Indeed, her unguarded comments in the diary proved to be an invaluable source, especially after I discovered that Dorothy's letters to Edmund from July 1916 until late October 1917 had not survived.

The unexpected windfall of my mother's correspondence also led me to recall a comment my father made in a late 1918 letter to Dorothy: "Won't it be interesting someday to fit the letters together ..." They never had an opportunity to undertake this themselves, but the story of *Mingled Souls* endeavors to carry out a variation of what he had in mind.

Harvard Law School

Waste no more time talking about great souls
and how they should be. Become one yourself.
— Marcus Aurelius (A.D. 121-80)

I f it hadn't been for Marion Rushton, there would be no story to
tell about Edmund and Dorothy, about the improbable way they
fell in love and how they dealt with obstacles everyone assumed
were insurmountable.

It was Marion who made the introduction on a rainy evening in
July 1916. The three of them were standing together in the ballroom
of the country club in Montgomery, Alabama. But even before that
dramatic moment, there had been a prologue. It all started in Cambridge, Massachusetts, the day Edmund and Marion crossed paths
for the first time, purely by chance.

In September of 1914, both young men were students at Harvard
Law School, and each had an urgent need to find a place to live before
classes began. They happened to arrive in the office for off-campus
living on the same morning, and after learning of a new listing near
Harvard Square, they decided to walk down Kirkland Street together
to take a look.

The first floor apartment in a grey clapboard house was conve-
niently located and had spacious rooms and large windows, but

there was one hitch — the rental contract had a joint lease. Edmund and Marion looked at one another — virtual strangers, on the verge of becoming housemates. Would it work? Or not? Who could predict? The clock was ticking. They took a chance and signed the lease.

Strangers living under the same roof discovered common interests. Both had majored in history in college and had an interest in Greek and Roman philosophy. They had independently discovered the pleasure of rowing on the Charles River, and each belonged to a different law school debate team. Before long, acquaintances were congenial friends.

Marion, like many a Southern lad, carried the name of General Francis Marion, renowned in the annals of American Revolutionary War history. The general was best known for his ability to elude capture when Loyalists were wading through the swamps of eastern South Carolina in pursuit of Colonial soldiers. Even British opponents acknowledged his cleverness, and dubbed him "The Old Swamp Fox." A hundred years later Southerners still remembered their hero.

Francis Marion Rushton was born in Montgomery, Alabama, in 1893. At a young age he went off to Marion Academy and then to Harvard College. After gaining a Master's Degree in History at the University of Virginia, he decided to follow in his father's footsteps and study law.

Edmund, one of seven children in an Irish Catholic family, grew up in the far north, on the shore of Lake Superior in the little town of Ashland, Wisconsin. He graduated from the University of Wisconsin in 1913 and was a second-year law student when he met Marion.

At the beginning of their first semester as housemates, Edmund, Marion, and Tommy Sanders, another law school student, signed up for a course in English corporation law. It was then that Marion noticed "Old Shea's" gift for taking impeccable notes. Writing in black ink on 4" x 6" cards, Edmund distilled the contents of an hour-long lecture down to its essential points, doing so with clarity and concision and no crossed-out words.

As the three of them soon learned in the course, a corporation was "an enterprise undertaken by a group of persons in order to achieve a result that a single individual could not carry out alone." But while their professor focused on the original corporations that were founded in seventeenth-century England to realize financial objectives, Marion, Edmund, and Tommy decided to form their own virtual corporation devoted to philosophic inquiry.

Using a format similar to the one Socrates used with his followers, the three directors of the Cambridge Christian Corporation met periodically to share dinner and hold roundtable discussions based on open-ended questions of perennial interest: Why did Aristotle distinguish practical wisdom from theoretical wisdom? How does one define virtues such as justice and wisdom and goodness, and how do virtues help one to lead a good life?

The directors of the Cambridge Corporation left no written accounts of the conversations that took place between 1914 and 1916, though Edmund's appointment books record the dates of several meetings. But their meetings likely gave Edmund at least one opportunity to share his reflections about a Roman philosopher who had become an important inner guide for him.

It was Edmund's father William who first introduced Marcus Aurelius to his son by presenting him with a copy of *Meditations* when he graduated from high school. By the time Edmund reached law school, he had read *Meditations* and had come to appreciate why his father held Marcus Aurelius in esteem.

In *Meditations*, Aurelius describes the rigorous and disciplined mental training he underwent with Stoic teachers in order to liberate himself from judgmental and ego-centered patterns of thought. By committing himself to a disciplined way of thinking, he discovered the gifts of inner peace. By keeping his thoughts and feelings under control, he could remain serene and grounded in the way of "wisdom-Sophia," even when chaos reigned in the outside world.

In Book Six of *Meditations,* Marcus Aurelius sums up his creed:

> Keep yourself simple, good, pure, serious, and unassuming; the friend of justice and godliness; kindly, affectionate, and resolute in your devotion to duty. Strive your hardest to be always such a man as Philosophy would have you be. Reverence the gods, succor your fellow mortals. Life is short, and this earthly existence has but a single fruit to yield — holiness within and selfless action without.

Though the *Meditations* were, in fact, Marcus Aurelius's private notes to himself in a journal, what he wrote spoke directly to Edmund's heart. He, too, was an inner-directed soul, and in many ways the values espoused by Marcus Aurelius coincided with the Christian ideals Edmund had grown up with. Aurelius's insight that "holiness is within" aligned with the core truth Jesus tried to impart to his disciples that "the Kingdom of God is within." Edmund's embrace of the mysterious and abiding spiritual relationship that lives between creator and creature helped him find the sense of self he possessed in the spring of 1916, his final semester at Harvard.

Edmund was one year ahead of Marion, and as his graduation in June approached, when they both began to realize that their time together was coming to an end, Marion came up with an idea. He invited Edmund to Alabama to visit his family in Montgomery as their houseguest.

Marion's mother had died a few years before and both grandmothers had come to live with the family to provide companionship for Mr. Rushton and Marion's four younger siblings. There was so much Marion wanted to share with his friend in the Deep South, a part of the country he loved.

The very idea sounded irresistible, and after consulting calendars, they agreed on a two-week visit. That would ensure that Edmund reached Madison, Wisconsin, by mid-July, in time to take the state bar exams.

Revelations in Dorothy's Diary

Add goodness to the faith that you have
and understanding to your goodness.
—2 Peter 1:5 (Motto of Agnes Scott College)

The diary Dorothy began to keep in June of 1916 consists of thirty 4″ x 6″ lined pages still held together with a twisted hairpin. She had just returned to Montgomery after finishing her freshman year at Agnes Scott College, and by writing down her thoughts, she hoped to clarify her mixed-up feelings regarding Tom Owen, a boyfriend from high school days. Dorothy had broken up with him six months before. But Tom had just made an unexpected and upsetting reappearance in her life.

As she explained in her diary, she broke up with Tom because he did not take seriously the ideals she believed in. Though conscious that she no longer admired Tom's character, Dorothy admitted that she still felt attracted to him.

When Dorothy had entered Agnes Scott in the fall of 1915, like her freshman classmates, she had signed a promise to uphold the school's honor code. The promise implied a student's willingness to act honorably in academic matters as well as in all aspects of her life. To uphold a written promise was a serious matter, and by December her conscience told her that she ought to end her relationship with

Tom. But she felt awkward about telling him she did not admire his character. Instead, during the Christmas 1915 holidays, she returned his fraternity pin, telling him that she no longer loved him. The truth was, she did love him, but in an infatuated way.

Six months later, shortly after Dorothy's return to Montgomery in June 1916, she was taken aback by a telephone call from Tom. He was in the army, stationed at nearby Camp Sheridan. He expected to leave with his unit to join General Pershing on the Texas-Mexico border. He was calling because he wanted to come say goodbye.

When Tom arrived at the front door and Dorothy saw him looking more handsome than ever in a military uniform, she later commented in her diary that she couldn't help but feel the strong pull of his charm. During the next two weeks, Tom kept in touch by occasional telephone calls, and listening to the familiar sound of his voice led Dorothy back into the old pattern of romantic daydreams.

On Thursday, June 29, rain poured down again, as it had nearly every day that month. She felt cooped up inside the house, and felt a strong desire to reread Tom's old letters. Inviting her younger sister Elisabeth to share the thrill, they climbed up on Dorothy's bed and propped pillows against the rosewood headboard. That evening Dorothy made a diary report:

Thursday, June 29, 1916

I was a goose and indulged in doing what I haven't done in about five months, reading over his letters. I wanted to impress Elisabeth (she is at a most impressionable age — 14) and I opened the box and read several of the most desperate of them and lived over several interesting incidents for her unsophisticated benefit. It was nice while it lasted but it hurt awfully when I had finished. There were things I just <u>can't</u> forget — I know in my practical heart they were not the kind of letters he or any other young man should have been writing to me. If I had been so awfully proper, I couldn't or wouldn't have read them. But I <u>loved</u> them, loved them. They were the most passionate things I ever hope to read and some things in them were plain <u>bad</u>.

I don't know what is wrong with my perfectly nice refined nature, but I love the places where he scrawled all over the page and said, "<u>God</u>, how I love you. I can't do without you. Isn't it hell for me to think that someday some other man will hold you in his arms and kiss your lips because they are his? Oh, God — my wife — my wife — say you will, my Dorothy."

Isn't it awful? I know my taste or heart or something is depraved, but reading over those things just had me so stirred up that I was almost weeping when Elisabeth was playing "In the Gloaming" on the piano last night.

The next day, Friday, June 30, Tom telephoned Dorothy, his voice sounding urgent. He needed to see her, he said, and asked if he could come by that evening.

After they had arranged their chairs in the usual place, outdoors near the pink oleander bush, he recounted the story of what happened after their tearful parting last December, the evening Dorothy had given back his fraternity pin while they were standing outside her house on the Perry Street sidewalk. Later that evening, Dorothy described the scene:

Friday, June 30, 1916

A thousand memories rushed back, and we talked sanely and calmly for some time, and then I asked him quite abruptly if I had hurt him much last Christmas. I shall never forget the way he looked at me as he said it. It seemed to me that he had grown lots taller and more manly looking. He was not near me when he answered. He was leaning back in his chair and he answered me very quietly, "You will never know how much, Dorothy. I think I have something of manhood and strength in me to have fought it out. I never gave up and I won, but even you can never know how hard it was ..."

... I felt like I couldn't stand it, I can't explain the feeling I had. I told him to tell me everything —

He loved me up until last Christmas. And then after that miserable night and the lie, he went back to fight it out alone.

Tom said the only way he knew to forget was to try to love somebody else, and he did. Her name is Dell O'Neal and she is very fine and straight and fair and more than anything, she gave him her love. He said it saved him when he was doubting everything good in the world. And he pushed out and crowded out every feeling he had for me. And, well, can you blame him? He learned to care for her a very great deal, so deeply that in all these months he has said the same things to her that he said once to me. And she loves him. And he fooled himself into thinking he loved her. He does, but not the right way. (He did not tell me that though).

When he had finished he reached over and took both my hands. "Will you promise me that if there is anything in the whole world that I can do, you will let me know, and I will come to you?" His voice was kind of husky and I could feel his hands trembling a little. "There is just one other thing that I must tell you before I go. Somehow I think it is your right to know. It is not very much to you, maybe, but I have known it for over a year ... It is very short ... I love you."

He did not try to touch me. He only said it with his face turned away, and with something like a sob. And I knew in that moment that he meant it, and that I loved him.

Neither of us spoke for a good while. We were both very near tears. I wanted more than all the world to say to him that I loved him. I shall never want anything more. I felt somehow that I must not. His voice sounded more than ever like a sob when he caught both my hands and said, "Dorothy, I will do anything in the whole world that you say. I am waiting for your answer. I love you."

... I do not know where the strength came from unless it was from God. It would have been weakness to tell him I wanted him above all else, and that I loved him, and that it could never have been. In the moment when he waited for his answer, I thought of a million things, my splendid father as he told me goodbye for college at Christmas with tears in his eyes. He was so proud of me and my mother. It would have broken their hearts, and I thought of that girl somewhere, very strong and square and fine, and loving him and trusting him with all her heart, and I knew I could answer only one thing in the whole world which would be straight to all of us and to my self-respect. And so I said, "There isn't but one thing, Tom, that we can do. You must forget me and love her. You must, you can, and you've got to ..." I do not know how I had the strength, but I sent him away. It hurts so. Only God will ever know. It is the hardest thing that has ever come to me, but I did not fail. I am glad for the strength. I believe in the end that he and I will both be better for it all, and I did not fail. He begged me oh, so hard for my love! He did not know that it was lying at his feet. I told him that I cared more than ever before but I did not tell him I loved him. Somewhere a mockingbird was singing the wildest sweetest song.

~ ~ ~

The next morning, Saturday, July 1, Dorothy's mother Daisy, noticing the moodiness of her usually vibrant daughter, knew better than to voice her skepticism about Tom. Instead she reminded Dorothy about the dance at the Montgomery Country Club that night. Just go and spend the evening with some friends, she suggested. And then, believing that parties never failed to chase away the blues, Daisy offered to invite some of Dorothy's close friends to a dinner party the next weekend. Once she had Dorothy's approval, Daisy began drawing up a guest list and planning the menu with Patsy, the cook. On the evening of Saturday, July 1, Dorothy followed her mother's suggestion to get out of the house and go to the dance at the club. That was the evening she met Mr. Shea.

Meeting in the Ballroom

The inspiration a writer takes from a predecessor is usually
accidental, like the inspirations of our lives; those individuals
met by chance who became integral to our destinies.
We meet — we "fall in love" — we are transformed.
— Joyce Carol Oates, *The Faith of a Writer*

Marion was waiting at Union Station in Montgomery when
Edmund's train arrived one afternoon in late June. With Edmund's suitcase in the back of the Rushtons' Ford, Marion headed
out of Montgomery toward Grandview, a little town about ten miles
north where the Rushtons had a summer place.

His parents bought the house years ago, he said, and added a pool
and tennis court as enhancements for their five young children. The
place was still a godsend during the heat of Montgomery summers.

Before long the Ford turned off the road and started up a long dirt
driveway, giving Edmund his first look at the majestic antebellum
house standing at the top of the hill. Marion said it dated back to
the 1840s. Before they went inside, he gave Edmund a tour of the
grounds, identifying tall loblolly pines and the handsome live oaks
that stood around the house.

That evening Edmund sat surrounded by members of Marion's
family at the long dinner table — Mr. Rushton, his mother, his mother-in-law Mrs. Wyatt, and Marion's younger siblings, Wyatt, Rachel,
Mary, and Graham. Soon he felt at ease in their midst, warmed by

their welcome and well nourished by the Southern dinner set before him of fried chicken, black-eyed peas, okra, corn pone, and home-made strawberry ice cream. That night in the guest room upstairs he climbed into a high four-poster bed and fell into a sound sleep.

A week later, the first of July, Marion and Edmund put on suits and ties and headed south toward Montgomery to a dance at the Country Club. On the way, Marion mentioned that he wasn't certain if Tommy Sanders would show up or not. Tommy had been thinking about making the trip from Athens, Georgia, and if he did come, the three directors of the Corporation would be together again.

There was another person he hoped they would run into, Marion said. He wanted Edmund to meet Dorothy Thigpen. When Edmund asked who she was and why he wanted him to meet her, Marion explained that Dorothy's mother, a close family friend who loved to entertain, had telephoned to invite Marion to a dinner party for a group of Dorothy's friends next Saturday, the eighth of July. When Mrs. Thigpen learned that Marion had a houseguest, she invited Edmund to come as well.

The Rushton and Thigpen families had been close friends for years, Marion continued, recalling that the Thigpens often drove out to Grandview on Sunday afternoons in the summer when the children were young. Dorothy's father, Dr. Charlie Thigpen, still took care of everyone's medical needs in Montgomery when anything went wrong with eyes or ears, noses or throats. And Marion said he had a clear memory of Dorothy years ago. She was four years younger, and Marion remembered the way she looked as a little girl running down the big hill at Grandview, hand in hand with his little sister Rachel, both of them gap-toothed girls in white pinafores. Then he went away to military school and didn't lay eyes on her for years, but last Christmas he glimpsed her at a club dance, and was surprised at how grown-up she was. "She has lots of verve, and charm, and she's plenty intelligent. And if you don't watch out she'll dance your shoes off!"

Before long the Ford turned in the driveway of the brown-shingle clubhouse. It was a warm, humid evening and a fragrant honeysuckle was in bloom near the front door. After walking up the steps and passing through the living room with its rough stone fireplace and rustic chairs, they heard the band playing "Alexander's Ragtime Band," but by the time Marion and Edmund had walked down the hall to the doorway of the ballroom, the musicians were preparing to take a break. That was when Edmund saw Marion waving to someone at the other side of the room, and they began moving through the crowd.

"Well, Dorothy Thigpen," Marion said, bending to give her a kiss on the cheek. "You're the very person I've just been talking about. I want you to meet my good friend, Edmund Shea."

Before them stood a young woman wearing a white, ankle-length dress and a broad-brimmed hat. The pale pink hat tilted, covering part of her face. When Edmund leaned forward a bit and lifted the brim, he encountered a pair of dark eyes filled with merriment, telegraphing their message: "We have just finished our preliminary evaluation ..." Then he heard a voice with its hint of laughter: "Why, Mr. Shea, what a pleasure to meet such a good friend of Marion's," and she held out her hand. For a moment he felt an undeniable connectedness with a complete stranger. He never succeeded in explaining how he seemed to understand who this person was in her depths. Intuitive moments were rare in his experience, especially after three years of law school, which had trained him to base judgments on reason. But he stored away the impression in his memory, hoping never to forget it.

"I'll leave you two to get acquainted," Marion said, waving to another group of friends. Just then the musicians returned and Edmund asked Dorothy to dance. But before their conversation could progress more than a few sentences, realizing the music was too loud, Dorothy suggested they step outside on the terrace where it would be quiet. When a light rain began to fall, Edmund spotted a touring car parked nearby and suggested seeking cover under its canvas roof. After opening the passenger door for Dorothy, he walked around to the other side, got in the car, and sat down.

"At last we have a chance to talk," Edmund started off. "Marion said your family and his are old friends."

"Yes, very old friends," Dorothy replied. She went on to say that of all the Rushtons, she knew Rachel best, and in fact was delighted that Rachel would be entering Agnes Scott in September, adding that she herself was looking forward to her sophomore year. She loved being in college, taking courses that were challenging and stimulating, and she spoke of Dr. Gaines, the college president, who was a strong advocate of liberal arts education. He wanted his students to become aware of their intelligence and discover the joy that comes from using it and from living their lives with meaning and purpose. It was refreshing to listen to him, Dorothy said. "He believes we have futures to look forward to. He is actually convinced that Southern women have capabilities, which is music to our ears. Traditionally, Southern women have not been encouraged to develop their minds. Only a few from my high school class decided to go on to college."

Dorothy went on to mention a boyfriend she was in the process of breaking up with. "He was actually one of the ones who discouraged my going to Agnes Scott. But no one could talk me out of it. Still, I haven't yet said a final goodbye to him, though I know I must, for he does not share the ideals I believe in."

When Edmund expressed an interest in hearing more about her ideals, she told him the motto of her elementary school she had memorized as a child: *non quantum sed quam bene* ("not how much but how well"), adding that she still believed in doing things well. Then she described how the coat of arms belonging to her mother's Bissell family ("Honor lies in right living"), coincided with the honor code that every Agnes Scott student had to sign and uphold, not just in the classroom, with papers and exams, but in every aspect of life.

Edmund said he believed that living up to ideals was crucial to finding happiness. He told her that he and Marion and another law school friend had started a round table discussion club, the Corporation they called it, in order to talk about philosophic ideas that concern meaning and purpose, and raise questions about how to live one's life. He said he found it helpful to share opinions and ideas with friends, and he wondered if she might be interested in becoming a member. We would certainly benefit from having a feminine perspective, he added.

Dorothy was taken aback by Edmund's interest and courtesy. Southern beaus often spent the evening boasting about their exploits — how many birds they bagged on the last hunting trip, or how well they did last week on the golf course. In general, she said, the young men she dated were less interested in discussing ideas, especially with a young woman, because they liked to feel more intelligent than their partner, and in control of the conversation.

Edmund said the best advice he could offer was that she hold fast to her ideals. Then he took the knife and pocket watch off the gold chain on his vest and handed the chain with its gold Phi Beta Kappa key to Dorothy. The key served as the Great Seal, a symbol of the Corporation, and he wanted to place it in her safekeeping during the next week while he was in Montgomery. He went on to say that the three Greek initials engraved on one side of the key stood for the words "love of wisdom is the path of life" or "the way of wisdom." Wisdom, the all-important virtue for the Greeks, he added, helps each of us to discern what the best choice is and guides us on the path we are meant to follow.

Dorothy fastened the key and chain around her neck, and thanked Edmund. Realizing how late it was, they got out of the touring car and made their way back to the ballroom. By then the musicians were packing up their instruments, and guests were saying their last goodbyes as they left the clubhouse.

Edmund and Dorothy Say Goodbye

Ships that pass in the night …
— Henry Wadsworth Longfellow, "The Theologian's Tale"

I t was humid in Grandview the Sunday afternoon in July when Edmund borrowed the Rushtons' car and drove to Montgomery to say goodbye to Dorothy. He had telephoned ahead, and after greeting him at the front door, she carried a silver tray with a pitcher of iced tea and glasses to the porch table. As they settled into wicker chairs, Edmund opened the conversation by mentioning Dorothy's dinner party the evening before and the dance that followed afterward at the club, commenting on how swiftly the whole time had passed.

Dorothy was curious about Edmund's long trip back to Wisconsin, wondering how long it would actually take to reach such a faraway place. The recent heavy rains had washed out sections of railroad tracks in southern Alabama, forcing him to change his itinerary, he said. Instead of visiting a friend in Gainesville, Florida, he would head northeast toward Georgia. After visiting Tommy Sanders in Athens, he would go on to Madison, Wisconsin, where the State Bar exams were scheduled to begin in a week's time.

Dorothy took Edmund's Phi Beta Kappa key and watch chain out of her skirt pocket and, reaching across the wicker table, handed them to him as promised. She smiled and thanked him again for entrusting her with the golden key during the past week.

After several more minutes of conversation, sensing that the time for departure was near, Edmund brought up the question that had been on his mind. He asked Dorothy if she would grant him permission to write to her. She did, and then they both stood up and shook hands in a brief goodbye. Just before turning to go, Edmund smiled as he delivered his last words, "You'll see me again," then walked down the steps to the driveway. A few minutes later the Rushtons' Ford turned onto South Perry Street and disappeared in the distance.

What Edmund surely felt at the moment of their parting was acute regret. He already loved Dorothy, and knew how unlikely it was that they would ever meet again. He left no written impression of their last visit, only noting in his pocket-sized appointment book that on Sunday, July 9, "he stopped at the Thigpens' to say goodbye to Dorothy." But later letters to her reveal his capacity to remember minute details about each of the four times they spent together during his Montgomery visit.

~ ~ ~

In her diary, Dorothy describes her impressions of Mr. Shea as if confiding in a trusted friend. Her first entry refers to the night they met at the Country Club, when she had been reeling over the shocking news that Tom had a new girlfriend.

> … I saw a great deal of Mr. Shea that night [July 1, 1916] and when I left, I was wearing his Phi Beta Kappa key around my neck on his watch chain.

Though she doesn't say so in her diary, Edmund's invitation to Dorothy to join the Corporation must have taken her by surprise. She had finished only one year of college whereas the other Corporation members were older, all college graduates and law school friends.

Over the next few days, she made several undated entries:

I had a date with some members of the Corporation for yesterday afternoon, and when yesterday came, no one appeared but Mr. Shea who seemed a little sheepish at my questions about Marion and Wyatt. I was glad they didn't come. He was most nice alone.

He is very bright and intellectual and learned, and to say the least, he was very much interested in me. Of course I don't mean anything more than a desire for my company, perhaps slightly amused at my views on things, and maybe my eyes which he likes.

He is not the kind of man who cares a snap for girls, and I was a little flattered at his preferring my society to anybody he had met, for he did. I do not mean of course in a sentimental way. He liked me and was interested and so was I.

~ ~ ~

He left for Wisconsin [Monday, July 10], which is all rather sad.

~ ~ ~

"Ships that pass in the night and speak each other in passing ..."

We did "speak each other in passing," for we discussed pretty nearly everything from Plato's *Phaedo* to the extreme brownness of my eyes. I am sorry he has gone and that I shall never see him again.

I have written all this about Mr. Shea because it precedes a very peculiar state of mind, which I seem to have possessed during the last twenty-four hours.

I had a date with Tom last night and towards evening I began to have the most peculiar feeling that I did not want to see him and that I did not care a snap. It was the funniest thing. So unusual. I do not blame poor innocent Mr. Shea in the least for the feeling I entertained which Tom never effects in me. By night I had come to a most strange conclusion for me. I discovered that the only time I cared for Tom was when he was "making sweet talk." He bores me when he is not. The love I have for him is fed on romance and physical attraction for each other, not on intellectuality. It rather scares me. I never realized it before. I know there must be some intellectual component to it somewhere. We couldn't go on admiring each other's looks and sit up in moonlit places ... [diary entry breaks off]

Dorothy's comments reveal that Edmund's intelligence impressed her, and suggest that their conversation about Plato's *Phaedo* left her feeling intellectually uplifted. But the twinge of regret she felt over their goodbye seems to have been fleeting. The next day her diary entry recounted the newest variation of torment she felt over her relationship with Tom.

~ ~ ~

When Dorothy returned to college in early September, she found that Lucy Durr, her congenial roommate, was already busy unpacking her belongings. Their Spartan quarters on the second floor of Inman Hall were furnished with two iron cots, two dressers, and a pair of kneehole desks. Dorothy's desk lamp had a pink lampshade with flowers, and that was where she sat each evening, completing assignments for courses such as Physics, the Tragedies of Sophocles, Modern European History, and French. With frequent quizzes, papers to write, and final exams to think about, she became a full-time motivated student again, engaged in a journey of learning.

The chief designer of the rigorous curriculum at Agnes Scott was Dr. Frank Gaines, the founding president. Born in 1852, a native of Tennessee and a Presbyterian clergyman, Dr. Gaines had always regretted the scarcity of colleges for women in the Deep South. When opportunity knocked in the early years of the twentieth century, he responded eagerly and played a key role in helping to found Agnes Scott.

While he believed in enriching the lives of his students by opening their minds to the joy of learning, he cared even more deeply about helping each one to find her particular calling, the vocation she would dedicate her life to. Dr. Gaines often encouraged his young women to look forward, not backward. When they did discover their true calling, he assured them, they would find inner joy and peace.

And though Dorothy felt moments of conflict over her memories of Tom, she found reassurance in the wise guidance of Dr. Gaines. Most of the time she felt convinced she was in the place where she was meant to be.

In the autumn months of 1916, letters from Edmund turned up every week or so in Dorothy's Inman Hall mail cubby. Marion's friend was turning out to be a dependable correspondent, she thought, and what Mr. Shea wrote about was straightforward and never trite. He was different from any young man she had met, and she found it a novelty to hear about the remote town in northern Wisconsin where he lived. She also assumed they would never meet again. The distance that stood between them was too great for that to ever happen.

5

Edmund's Letters Begin
July 1916

Please pray for me, but I would rather have you write to me.
— Edmund Shea, letter, July 15, 1916

T he day after his goodbye to Dorothy, Edmund left Montgomery. As the train pulled out of Union Station and travelled northeast toward Georgia, he could see signs of widespread damage from the heavy rains of the last month. The Alabama River had overflowed its banks, and red clay fields lay submerged under water as far as the eye could see.

He spent some time jotting down notes in his pocket-sized appointment book, thinking back to his visit with the Rushton family. When he closed his eyes, it took no effort to call up his first glimpse of Dorothy in the ballroom. He was standing next to Marion when he heard her voice: "Why, Mr. Shea, what a pleasure to meet such a good friend of Marion's ..." It was no more than a simple declarative sentence, yet he never tired of listening to it again.

When Edmund awakened from a doze, he noticed a copy of the *Saturday Evening Post* lying on the seat next to his. Glancing through it, he was quickly drawn into the opening scene of a story by Earl Derr Biggers entitled "The Agony Column."

In it, a young American playwright, Geoffrey West, is in London to see a production of one of his plays. It's the summer of 1914, and as he walks into the breakfast room of the Carlton Hotel, a waiter seats him, recommending a plate of fresh strawberries. Geoffrey accepts, and then opens the morning edition of the *Daily Mail*, turning to his favorite page, the *Agony Column*, a section devoted to messages written by the lovelorn or love-struck, who are desperate to forge a connection with a stranger:

> Great Central: Gentleman who saw lady in bonnet 9 Monday morning in Great Central Hotel lift would greatly value opportunity of obtaining introduction.

Suddenly, Geoffrey's attention is riveted on a vision of feminine loveliness. She and a white-haired man have just walked into the breakfast room and sit down at the table next to his. The young woman opens her own copy of the *Daily Mail*, and he watches a smile come across her face while she reads the *Agony Column* with relish.

Protocol in 1914 England prevents Geoffrey from introducing himself, but after he returns to his nearby flat, he has an idea: First, he writes a message to the *Agony Column*, addressed to the young woman with violet eyes. Then, he delivers it to the *Daily Mail* office.

> Will the young woman in the Carlton Hotel who preferred grapefruit to strawberries permit the young man who had two plates of the latter to say he will not rest until he discovers some mutual friend, that they may meet and laugh over this column together?

Several days pass and no reply appears in the *Daily Mail*. His hope sinks. Then the next morning he opens the paper:

> Strawberry Man: only the Grapefruit Lady's kind heart and her great fondness for mystery and romance move her to answer. The Strawberry-mad one may write one letter a day for seven days — to prove that he is an interesting person, worth knowing. Then — we shall see. Address: M.A.L., care Sadie Haight, Carlton Hotel.

Edmund finished reading the first installment of the *Post* story, perhaps with a smile, wishing he possessed some of Geoffrey West's literary prowess. All he could do was hope that what he said in his letters to Dorothy would motivate her enough to send a reply.

After visiting Tommy in Georgia, he continued travelling north, arriving in Chicago "after a long and tedious ride." Then he took the overnight train to Madison and settled into familiar quarters in the Alpha Delta house. There he would spend the next two days preparing for the Wisconsin State Bar exams, conscious that all he had invested in effort and learning for the last three years in law school would be put to the test. That evening he took a canoe ride on Lake Mendota, and then just before retiring, he sat down and began his first written conversation with Dorothy Thigpen.

Alpha Delta Phi House
Madison, Wisconsin
July 15, 1916

Dear Dorothy:

There I up and called your name just as though it didn't take all of my nerve to do it. There are many things possible to be done in a Corporation that the world little dreams of. If it weren't for the Corporation and probably Lord Rushton I fear you would have forgotten me before now, but with those important aids ever present I rashly hope to remain yet a little while among your memories. But here I wander along talking about myself when my reason for writing to you is to ask what the fortune-teller told you. Was her name Leota? And do you remember that you said you would tell me about the results of your visit? I believe you hardly heard what I said when I asked if I might write to you. Please don't flatten out my rising hopes. That whole Montgomery visit passed like a flash and I saw so little of you — all too little.

Still I wonder. It is only a week ago tonight that we all had dinner with you, and our gracious hostess made her partner extremely miserable for what seemed a long, long time, and yet altogether very happy. That was a memorable impeachment — my corporate privileges and immunities hanging by the merest thread.[1] How it stormed! And the dance was such a brief affair — especially the snatches that we had together. I am so sorry it all ended so soon. And yet it may be only fairly begun, for as we have before observed great things may be accomplished in a Corporation.

The bar exams begin next Tuesday. I got here this morning and began to work on the statutes. It is very dull to come back to such drudgery, but one gets used to it. And one has memories. Please pray for me, but I would rather have you write to me.

Yours,
Edmund Burke Shea

~ ~ ~

Dorothy continued to occupy Edmund's thoughts during the next several days. Even in the midst of grueling bar exams, he found time to compose a two-part letter.

---

[1] Edmund is referring to a scene at Dorothy's dinner party the week before. Unbeknownst to her mother, who had set the table, Dorothy switched the place cards so that Edmund would sit next to her. According to her diary entries, she still felt vulnerable and humiliated over the recent news that Tom had a new girlfriend. Dorothy had not yet broken up with him. At one point during the dinner party she misinterpreted Edmund's hearty laughter, fearing it was directed at her. Invoking her newly acquired authority as a director of the Corporation, she insisted that he be put out of the Corporation. Fortunately Marion Rushton and other guests rushed to Edmund's defense, pleading his innocence, until Dorothy understood that he had actually been laughing *with* her, not at her.

Madison, Wisconsin
July 20, 1916

Dear Miss Dorothy:

Last week coming north on the train I read a story in the *Post* about a man who saw a girl in a distant country who impressed him very deeply. He finally got word from her that he might write seven letters to her, one each morning for a week, and from these letters she would decide whether she wanted to meet him or not. I know exactly how he felt, and would that I had some of his cleverness in writing! He could have convinced even you, I believe. The story wasn't finished and has been on trial all of this week. I must get the new *Post* and find out his fate and perhaps draw encouragement from his success. Sometimes I think my judge is inclined to liberality but then I remember that Saturday night trial in which the Chancellor seemed to have forgotten the principles of equitable relief and narrowly avoided convicting an innocent person. Don't you know that the equity courts were designed to mitigate the rigors of the common law rules and give a remedy where the law had none? That is why I wanted an equity hearing and why you were appointed Chancellor. Members of the Corporation ought to know such simple matters as that. I can see that you need some further instruction.

You would like this place. Did I tell you about it before? The university campus is on the shore of the lake — Mendota — and beyond the campus is a long row of fraternity houses that monopolize the best shore frontage in town.

July 21 ... A long series of interruptions has made this letter older by a day and a half than when it was started. It seems a bit incoherent — that part up there about the courts and perhaps you will understand it better when you know that it was written at noon between two agonizing sessions with the bar examiners. If they stuck to simple matters like the rule in Shelley's case and corporation law, all would have been comparatively safe and pleasant, but they seemed to have a consuming desire to know about Wisconsin statutes. But I keep roaming away on these legalistic tangents and I fear they don't interest you. Probably I have already said too much so I will tell you about Madison and the people whom one meets here some other time—perhaps. It might be said though, in passing, that this lake with the moon shimmering across it is enough to make a poet out of a hangman. You would love it.

Good night.
Yours,
Edmund

6

Edmund Returns Home
Summer 1916

Welcome home, son.
— William Francis Shea

After handing in his blue book for the last State Bar exam, Edmund walked to the Madison station and boarded the train for Ashland. He felt exhausted and was grateful for the chance to relax in a comfortable parlor car seat.

From the window, he watched the university buildings disappear in the distance. How imperturbable and stationary they were, he thought. And how different he was from them, for his own human journey involved moving from place to place, as well as adapting to change. Change was what he felt most keenly and sadness, too, suddenly realizing that never again would he be a student, an identity he had relished for almost twenty years. But even stronger than the pull of nostalgic thoughts was a fatigue that soon led him to drift off to sleep.

An hour later when he opened his eyes, the train was moving north, rolling along through central Wisconsin where green pastureland stretched to the horizon, and Jersey cows grazed near an occasional farmhouse. How different the landscape looked from the flat red-earth cotton fields in Alabama he had seen two weeks ago. But it was not the outdoor scenery that interested him; what he longed to do was remember the sound of Dorothy's voice, and the way she looked, and what they had talked about during the time they spent together.

His recent visit in Madison also stirred memories from his undergraduate years. The first one swept over him the morning he walked into the State Capital to take the first bar exam.

In the spring of his junior year, four years before in 1912, a letter from William Shea, Edmund's father, brought news that he was coming to Madison to try a case before the Wisconsin Supreme Court. On the appointed day, Edmund walked from the campus to the Capitol and was sitting in his perch in the gallery when the lawyers made their entrance into the courtroom. The justices were already there, sitting together on the bench, looking impressive in their black robes. Edmund had never seen his father try a case, and according to his 1912 journal, watching him pace back and forth across the room, cross-examining the witness in a thoroughly dramatic fashion, was a thrilling experience. He glowingly reported that his father had outshone his opponent "as the sun the moon."

Another indelible memory, from his senior year, involved a letter Edmund had written to his father in May 1913, just a few weeks before graduating. The past year had been the happiest in his life, he said, and he regretted leaving the university and saying goodbye to his friends. After signing his name, Edmund added a brief postscript: "P.S. I see by the Madison newspaper that I was elected to Phi Beta Kappa."

One sentence was all he needed. Election to the society was something they both acknowledged as a coveted academic honor, but boasting about it or any other worthy achievement would violate the ideal of modesty they believed in upholding.

~ ~ ~

When the train finally pulled to a stop in the Ashland station, Edmund caught sight of William's white hair from the window. Standing next to him was Isabel, now almost as tall as her father. Isabel was sixteen, Edmund's youngest sister.

Moments later father and son shook hands, and smiled in shared understanding while William put his other hand on Edmund's shoulder, delivering his customary greeting: "Welcome home, son," words that never failed to touch deep.

It was suppertime when they reached home and opened the front door of the house and Edmund smelled homemade bread. Edmund's mother Nora and his other younger sister Edith rushed from the kitchen to welcome him and within moments, the family gathered around the table to share a dinner of pot roast with all the trimmings.

After spending some time with the family after dinner, Edmund pleaded fatigue and went upstairs, looking forward to the luxury of a full night's sleep. His bedroom on the third floor at the end of the hall looked reassuringly the same — a single bed covered with his mother's homemade quilt, a chest of drawers, a floor lamp, and a kneehole desk, its top covered with an ancient green blotter. It was the north-facing window he liked best, for it looked toward Chequamegon Bay and provided him with a direct view of Lake Superior.

He liked it best when the water was cobalt blue, but he also loved watching its unpredictable variations. When it was windy, whitecaps raced to the beach all day. Other times the water was greyish-blue, its surface showing only faint ripples.

As he unpacked, he took out a navy three-piece suit and put it on a hanger. He had found it on sale in Boston, just in time to wear to his law school graduation. The suit had travelled to Montgomery too, and Edmund felt kindly toward it, recalling that he had worn it the Saturday evening he met Dorothy Thigpen.

But wasn't it absurd to go on assuming that he would see her again? Montgomery was over a thousand miles away, and he had

33

no viable prospect of returning. While he continued to put away his belongings, he admitted how unlikely it was that they would meet again. Yet hadn't he already expressed the exact opposite of that gloomy point of view? He thought of what he had said to Dorothy just before he turned to leave: "You'll see me again." What made him so bold? He didn't know. But he had no intention of giving up hope.

~ ~ ~

With five sisters in the family, Edmund grew up with ample opportunities to spend time with girls and young women. His sisters' friends were in and out of the house continuously it seemed, coming to visit, listen to the Victrola, play the piano, or do homework with Catherine or Edith. Often one or two friends stayed for dinner or spent the night. As a result of countless interactions, Edmund felt at ease in feminine company.

Yet in his growing-up years, only once did he develop a crush on a girl. Ruth Ellis was a dark-haired, serious-minded friend and classmate of his older sister Catherine. Ruth's family lived in the same neighborhood, and she caught Edmund's fancy when he was fourteen. He remembered how tenderly he felt toward her when he was in high school, and what anguish he suffered, wondering if she would ever glance in his direction. But Ruth never did. Edmund gradually came to realize that in Ruth's imagination, he would always be branded "Catherine's little brother." Even so, it was years before he stopped daydreaming about her.

~ ~ ~

After Edmund put on his pajamas, he stood in front of the mirror above his dresser. He did look like a serious young man, he thought. In high school and college his friends often told him he seemed older than his age, and they tended to look up to him, for he was never wild or foolish. Now, at twenty-four, he still wore his hair parted on the same side. He liked his grey-blue eyes, for he felt their direct gaze communicated the kind of person he aspired to be, a person who had nothing to hide. But suddenly for the first time in his life, he realized there was actually something he needed to conceal.

He had no intention of mentioning to another soul—and that included his closest confidant, his father—anything about his feelings concerning Dorothy Thigpen. He had already given his heart away. Without any assurance that she would ever answer his letters, he preferred to bear the agonizing uncertainty in silence.

Then he studied his face in the mirror again, wondering if he looked mature enough for clients to place their confidence in him. The truth was he didn't know. But he would soon find out. Tomorrow would mark the first day of his legal career as an apprentice in his father's office, and he would do his best.

Meanwhile, Back in the Deep South...

We are betrayed by what is false within.
—George Meredith, *Modern Love: XLIII*

Several days after Dorothy and Edmund said goodbye on the porch of the pillared house, Tom called asking to come by for the evening. He brought with him a letter from his girlfriend Dell and after Dorothy read it, Dell was suddenly no longer an abstract name: she became a real young woman who had fallen in love with Tom. Dorothy felt mortified and told Tom it was wrong for her to continue seeing him. Yes, she was right, he agreed. But then, at the end of their visit, as Dorothy described the scene in her diary, Tom caught her by the hands. He wanted her to remember just one little thing: "It's not much, but you have a right to know. I love you," he whispered. Then he left.

Dorothy's summer 1916 diary ended abruptly a few pages later. Once again she plunged her "gentle reader" into suspense, as she did in her 1913 memory book. And she herself seemed confused and stirred up, for as she admitted in her diary, she still felt attracted to Tom in spite of her reservations about his lack of integrity.

The next day Dorothy had lunch with some Montgomery friends, and when she returned home, a letter was waiting on the hall table near the front stairway. She picked it up and headed up to her room, slipped off her shoes, and arranged the pillows against the headboard of her rosewood bed. The front of the envelope showed her name in unfamiliar handwriting. Then she noticed the postmark: Madison, Wisconsin. It was a letter from Edmund.

When Dorothy read the sentence that referred to her dinner party, she felt another twinge over her mistaken assumption that Edmund's laughter had been directed at her, and she felt relieved all over again that he had forgiven her so easily. Southern women were expected to keep their poise regardless of the circumstances, and she had clearly failed to control her feelings for several minutes. As far as Edmund's question about Leota the fortune-teller, the answer was complicated, for giving it would mean disclosing Leota's prediction.

Memories of the visit with Leota were still fresh because she and Susie Lovejoy had seen her just a few days ago. Leota lived in a gypsy wagon outside of town. While a visitor waited expectantly in the dim interior of her wagon, she examined the pattern of tea leaves in the bottom of the cup before making her predictions. Looking with dark eyes directly across the table at Dorothy, Leota had delivered her declaration: Dorothy was going to fall in love and marry some-one her parents would disapprove of. Dorothy assumed Leota was referring to Tom and felt thoroughly let down. "Well, of course," she thought to herself, "my father and mother have always disapproved of him. I already *know* that!"

Conscious again of the letter she was still holding in her hand, Dorothy began to wonder what good could come from starting up a correspondence with someone she had met so briefly, especially since she never expected to see Edmund again. She'd never engaged in a conversation with a Yankee before, and she had to admit she enjoyed their long talk, especially the open-ended questions Edmund had raised about Plato and Aristotle.

But Dorothy was also aware that her father's opinions concerning Yankees were negative. She'd grown up listening to him expound at the dinner table, using phrases she knew by heart: "Yankees are a race apart—uncouth and untrustworthy, every one of them!" And her mother, though less verbally overt, was fiercely Southern in her views, having grown up in South Carolina. In Charleston as in Montgomery, Yankees were automatically placed outside the accepted circle. But why, Dorothy wondered, would Marion Rushton develop a close friendship with a Yankee when he was the most dyed-in-the-wool Southerner she had ever known, outside of her father? It didn't make sense.

It was from her mother that Dorothy had learned to follow the elaborate code of Southern manners, including the correct way to word an acceptance to a wedding invitation or some other social event or how to regret one, if necessary. She wondered if she should send Edmund one of those, nicely worded. It could almost compose itself:

Dear Mr. Shea,

Thank you very much for your kind letter of July 15. I have been giving some thought to the fact that when I return to Agnes Scott in a few weeks, the press of college duties will fill up my time and attention to an extreme degree. I fear that the demands connected with my academic courses will render it impossible for me to enter into an ongoing correspondence with you.

With every good wish and with kind regards,

Sincerely,
Dorothy B. Thigpen

It sounded gracious enough, she thought. But it did not express what she wanted to say. She was old enough to make up her own mind about such matters. She put Edmund's letter back in its envelope, planning to answer it tomorrow. Right then she needed to take a nap. There was a dance at the club that evening and she wanted to be rested.

8

Dorothy's Early Years

Non quantum sed quam bene.
—School motto, Montgomery School for Girls

What were the ideals Dorothy referred to in her 1916 diary, the ones that meant so much to her? And when did she first become aware of boys and long to have them take notice of her? Fortunately, Dorothy's mother's early records and the memory books Dorothy kept from age twelve to fifteen contain a treasure trove of details that shine light on these questions. They also allow the reader to catch glimpses of a child who showed a strong desire to do her best at an early age, a young person who never seemed to run out of enthusiasm while she was growing up in the Deep South in the beginning years of the twentieth century.

Dorothy was born in Montgomery, Alabama, on August 23, 1897, thirty-two years after the Civil War ended. By the turn of the century the South had barely begun to recover from the collapse of its economy. The version of recent American history Dorothy absorbed from her parents and teachers was still intensely loyal to antebellum values and traditions. The town of Montgomery acquired the name Cradle of the Confederacy in 1861 after Jefferson Davis stood in front of the Alabama state Capitol and took the oath of office to become President of the Confederacy. In Dorothy's growing-up years, Montgomery residents took fierce pride in their town's claim to Southern fame.

When Dorothy was two years old, she and her parents and her black nurse moved to their newly completed house on South Perry Street, a neighborhood opening up on the southern outskirts of town.

The architect Frank Lockwood designed the house with tall Ionic columns that evoked the grandeur of ancient Greece as well as a nostalgia for the vanished world of the old South. Spacious high-ceilinged rooms, crystal chandeliers, and parquet floors contributed to the formal elegance of the house Dorothy lived in until she went away to college at seventeen.

Dorothy's father, Dr. Charles A. Thigpen, was a hard-working and dedicated physician. Born in Greenville, Alabama, he grew up in a devout Southern Baptist family. Dr. Charlie had a gruff and rather stern outer bearing, but he also had a tenderhearted side, and Dorothy grew up blessed with the gift of inner confidence, certain that her father's love for her was abiding and unconditional. She was also aware of his strongly held opinion concerning Yankees and knew better than to disobey him.

Unlike Dr. Charlie, who despised small talk and parties, Dorothy's mother was a born social creature. When Daisy Lee Bissell Thigpen arrived on the scene in Montgomery as a slim-waisted bride in 1896, she brought with her from Charleston an air of elegance along with a love of stylish floor-length dresses and a collection of hats flourished with feathers and veils.

In addition to passing on to Dorothy her dark-eyed beauty, Daisy also taught her daughter how to be gracious to others and feel at ease in a room filled with guests. But Daisy was more than an accomplished hostess who loved to plan dinner parties and garden teas. She was a devoted wife and mother, someone who lived her life "as if a kingdom cared." A devout Episcopalian, it was she who took the initiative in Dorothy's spiritual upbringing. When Dorothy was old enough, mother and daughter walked together to the near-by Episcopal Church of the Ascension each Sunday to attend the weekly Eucharist. Choral music, the solemnity of the Communion service, and listening to cadenced passages read aloud from the King James Bible all helped to create a setting that stood apart from the everyday world, a place where Dorothy first learned to encounter the presence of the Holy.

In 1902, Dorothy's younger sister Elisabeth was born. Two years later in 1904, Charles junior came into the world. While Charles was a toddler, he suffered a bout of infantile paralysis, as polio was called then. The illness that affected the muscles in one leg left him permanently lame.

What caused polio and how the disease was spread were questions that doctors were unable to answer in the early 1900s. Parents of afflicted children and attending physicians felt powerless to prevent the spread of the disease or to restore damaged muscles. Though its contagious nature was recognized and feared, no one understood how the virus was transmitted.

In addition to bearing the distress of not knowing what caused the disease, families also lived under a taboo that prevailed in the early part of the twentieth century, an ironclad prohibition that for-bade verbal allusions not only to polio but also to afflictions such as tuberculosis, cancer, Parkinson's, and alcoholism.

There is no mention of Charles's crippled leg in the memory books Dorothy kept from 1911 to 1913. Surely the illness of her young brother and its unfortunate crippling effect caused deep and ongo-ing sorrow for her and for every member of the Thigpen family. Yet the cultural imperative, a leftover from the Victorian era, prevailed. One did not speak about such subjects or even write about them in diaries. Instead, one bore the pain in silence.

~ ~ ~

In September 1904, Dorothy entered first grade at the Montgomery School for Girls. Encouraged by Doctor Charlie to look up new words in his Webster's unabridged dictionary, she discovered the joy of learning and brought home nearly perfect report cards in subjects such as spelling, rhetoric, geography, writing, and arithmetic.

The twenty-five surviving school reports in Daisy's collection, from 1904 to 1908, show that Dorothy's average stayed between 97 and 99. Twice, according to Daisy's diary, she won gold medals for being the top student in her class.

Among the report cards Dorothy's mother saved is one from the winter of 1907. To the left, in the non-academic section near the top of the list is a drawing of a hand with one finger pointing to "Deportment." Above the hand, the word "Pity" is written, followed by an exclamation point. One wonders what infraction precipitated Dorothy's minor fall from grace.

It was also in 1907 that Dorothy sat for a formal photograph. Ten years old that August, she studies the viewer with polite regard, her black hair parted in the middle, standing out against the white expanse of a high-necked Victorian dress with panels of lace set in horizontal rows across the front.

Her expression, solemn as well as lively, suggests that she may have already discovered the enjoyment that arises from spending time in one's own inner world. While she was obliged to sit immobilized in a chair longer than she must have wanted to, any number of thoughts and ideas undoubtedly passed through her mind, including making her own plans for how to spend the rest of the afternoon after she had taken off the confining dress and changed into comfortable overalls and Mary Janes.

~ ~ ~

The succinct motto of Dorothy's elementary school appears at the top of her 1907 report card: *Non quantum sed quam bene.* The Latin translates into "not how much but how well," and the wisdom saying leads one to speculate that it may have played a part in inspiring Dorothy to do a job well, to do her best.

The *quam bene* maxim encourages a focus on the adverbial quality rather than on outer measurable quantity. Someone acting from a *quam bene* perspective presumably does so without an ulterior motive in mind — without seeking to gain profit or merit, for instance. Acting from a *quam bene* perspective becomes its intrinsic reward, the way virtue is its own reward. Clearly Mr. Starke, the school's founder, chose the motto to encourage students to live according to a *quam bene* perspective.

The school motto may have reinforced an inborn gift. Dorothy's academic record from grade school through college reveals both her ability and her achievements — and time and time again she comments in her memory book: "I'm going to do my very best."

9

Dorothy's Memory Book, Volumes 1 & 2
1911–13

I've got the mumps … I'm nearly dead.

—Dorothy Thigpen, memory book, March 1911

In February of 1911, like many of her thirteen-year-old friends, Dorothy began to write down details of her life in a memory book. Making periodic entries, she kept at it until 1913, compiling two sizeable volumes, each one bound in a maroon cover.

Using a pen dipped in ink and good-sized sheets of lined paper, she created verbal glimpses into her life, especially outside of school. Her spontaneous comments also throw light on what it was like to grow up in the Deep South in an era when Victorian formality still ruled. Women wore floor-length dresses, elaborate hats with veils, and kid gloves, and left an engraved calling card when the friend they went to visit was not at home.

In March 1911, a month after she had begun her first memory book, Dorothy was atypically at home on a school day, confined upstairs to her bedroom on the northwest corner of the house. Two west windows looked down on South Perry Street and the clops of horse hooves signaled the passing of an occasional carriage. At other moments the whirr of automobile tires was heard.

Usually she wrote in her memory book at a small mahogany roll-top desk that stood between the west windows. Its leather-topped panel slid in and out to provide writing space as needed, but on this day, she was sitting in bed with pillows propped up against the high rosewood headboard, intent on her task. Careful not to spill the black ink when dipping the pen in and out of the bottle, she described her plight:

> I've got the mumps. And on both sides, too. I'm nearly dead. I have had a miserable day. Mumps is no joke! It's perfectly awful. I got up Sunday and went downstairs. Today I am up. I'm just crazy to get out and play.

Once restored to her energetic self, Dorothy was free to play after school with her closest friends, Susie and Virginia. They roller-skated up and down the Perry Street sidewalk, spun tops, and played countless games of "I Spy," "Rock, Paper, Scissors," and "Stealing Sticks." Often they spent the night at one another's house, remembering to pack their memory book in a suitcase along with nightgown, slippers, and toothbrush.

As important as compiling the written text was the adornment of almost every page of their books with an emblem—a feather, a sprig of fern, or a twig. Sometimes a theater program, a movie ticket, a postcard, or a letter was pasted on the page. No doubt the inclusion of concrete objects helped to evoke an experience in all of its felt details.

~ ~ ~

In the inscription inside the cover of her new 1912 memory book Dorothy dared to look ahead into the distant future and imagine her destiny as a mother and grandmother:

> Memory book of Dorothy Bissell Thigpen
> (Age 14 years)
> Montgomery, Alabama June 1, 1912
> Dedicated to
> "The little grandchildren that are to be!"

Page one begins with her commentary on a piano recital and a copy of the program. In spite of an attack of nerves beforehand, she pulled herself together and once again rose to the occasion and did her best.

June 1912

Miss Annie May's recital was tonight and I played in two things. I never <u>have</u> been so scared as when I went to play "Good Night." My legs were trembling so that my slippers would hit against the pedal, and I felt my face getting redder and redder and my hands getting colder every minute. I did not make a single mistake though.

Once her eighth-grade school year ended, Dorothy went shopping with Daisy to assemble her wardrobe in preparation for a two-week visit to Asheville, North Carolina. Thanks to the kind invitation of Virginia and her parents, Dorothy was about to embark on her first train trip without her family. She packed her memory book and made a report the following day:

July 9, 1912

Well, I got here! It's just beautiful and I like it <u>very</u> much. I am <u>so</u> homesick though. Mrs. Tyson and Virginia met me at the train and they are so kind ... The mountains!! They are perfectly beautiful and I am charmed with Asheville, but ... there's no place like home ...

During her stay in the cool mountain air of North Carolina, Dorothy visited the house and gardens at the Biltmore estate, and enjoyed suppers, dances, and movies, all in the adolescent company of Virginia and her friends. On July 20, the Tysons took the girls on an all-day excursion to the highest mountain in the state.

I saw "my friend Pisgah." The mountains were the most beautiful things I ever saw. We got green apples, blackberries, and huckleberries. The woods were simply lovely. Just trees and flowers ... we were 5000 ft. above sea level.

In the latter part of July, Dorothy waved goodbye to the Tysons, and feeling like an experienced traveller, took the return train to Montgomery and settled back into the rhythm of her daily routine at home.

~ ~ ~

Attending the weekly Sunday service at the Church of the Ascension suddenly took on new appeal when she noticed a handsome young man sitting in the sanctuary with the choir. Tall, brown haired, and good-looking, he was probably in his twenties, and she felt certain that he had glanced at her more than once! In fact, as she confided to her memory book, she was convinced he had noticed her while she sat in one of the pews near the altar. By early autumn, not long after her fifteenth birthday, she needed to release some pent-up feelings:

Sept 10, 1912

About J.B.!! I don't see what makes me like him so much when he hasn't shown by word or sign that he likes me. I will stop liking him and being so silly until he makes some advances. It's so <u>absolutely silly</u> I have been sitting on needles all day for fear some of the things I have said would get to his ears. If they <u>would</u>! I could never look him in the face again. Oh! Do you think anything will? I have talked entirely too much about him to too many people, and if anything I said about liking him so much would ever get to him, I would "<u>bust</u>." I started to burn this <u>silly</u> book, but it has so many good times in it that I know I would be sorry afterwards. I <u>will</u> stop talking and thinking and dreaming about him so much ...

Not long after this, J.B., who had been away on a trip, returned to Montgomery and took his customary place in the sanctuary with the choir members. Then, through a friend, Dorothy heard some unwelcome news.

Sept 21, 1912

Positively last appearance of J.B. Well, the end has at last arrived to this silly affair ... the girl is visiting his sister ... I never thought he would fall in love with anybody that wasn't beautiful. But it seems as if I was mistaken. She is extremely stylish and good-looking but not pretty. She is small and very cute looking and had on very stylish clothes ... After church, J.B. came outside. I have never seen him look so grand. He had on a tie just the color of his eyes, and his hair looked so smooth and brown. (I declare, I am very sentimental) ... I walked on with some people, and I knew he was looking at me. In church he looked at me about as much (and maybe more) as he looked at her ... This is the end, and I hereby bid him goodbye forever. The theme is dead. (Tragic). It is the end.

But it was not quite the end. Six weeks later on the morning of November 3, 1912, an article in the *Montgomery Advertiser* announcing J.B.'s engagement to P.M. ended with a brief encomium: "Mr. B. is a member of a distinguished old family and is a young man of sterling qualities." Dorothy added her own inimitable comment next to the newspaper account she pasted into her memory book:

Mr. and Mrs. J.B.! Well he's buried and the grass is growing nicely on his grave, and my only regret is that I was so "dog-goned" silly about him.

She handled the end of her first crush gracefully, but actually, J.B. wasn't the only person who was spending time in Dorothy's romantic thoughts.

For the last few months, she and Susie and Virginia had been going together to the Saturday afternoon matinee at the Empress Theatre, and it was not just to take in exciting adventures. What they enjoyed most was gazing at their new "heroes," the current silent film stars who were already exerting a magnetic pull on their hearts. It wasn't long before Wallace Reid, one of the best-known actors and one of the most dashing looking, became Dorothy's declared favorite.

Motivated to prove her loyalty as a fan, she wrote to Carlton Motion Picture Laboratories, enclosing a dollar bill in the envelope, and requesting photographs of several well-known actors. When the pictures arrived, she trimmed a small one of her hero to fit inside her gold locket. Then she sat down and composed a nicely turned lyric.

Nov 3, 1912

> *There's a handsome face I've often seen*
> *Focused on the picture screen*
> *A figure tall and firmly knit*
> *And clothes that most divinely fit*

> *O, Wallace Reid, the hearts you've smashed*
> *I fear to tell the number —*
> *If you could know the hopes you've dashed*
> *T'would spoil your peaceful slumber*

> *When in your arms the heroine lies*
> *My own heart gets into a whirl*
> *And as you gaze into her eyes*
> *I wish I was a picture girl.*

DTS, Age 15

Two weeks later it was not the thrill of watching a silent movie but a live production with an acclaimed actress that stirred her imagination and sent her into rapture.

Nov 20, 1912

I'm joy, joy, joy!!! *Peter Pan*! The most wonderful, wonderful thing that I have <u>ever</u> seen. And Maude Adams is the most <u>beautiful</u>, lovely and <u>simply</u> exquisite thing there ever was. Oh! I never, never have seen anything or anybody that walked right into my heart without even knocking as Maude Adams in *Peter Pan* did. I'll never forget when she said, "She's dead" or "<u>If</u> you believe in fairies, <u>wave</u> your handkerchief and <u>clap</u> your hands, oh, if you <u>do</u> please wave!" The Montgomery people (I'm ashamed to say) took an age to decide whether they did or not and then, <u>such</u> clapping!

The next week Dorothy was beside herself with excitement over a weather event that practically never happened in the Deep South. Once again, she dared to look into the distant future, and then prophetically expressed her feelings to her own grandchildren, longing to share with them a miraculous moment:

Oh, "little grandchildren that are to be," what do you think? It snowed tonight!!!! Isn't that wonderful? If you are Yankee "little grandchildren that are to be," you will laugh, but to us it was simply wonderful! We all wrapped up (the whole neighborhood) and yelling and shrieking, walked down to the Ligons and all around. Mrs. K. said we looked like a picture with the snow all over us.

I never saw or heard of anything so wonderful and I had a grand time!

~ ~ ~

The festive mood that energizes the Christmas season was in full swing one evening in December 1912 when Dorothy and a group of Montgomery girls made their debut in the old-world elegance of the Exchange Hotel.

It was in that large and elegant ballroom decorated with holly, smilax, and mistletoe that Dorothy first met Tom, a broad-shouldered college freshman who would soon begin to transform the way she thought about herself. Tom, according to Dorothy's memory book, was smitten from the moment of their introduction, and once he had led Dorothy onto the dance floor, he wasted no time in attempting to win her affections, launching a campaign that moved at roller-coaster speed.

December 1912

Friday night I made my debut at the Exchange Hotel at the Elmore's dance and had a grand time. A certain person (no names to be mentioned hereafter) was lovely to me. The sweetest boy I ever saw, but such a flirt ... I had four dances with the blue-eyed fellow. He's terribly silly and personal but his eyes!! They look right through you and he asks such strange questions ... Oh, you tobacco smoke! When he dances with you, he simply <u>crushes</u> you up close. I had a perfectly dandy time.

On Christmas night he asked me to wear his fraternity pin as soon as it comes and he just went on! Then Sunday he called me up and talked for an age, asked me to a supper at his house and also asked me to go to the fraternity dance with him next Friday. Said he had something pretty to give me. <u>What</u> do you think it was? Promise me you won't tell, gentle reader? It was a beautiful diamond ring! For once in my life I had my wits about me and told him <u>of course</u> I couldn't ... He called Sunday and oh, such a tearful goodbye. He made me promise to write to him.

Tom's first letter arrived in the mail in January 1913.

He has written me something which almost verges on a really truly love letter, begging me to let him wear my Delta Sigma Phi pin.[2] Would you, gentle reader? I know he was pawing the earth with impatience, for it has been nearly a week since I got his last letter and I haven't let him know I ever got it. It won't hurt him though. I believe he really likes me. His name, gentle reader, is T.O.

This was the final entry Dorothy made in her Volume II memory book. She was fifteen and a half years old, halfway through her freshman year at Sidney Lanier High School.

After their tearful goodbye at the end of the Christmas holidays, Tom returned to the University of Alabama to pursue his career on the football field and in his fraternity house, leaving Dorothy behind in Montgomery with her heart caught up in an unprecedented whirl.

Perhaps feeling too grown-up to begin another memory book or else finding that she was too busy to commit to a new one, Dorothy gave up the practice of writing down the details of her life in a

---

[2] Dorothy's high school sorority.

journal. Her decision left her reader stranded, with no opportunity to find out about her innermost feelings or learn anything more about the romantic adventure she had just begun with Tom, the impetuous suitor who had recently swept into her life with dramatic suddenness.

10

Edmund's Childhood Years

Tomorrow I am not going to fight with any of my sisters
or call them names …

—Edmund Shea, diary, February 1905

While Dorothy was growing up in a land where crops of cotton, peanuts, and corn thrived in red clay soil, and purple wisteria and pear trees filled the month of March with fragrance, Edmund was spending his early years in the upper reaches of Wisconsin, in the little town of Ashland that lay on a latitude so far north that some years snow covered the ground from November to April.

Ashland sat on a bluff overlooking Chequamegon Bay, an arm of Lake Superior in the northwest corner of the state. The winters there were long and cold but even when the temperature hovered below zero for days on end, Edmund relished the chance to climb onto a toboggan and hurtle at heart-stopping speeds down snow-packed slopes on the outskirts of town. On moonlit nights he walked to the nearby lakefront with his sisters Edith and Catherine to skate on the bay, skimming across the glassy surface for several miles before turning around to return home. Then, pink cheeked and breathless, they clustered around the fireplace, sharing details of the excursion with the family, while warming their half-frozen fingers.

Like tobogganing, skating on the bay was an exhilarating sport that included possible danger. Sometimes without warning a loud boom like a rifle shot broke the silence and signaled a nearby crack in the ice. It was an ominous sound and sometimes foretold the fate of a hapless child, if one passed over the wrong spot at the wrong time. Death followed moments after an unexpected plunge into the icy water.

In the long days of summer, the lake offered swimming, sailing, and canoeing. The Sheas had a cottage on nearby Madeline Island, one of the dozen Apostle Islands that lay scattered across the water in Chequamegon Bay. Edmund and family members often took a small boat called a skater or a larger ferryboat from Bayfield, a town to the west of Ashland, to reach La Pointe, the main town on the island.

Six Gables, the Shea's rustic cabin, perched above the steps that led from the dock, nestled in a stand of balsam firs. On cool summer evenings kerosene lamps lit the porch after supper, and chairs and a hammock gave family members and friends a place to relax and watch the western sky as daylight faded and stars began to appear above the bay. Better still, on evenings when the right weather conditions prevailed, the aurora borealis, the northern lights, put on an eerie display, one that lasted for hours and sent long bands and arcs of red and green and yellow light that pulsated upward toward the heavens.

In his teenage years, Edmund looked forward each summer to taking at least one canoe trip with his sisters Edith, Louise, and Catherine, and a few friends. They paddled fifty or sixty miles up the shore of Lake Superior, bringing along tents, fishing rods, sleeping bags, and provisions to last for several days.

There were five girls and two boys in Edmund's Irish Catholic family. Will, the eldest child, told his younger brother many years later that he could still remember the day in late March of 1892 when he was playing outside in the snow and his father William came out of the front door to announce the happy news that a baby boy had come into the world. Even before the baptism, William decided to name his second son for Edmund Burke, so highly did he esteem the Irish statesman and philosopher. Will was ten years old at the time and said he realized then how much he had been hoping for a brother. He was already outnumbered by his younger sisters, Eugenie, Louise, and Catherine, but before the family circle was complete, he would gain two more sisters younger than Edmund — Edith and Isabel.

Just as Lake Superior stood out as a favorite geographical feature in Edmund's boyhood memory, the person who imprinted his young personality most deeply was his white-haired father William Francis Shea. For Edmund, William was his first and most influential teacher, the one who inspired him to do his best under all circumstances.

William had grown up on Wisconsin's frontier, a rugged setting in the 1870s and 1880s, where he developed habits of thrift, resilience, optimism, and hard work. He had to leave school at age eleven to work in a shingle factory, so he knew how important the gift of an education was, recognizing that it provided the best way out of the trap of poverty. Even in adulthood when he was earning a steady income as an established lawyer, William regularly set aside money in order to provide a college education for all his seven children.

Edmund and his siblings had assigned chores for which William paid wages. He also opened a savings account for each child, to give them practice in conserving a nest egg. An example of how William's philosophy of thrift was put into action turns up in Edmund's 1905 diary. He was thirteen then and expressed delight over finding "a peach of a nail file" to give his sister Catherine for Christmas. He understood from his father's example that what mattered most was the loving thought behind a gift, not its monetary value.

William loved books, and from the time Edmund began to read, he enriched his son's literary diet above and beyond school assignments. Starting him off with Greek and Roman myths, he then supplied Edmund with the *Iliad* and the *Odyssey*, with tales of Siegfried and King Arthur. Reading the stories and talking about them with his father made Edmund long to be like their heroes and accomplish deeds of courage and valor. The stories also provided indelible models that shaped Edmund's values and inspired him to want to live up to heroic ideals.

After Will went off to college, Edmund took on some of his older brother's household duties, such as carrying buckets of ashes up from the basement. When he grew old enough to take on more, he beat rugs, sold springwater to neighbors, tended the rose bushes, cut the grass, and chopped and stacked wood.

Nora, Edmund's mother, a soft-spoken soul, found joy in her role as devoted wife and mother. A natural homemaker who enjoyed baking bread and pies for her family, she also willingly shared with her five daughters favorite recipes and all she knew about the domestic arts.

Her piety, quickened by her younger brother Eugene's decision to become a diocesan priest, also deepened her sense of loyalty to the Catholic Church. At the turn of the century the Vatican I church made proclamations with militant authority, drawing strength from a recent papal teaching that re-emphasized the doctrine, "Outside the Catholic church there is no salvation."

St. Agnes' Church, the parish where the family worshipped, stood only a few doors away from the Shea house on Front Street, and it became their weekly destination when Nora and the children walked to Mass each Sunday morning.

For much of his adult life William did not attend Sunday Mass, preferring to spend Sunday mornings at home communing with the authors of his favorite books. Thus, it fell to Nora to take the initiative in church matters. When Lent came around each winter, she revived the practice of saying the rosary after dinner each evening while family members knelt around the dining room table. Edmund's two younger sisters, according to a letter he wrote years later, struggled at times to control their impulse to giggle while engaging in the lengthy repetitions of Our Fathers and Hail Marys.

In January 1905, when Edmund was a twelve-year-old freshman in the Ashland high school, he began to keep a diary. One gathers from his brief entries that he got along amicably with Catherine, Edith, and Isabel, who still lived at home. Still, peace did not necessarily reign at every moment, as he revealed one frigid February day when the temperature hovered at minus nineteen degrees.

It is very cold today. Tomorrow I am not going to fight with any of my sisters or call them names, etc. I am not going to swear once either. If I correct one fault every day and keep it up that way, I will be a saint after awhile.

The next day, Saturday, dawned mercifully free from thoughts of reform.

This was just a dandy day. The sun was warm and bright. I feel glad that I am alive on a day like this has been. I began to saw some Norway pine 4 foot slabs. I am going to get $2.00 a cord for sawing them and putting them in the cellar. They are wet and frozen so they don't saw very hard. I will be through in 2 weeks. I stayed home all day.

In an entry later that year Edmund expressed intense dislike of short pants, and objected to the school rule obliging freshmen to wear them. He had also begun to suffer a new, excruciating adolescent torment when his voice broke for the first time during a recitation in Latin class. His embarrassment led him to comment that he "guessed he'd give up talking" until things came under better control.

~ ~ ~

On Valentine's Day of 1905, Edmund's maternal uncle Gene Madden and his sister Aunt Louise Madden arrived in Ashland for a short visit, and while family and guests gathered around the dinner table the first evening, a new idea was broached—that Edmund would go to visit his uncle and aunt and spend the next four months with them. His first diary comment was noncommittal: "Maybe I am going to Minnesota with them."

Uncle Gene and Aunt Louise lived in Fairmont, a small town in the southern part of the state. Father Eugene Madden had recently been named the pastor of St. Paul's Catholic Church and Aunt Louise lived in the rectory, serving as her brother's companion and house-keeper. Though specific reasons for the visit are not spelled out in the diary, Nora and William may have envisioned it as an opportunity for Edmund to receive guidance from his uncle while he mastered the contents of the Baltimore Catechism. He was to make his First Holy Communion in June 1905. Edmund's next diary entry reveals his growing enthusiasm over the prospect of a visit:

> I am sure I am going to Fairmont. I won't come home until after school lets out. I am going to get a kid to carry out the ashes and get the wood. Ma always used to say, "If you don't like it here, pack up and go away someplace." But now she almost won't let me go ... I bought a new suit of clothes this afternoon ...

The next morning Edmund waved goodbye to his family, and travelled westward by train with his uncle and aunt across Wisconsin, and over the Mississippi River. They changed trains in St. Paul and turned southward, finally reaching Fairmont that evening.

The next morning when he got up and looked out of the front window of his second floor bedroom in the rectory, flat Minnesota prairie-land spread out under a thick blanket of snow as far as the eye could see.

February 18, 1905, Saturday

> I slept like a log last night and didn't get up until 9 o'clock. After dinner I went downtown with Uncle Gene. All along the main street farmers had their big green sleighs tied. They only come in on Saturdays. We went to see the principal of the school and then went to the church. They have a dandy church here. No saloons run on Sunday ...

The white clapboard rectory stood next to St. Paul's Church and Edmund soon found that within his new home the pace of life moved more quietly and slowly than it did in his bustling Ashland household.[3] There were fewer conveniences too, he noted, without realizing at his age how much the absence of a water tank added to the time and effort his aunt made in carrying out her duties as laundress.

There is about 10 inches of snow today. Aunt Louise has been melting snow all day with which to wash tomorrow.

~ ~ ~

Occasionally on Sunday Father Gene's friends Father Mikoli and Father Murphy joined them for the meal at noon, for which Aunt Louise created special feasts such as fried chicken with rice and gravy and homemade biscuits followed by homemade sponge cake, repasts that led Edmund to comment wistfully: "I wish priests came around here oftener."

Did Catherine and Edith predict before he left Ashland that their brother was going to fall prey to severe bouts of homesickness? Edmund brushed off the thought in a diary sentence: "I won't be because I haven't been yet."

A few weeks later though, he received a notice in the mail that a package was waiting for him at the post office. After racing down Blue Earth Street and presenting the slip to a postal clerk, Edmund took the package outside and sat down on the curb to take a look.

---

[3] In 2012, when I began to work on this chapter, motivated to learn as much as I could about St. Paul's Church, I telephoned the Fairmont, Minnesota, Historical Society, explaining to the woman who answered that my great-uncle had been the pastor of the church in the early 1900s. I asked about the rectory and whether any photographs of the church were available. After a long moment of silence, the woman replied, "Well, you won't believe this, but I am actually sitting here right now in one of the front second floor rooms of the house that many years ago *was* the original rectory of St. Paul's Church! Now it belongs to the Historical Society."

Inside the wrapping was a note from Catherine saying she had made the gift, and within the tin box lined with wax paper lay a luscious looking double layer supply of fudge squares. The first taste of sweetness led to a succession of other memories that filled his imagination, materializing in detail — the crate that stood in the corner of the kitchen in Ashland, the one that held the wood he always split to the right length to fit inside the black stove, and the smell of bread in the air, the loaves cooling on the rectangular wood breadboard where his mother always placed them. He could hear Edith and Catherine laughing as they sat near the fireplace playing cards, and see the trace of a smile coming across his father's face while he sat at the dining room table looking over Edmund's latest report card.

Not one fudge square was left in the tin box when he got up from the curb, and as he walked back to the rectory, he had already made up his mind to write to Catherine and thank her for the fudge. He was determined to be strong the way his father was; there would be no mention of homesickness.

~ ~ ~

During many evenings in the next four months, Edmund and his uncle Gene sat in the rectory living room, working through the chapters of the Baltimore Catechism. In addition to memorizing the Our Father, the Hail Mary, and the Apostles' Creed, Edmund learned the essentials about the seven sacraments and the Ten Commandments. With his uncle's encouragement, he also began wearing a scapular and attended daily Mass during Lent as ways to prepare for his first Communion in mid-June.

In the Catholic Church in 1905, children received first Communion when they were twelve or thirteen, an age that signaled a passage from childhood into adolescence, a time when the Church deemed a young person mature enough to understand that receiving the Eucharist meant taking the reality of Christ's presence into his heart.

In addition to helping with catechism lessons, Father Gene also taught Edmund to serve Mass, a training that involved mastering a number of detailed duties, such as memorizing Latin responses to prayers, carrying the missal from one side of the altar to another, bringing cruets of water and wine to the priest at the offertory, and ringing the silver bell at the moment of consecration. At High Mass, an acolyte also assisted the priest in the use of the censer, the silver or brass receptacle on a chain that contained glowing coals. When the priest added grains of incense to the coals and swung the censer, fragrant smoke, reminiscent of balsam firs, ascended upward in the sanctuary. Father Gene explained that the use of incense was ancient, going back to Old Testament times when it was used in Jewish temple rites.

Edmund's responsibilities as an altar boy also included lighting candles on the altar before each Mass and pouring oil into the red sanctuary lamp that stood near the altar. The burning light was a sign that the reserved Sacrament, the Eucharist, was there in the tabernacle. As Edmund learned from his uncle, a lamp lit with oil also stood before the Holy of Holies, the Ark of the Covenant, in ancient as well as in modern Jewish temples.

Edmund's duties in the sanctuary required alertness at all times. Gone were the days when he might have dozed in the family pew during Mass in St. Agnes' Church in Ashland. At St. Paul's, he learned to pay close attention, and by observing his uncle's reverent attitude whenever he genuflected or made the sign of the cross, Edmund came to understand that every gesture one made in the sanctuary was done in order to honor and acknowledge the presence of the Holy.

The sound of the men's choir singing Gregorian chant during High Mass provided another sensory experience that drew him into the beauty of the liturgy and led him to write in his diary, "I hardly know what to do with myself when I'm not serving Mass on Sunday." Edmund's experience as an altar boy in the sanctuary during the winter and spring of 1905 served as preparation for his First Communion, a genuine rite of passage that led him to encounter the reality of the Holy for the first time.

By late April, spring finally arrived in Fairmont and Edmund traded his wool underwear for cotton. One afternoon when he returned to the rectory from school, he found a gift sent from his uncle John Madden, a book by Howard Pyle called *Men of Iron*.

Set in fourteenth-century England, Pyle's stirring tale brings to life a medieval world where Myles Falworth, a likeable young knight-in-training, is engaged in an arduous program to gain proficiency using a knife, sword, and lance. In addition, he is also developing disciplined habits in order to internalize virtues such as courtesy, humility, and loyalty, all in preparation for the lifelong promises he will make to God and the king. The night before taking his vows, Myles remains in the castle chapel during an all-night vigil, with his suit of armor piled up near the altar, praying to the Lord for the strength he will need to live as a faithful and devoted knight.

The convergence of Howard Pyle's gift as a novelist with the moment of time that this particular book came into the hands of a boy on a Minnesota prairie meant that Edmund entered fully into the imaginative world of medieval England, and connected on a profound level with the core meaning of the story. Perhaps he began to understand then that like Myles, he too belonged to a fellowship of souls that felt called to live up to an inner ideal. Years later in letters to Dorothy, Edmund sometimes referred to himself as "a knight in a faraway country," suggesting that his desire to live as a single-hearted hero like Myles was still very much alive in his consciousness, years after he had finished reading the stirring story in *Men of Iron*.

A few days before First Communion Sunday, Edmund helped Uncle Gene sweep out the church. He took up the rug in the sanctuary and beat it and helped his uncle place a fresh linen cloth on the altar.

William and Nora arrived in Fairmont on Saturday and were

sitting with other parents of first communicants in one of the front pews at St. Paul's the next morning. At Communion time, Edmund knelt at the altar rail with his classmates, waiting while his uncle moved down the line, stopping before each child. When Edmund's turn came he listened to the words he knew by heart: *Domine Jesu Christe, santificatur animam tuam in vitam aeternam. Amen* ("May the Lord Jesus Christ keep thy soul unto life eternal, Amen"). Edmund's characteristically brief diary comment conveys much in a few words: "I went to First Communion. I was very happy."

Edmund returned to Ashland with Nora and William and spent the rest of the summer days at home, enjoyable ones that included visits to the island with the opportunity to swim, repair the dock at Six Gables, and plan another camping trip with Catherine, Edith, and his good friend Charlie Gardner. Then school began, and the next three years at Ashland High School passed by, but unfortunately for posterity, they passed without the aid of another diary to provide daily details.

After skipping two early grades and making enviable marks each year, Edmund graduated from high school in June 1908, three months after his sixteenth birthday. He gave the class address at his graduation ceremonies as a final flourish, and William, ever ready to bestow an appropriate book at the right moment, presented Edmund with one of his favorites, Marcus Aurelius's *Meditations*. Father and son had always enjoyed a close bond, one that did not depend on detailed verbal exchanges. It is likely that William handed Edmund the small volume after commencement and smiled when he congratulated him on a job well done. It would be up to Edmund to read the book carefully, and then figure out why his father would hold a pagan emperor in such deep admiration.

Edmund's Education Within and Beyond University Walls
1908–13

Accept whatever befalls you without resentment.
—Marcus Aurelius, *Meditations*

S mooth sailing describes the voyage Edmund had made all the way through the Ashland schools. But his journey through college included unexpected twists and turns, and at times presented challenges that tested his mettle. A major crisis rose up in his sophomore year when the threat of serious illness led him to drop out of school.

Edmund's undergraduate career began in 1908. Swayed by his older brother's glowing endorsement of his school days at Notre Dame, he followed in Will's footsteps. But it wasn't long after Edmund's arrival that he found his feelings about Notre Dame bore little resemblance to Will's.

An early entry in the sporadic diary he kept that year sheds some light: "I suppose I'm in the grip of homesickness but no one will ever know about it." He intended to make the best of it without complaint, aware of the sacrifice his father was making to send him to a private college. But in the surviving letters he wrote home, though he steered clear of the subject of loneliness, he betrayed a minimum of enthusiasm.

After spending the Christmas holidays at home, a time when he was buoyed up by the fellowship of family and the luxury of home-cooked meals, he returned to the gloom of Sorin Hall and sat down to write to his mother:

Dear Ma,

Once more we convicts are assembled on the historic and beautiful spot of Notre Dame ...

The word "convict" says volumes about how he felt to be in the "beautiful spot," in the penetrating damp of South Bend's climate while he chafed against the rules and monotony of an all-male community. But it was during those months that he began to appreciate for the first time the courage his father William had shown in facing his own version of adversity at a young age.

Had he [William] been better cared for, he would now be a big well-developed man. But working from twelve noon to midnight, beginning at age eleven and weighing eighty-five pounds, living on sour milk and potatoes, he is a living example of what a man can do when his will is strong.

On rare occasions, William had shared with Edmund some stark facts of his growing-up years, and how he derived strength from the example his own parents embodied. For in holding onto the faith and courage of their Celtic forebears, Patrick and Eliza Shea never abandoned their conviction that God was with them, even in the midst of the grinding poverty and discrimination they endured as Irish immigrants.

By the beginning of spring in 1909, Edmund's diary comments reveal that the way he perceived Notre Dame classmates was also evolving. He "no longer felt envious of the rich kids around here" and "didn't mind not having two pennies to rub together." In the spring, he mentioned two teachers, both Holy Cross priests he had come to know and admire, and by the end of the school year, his diary comments sound like those of a fairly contented college student. But when Edmund returned to Ashland for the summer, after he presented the pros and cons of his experience at Notre Dame, William and Nora supported his desire to transfer to the University of Wisconsin at Madison.

This time the transition was easy. Not long after settling into off-campus housing in Madison, Edmund joined a sophomore class debate team and decided to major in history. By the time he returned home for the Christmas holidays, everything had fallen happily into place. But his upbeat mood was cut short, for in February he began to feel under par, bothered by a cold and sore throat and by a troublesome cough he could not shake, despite repeated doses of Doc Sullivan's cough "dope."

~ ~ ~

A goldmine of information revealing what happened next in Edmund's life came to light in late 2011, when my son Edmund Shea Harvey discovered a journal his grandfather kept from 1910 to 1913. The buried treasure found in the garage of my son's house in Hanover, New Hampshire, begins in January 1910, around the time Edmund returned to Madison for his second semester. The diary provides details about his life in the outer world, as well as glimpses into the way its teenaged author confronted adversity in the spring of 1910.

In late February Edmund's cough was still "knocking the tar out of him," and he wondered if the sound of it in the middle of the night "would wake everyone in the house" (the off-campus lodging where he lived).

Occasional comments about Edmund's poor health reached home through his letters, and by the latter part of March, William's concern over his son escalated, for they triggered haunting memories of illness and death in his own family in the late 1870s.

William was in his mid-twenties in 1877 when his father Patrick Shea died of consumption in the family house in Kewaunee, Wisconsin. Also living at home then were William's mother Eliza, and his younger siblings Eliza, Catherine, John, Patrick, and James. Eliza and Catherine, both schoolteachers in their early twenties, also died from the infection they caught from their father. Within two years, tuberculosis carried off three members of the Shea family.

William called his son-in-law Mike Flatley for advice. Mike, married to Eugenie Shea, was a general practitioner living in Antigo, Wisconsin. He advised his nephew to come see him for a checkup, and though Edmund stalled for several days, reluctant to leave school in the middle of the term, he took the train to Antigo on April 11.

Mike's first step after examining Edmund's throat, which was "covered with little white spots," was to paint it with iodine, a highly disagreeable experience that caused Edmund to feel he "was going to die of strangulation for about five minutes."

Next came a skin test for TB on Edmund's stomach, but it was a "fizzle," so a few days later Mike put some serum in Edmund's eye. The next day it "was sore as the dickens which was evidence of TB germs. Mike says the best thing to do was see Doc Murphy in Chicago to make sure. There is no hope of going back to school."

Mike sent Edmund to bed and dosed him with cod liver oil and whiskey, a vile tasting mix designed to make him strong but instead he felt "rotten." A blizzard descended on Antigo, a most unusual event in mid-April. The Antigo newspaper attributed the cause of the storm to the appearance of Halley's comet, but the freak snowstorm may have confirmed Edmund's sense that the whole world was falling apart.

Still, he wrote that he "shook off the blue, for that was not 'philoso-phia'" (i.e., not the way to follow a love of wisdom, the way of life espoused by Marcus Aurelius. The Stoic philosopher-emperor firmly believed that by practicing disciplined habits of thinking, living in the present moment, and not yielding to negative feelings, one could achieve inner serenity, even while chaos raged in the outside world. Both William and Edmund considered Marcus Aurelius a wise and reliable inner guide).

Edmund's diary reflection continued:

I want to learn something definite ... I hope there is no TB but if there is, there is going to be a fight and I expect to win out. Mrs. Scott Ellis is a good example of nerve. She lived at least two years by sheer willpower. But she went at last. It was hard on Scott and Ruth but they stood it well.

The Ellis family lived near the Sheas and Mrs. Ellis was the mother of Ruth, a classmate of Catherine Shea and a girl Edmund had been fond of in high school. He had known Ruth's mother for years and so could remember the way she faced her fatal illness with willpower and "nerve." But Edmund was a whole generation younger than Mrs. Ellis. He had turned eighteen only a month before Mike delivered his sobering diagnosis. Yet in a few words, Edmund showed remarkable maturity by declaring his willingness to take on the shadowy opponent of serious illness without a trace of self-pity.

At the end of April Edmund left Antigo and returned home to Ashland, and as soon as William scheduled an appointment, he and Edmund went to Chicago to consult Dr. Murphy. In agreement with Mike's diagnosis of Edmund's primary TB infection, Dr. Murphy advised him to drop out of college, live in a temperate climate, and spend as much time as possible outdoors. In an era before medication existed, doctors could only hope that a combination of fresh air and a warm environment would increase the chances for their TB patients' recovery.

During the early summer of 1910, Edmund felt well enough to take on part-time surveying jobs in and around Ashland. He and his parents also talked over where he would spend the coming year, and settled on a plan that included stays in Colorado, Oregon, and California. On July 11, with a trunk and suitcase packed for adventure and with William, Catherine, and a few friends to wave him off, Edmund began his train journey westward, headed toward Loveland, Colorado.

Loveland, a small town about fifty miles north of Denver, lay under an open sky to the east of the Rocky Mountains. An Ashland friend of Edmund's, Avery Clark, had recently settled there while he worked his way up through the ranks at the local sugar mill, a factory where sugar beets were refined and processed. The combination of the Colorado mountain air and knowing someone there attracted Edmund, especially after Avery encouraged him to inquire about jobs at the mill.

Once Edmund found a place to stay in a rooming house, he walked to the employment office at the sugar mill and was hired on the spot for the only job available—that of a day-laborer painter.

At least the work site itself conformed to Dr. Murphy's guidelines, for it was outside, on the roof of the factory building. But the work involved scraping old paint off a 24' x 25' water tank and then applying a fresh coat. In the midst of a ferocious heat wave, working outside in temperatures that stayed in the nineties day after day was exhausting. To make matters worse, the paint fumes irritated Edmund's throat and stirred up his cough.

The image of Edmund carrying a lunch pail, trudging to the mill each morning, and putting on overalls before starting to work on the hot roof contrasts sharply with the life he had keenly enjoyed until recently as a student at the University of Wisconsin. There he walked up the hill toward Bascom Hall carrying a book bag and looking forward to courses in English medieval history or the poetry of Horace. Yet in spite of the calamitous changes in his life, Edmund's diary entries about Loveland are virtually free of resentful or discouraged comments.

At least weekends brought respite from the water tank. Mr. and Mrs. Swan, the owners of the rooming house, sometimes invited Edmund to join them on rides to the surrounding countryside to take in the beauty of the mountains or views of the brilliant stars and moon in the western heavens. He also dropped by to see Doc Forbes each Saturday to get his lungs checked or to get more cough dope.

One afternoon in late August Edmund arrived at the Swans' to find a letter from his brother Will. Now a general practitioner in Portland, Oregon, Will encouraged him to come spend the month of September with him and his wife Olga. Edmund jumped at the invitation and sent his acceptance by return mail.

It was surely without regret that Edmund gave his resignation to Mr. Nugent at the sugar mill. And when he stopped in to say good-bye to Doc Forbes, he was relieved to learn that his lungs sounded better and that he had "only a suggestion of congestion in one tube."

Then he made arrangements for his train trip westward, and while he packed his belongings, he must have felt tremendous relief as well as a sense of accomplishment. He had spent part of the summer in a dry climate to improve his health and had managed to survive monotonous work and support himself almost completely on his own slender earnings. To sum up his feelings about the desolate town where it all happened, he used a single understatement: "Loveland is not a place where one is in great danger of dying from excitement."

~ ~ ~

After leaving Loveland, Edmund's train stopped at Estes Park. Bowled over by the grandeur of the scene, he took time to write a letter to his father.

Estes Park, Colorado
August 26, 1910

Dear Pa,

This trip to Estes Park is an experience which I will never regret or forget. The mountain scenery is beautiful and majestic beyond my powers of expression. The drive up the canyon, which is the keyhole to this mountain park, is along a twisting road blasted out of the rock wall, and in many places it fairly hangs over the brawling torrent, known as Big Thompson. The river supplies all the irrigating water used in this region. It was a strain on the neck to look up to the top of the cliffs hanging above the trail and before we finished, my neck felt like Michelangelo's used to when he first began painting ceilings.

The park is a grassy valley in the midst of the Rockies. There is a settlement of a few buildings around the post office, and on the neighboring hillsides are scattered the cabins of the summer folk. This morning I rode a horse out the trail to Long's Peak. From the foot of the peak the view was wonderful to behold. In this clear air one can see great distances, and often you would swear you could spit on a mountain ten miles away. On all sides were the mountains piled up, one range above the other; they are partly covered with pine, but the tops are as bare of vegetation as a billiard ball. The creases in their sides are filled with ice and snow … Long's Peak itself as it towers up into the blue is the most inspiring sight I ever saw …

Your loving son,
Edmund

The train then headed westward via Salida. After going up over the crest of the continent at Marshall Pass, an exhilarating elevation of eleven thousand feet, Edmund got off in Salt Lake City and took time to visit the Mormon Temple and swim in the buoyant water of the lake.

12

Life in the Far West
1909–10

Who will believe that the Kingdom of this world not less
than the Kingdom of Heaven lies within?
—Bishop Spaulding, *Education and the Higher Life*

Will Shea was waiting for him on the platform in the Portland
train station, Edmund reported, and after they drove home in
his Hupmobile, he offered to give Edmund a checkup. "He thumped
my chest and declared the tuberculosis was cured sure enough."

Tipping the scale at 156 pounds, Edmund showed a gain of ten
pounds since his visit with Mike five months before. Will was pleased,
and confirmed the wisdom of taking a year off from school. Then, to
show his faith in the value of outdoor living, he helped Edmund set
up a tent in the front yard. With a card table and chair to enhance his
quarters, Edmund spent the majority of each day outside, enjoying
Portland's warm autumn weather while he caught up on correspondence and savored the gift of free time.

His new freedom allowed him to take long walks to explore the
city, look up an Ashland friend who was living there, and make
contact with his Notre Dame French professor who had moved to
Portland. Finally he had time to read the books his father William
sent him from time to time. Recent arrivals included Froude's biog-
raphy of Caesar, Thomas à Kempis's *Imitation of Christ*, Newman's

Apologia, and a pocket-sized book by Bishop Spaulding, *Education and the Higher Life.*

An indefatigable reader himself and an ongoing supplier of books to his son, William was also a reliable correspondent. His letters, usually several pages long, arrived on sheets of crisp white paper. Composed with a pen dipped in black ink, William's forward-slanting words in billowing script bounded across the paper to deliver the news: "Mae is back in the hospital. Not long for this world." Or, "Mr. D. was fired from his company job last week. Skimming the coffers. Mrs. D is understandably inconsolable." William also encouraged Edmund to cultivate the habit of reading a few pages of *Education and the Higher Life* each day, even when workdays were long. In it, Bishop Spaulding of Peoria, Illinois, encouraged young men to hold onto lofty ideals, to realize that "conduct and not culture is the basis of character," and to consider the following: "Who will believe that the Kingdom of this world not less than the Kingdom of Heaven lies within?" With a caring father who supplied books that nourished and fortified the soul, Edmund's spiritual journey would continue to deepen in the coming year as he lived in the midst of new challenges.

In early October, a long-awaited meeting with Mr. John Joyce took place. Mr. Joyce, an old friend of William's who formerly lived in Ashland, was in Portland for a brief visit before continuing on to Tuolomne, California, where he was one of the managers at the West Side Lumber Company. William had written to him to ask if he might help Edmund find a job at West Side, and Mr. Joyce assured him he would. When Mr. Joyce met Edmund, he confirmed his willingness to help and suggested that he come soon to Tuolomne.

A few days later Edmund travelled to San Francisco by boat, swayed by the fact that going by water cost fifteen dollars — a lot less than the thirty dollars needed for a train ticket. His diary includes a description of the beauty of Oregon's coastline in late afternoon light.

Unfortunately, during the night his susceptibility to seasickness manifested itself, a sensitivity that would stay with him the rest of his life. After arriving in San Francisco, his diary entry opened with a lament:

> Good Lord, how rotten I felt. Even a glass of water would not stay down for more than ten minutes ...

A ride on the Santa Fe Railroad later that day took him through Oakdale, and then eastward to Tuolomne, a little town with an elevation of 2,600 feet, the place that would become home for most of the coming year. Edmund had learned from Mr. Joyce that he would begin work as a teamster, and that the best living quarters to be found were at Mrs. Bishop's Rooming House. Accordingly, Edmund signed up for a room there and unpacked his belongings.

The next morning he reported to his boss, George Kennedy, another man with Ashland connections. It was George who showed him around the enormous lumberyard and introduced him to his teamster co-worker Ed, an Englishman with a clipped mustache and an unmistakable British accent.

Edmund's first job at West Side involved mastering new skills, such as putting the horse's harness on right-side up and learning how to attach his horse to the wagon. Basically, a teamster made his way to the supply center of the yard, picked up specific orders, and then delivered long planks of lumber to other parts of the yard or to customers in nearby Tuolomne.

Ted, an elderly horse, was usually compliant, but on mornings when the load felt too heavy, he gave in to an urge to lie down in the shafts and refused to budge. Edmund learned from Ed that a whack on Ted's rump would usually rouse him from a prone position.

There were other new experiences. He took a weekly bath in a "slimy half barrel," and at Mother Bishop's house each day during breakfast, lunch, and dinner he rubbed shoulders with other roomers, an assortment of rolling stones, misfits, and colorful itinerants who made up the work force at West Side Lumber.

While he met some who were good-natured and large-hearted souls, many of the men were "extremely smutty-minded and swore so needlessly." Some were "hooked on women or booze and shot their entire weekly stake on a Saturday night binge," habits Edmund had no desire to take up, especially when he was struggling to save every penny possible from his daily wage of $2.15.

Edmund witnessed the effect addictive habits had on the lives of a few men he knew who took laudanum to "fix the jimmies." One worker shot and killed himself the day he learned he had cancer of the mouth. Another co-worker died of TB. And several lumberjacks who lived in nearby West Side camps lost their lives in work-related accidents while Edmund was in Tuolomne. What Edmund internalized in the autumn months of 1910 were life-changing lessons unlike any he might have learned in a university classroom.

On those sunny days in October and November, while Edmund delivered supplies in the open air and bright autumn leaves covered nearby hills, a teamster's life was a happy one. But by December the rainy season arrived. Forewarned, he bought a secondhand slicker and brimmed hat, but even so, water found devilish ways to trickle down the back of his neck, giving him a new understanding of the word misery. Rain continued to fall on an almost daily basis, but then one day in mid-December, Stuart Ingalls's letter arrived, bringing news that must have felt to Edmund like a gift from heaven.

Stuart and Edmund had met at the University of Wisconsin, and like Edmund, he was taking a year off from college to recover from a touch of TB. Stuart sounded well settled in southern California; his reports exuded enthusiasm, especially the one describing his cabin outside of Upland, a town east of Los Angeles where vast citrus groves flourished. Even better, Stuart invited Edmund to come and spend the winter. They could share the rent, he suggested, and he felt certain that Edmund would easily find work picking oranges and lemons, as he was doing.

Fortunately George Kennedy, Edmund's boss, gave his blessing to Edmund's request. He suggested that Edmund return to Tuolomne at the end of March. When enough snow had melted in the higher elevations, George planned to send him with a group of West Side surveyors to measure the company's boundaries where they abutted Yosemite National Park.

Both Edmund and Stuart spent the winter months in Upland working as day laborers, picking citrus fruit. In late March Edmund returned to the rough and tumble crowd at Mother Bishop's boarding house in Tuolomne. At least this time he was coming back to a familiar environment.

In late June, the group of West Side surveyors arrived at their campsite near Yosemite. They pitched tents and slept on canvas cots. John Muir's new book about his summer in the Sierras had just come out, and as soon as William read it, he sent a copy to Edmund. This prompted Edmund's letter of thanks:

> As you say, Muir's book certainly helps one to appreciate the Sierras. Of course he perceived many things invisible to the ordinary mortal, and his power of expression is not comparable to that of everyday folk, but this satisfaction at least I have, that many of the plants, animals and natural phenomena of various kinds which he describes I was already familiar with from observation. And the mountains in general exhilarate me almost as much as they do him.

In addition to the chance he had to live in the sublime beauty of Yosemite, Edmund also gained experience in the field of surveying. He wrote to William on July 30, 1911:

> The past two weeks we have run section lines, blazing the boundary of West Side lands for the timber fallers ... In many places the steep slopes will not permit a measure of more than five feet horizontally, and sometimes when we encounter a per-

pendicular wall of rock it is necessary to put out a measuring pole from the top of the cliff until its end is directly above a certain spot at the base from which the measure is then continued. It is a curious fact that owing to these steep hills and deep canyons, a section of land really comprises much more than 640 acres because, as you know, the survey lines are horizontal to the earth. Hence if a ¼ section lies on a ridge half a mile broad at the base and a thousand feet high, the owner has possession really of some eight hundred acres. At present we are laboring on a section described in the gov't notes as perfect, but which is found to be wide by two hundred feet. According to our survey a considerable trespass has been made on the West Side Co., and to make assurance doubly sure we are going around the section again, running the line by observation on the North Star ...

By mid-August when the survey work had been completed, Edmund and his co-worker Con began their return to Tuolomne on foot. In his journal, Edmund described their journey:

Wednesday Aug 16, 1911

On Sunday last Con recovered from his chill and fever so as to be able again to take to the trail. From Tilltill, elevation 5,600, we dropped into Hetch Hetchy, 3,600.[4] The trail was very stony and six miles long ... In Hetch Hetchy the Tuolomne is a sluggish stream giving no hint of its fearful rapids just above and just below this point. We were much impressed by a waterfall

---

[4] The days of Hetch Hetchy's pristine beauty were numbered, unbeknownst to Edmund. Two years after his journal entry, following Congressional meetings in Washington, D.C., authorization was given to the City of San Francisco to proceed with plans to flood the valley and create an enormous reservoir to provide additional water for an increasing number of San Francisco residents. Strong objections raised then by John Muir and members of the Sierra Club were overruled, and in 1923 the entire Hetch Hetchy Valley disappeared from sight, submerged under three hundred feet of water.

that tumbled perhaps seven hundred feet from the cliff. The stream was of considerable size and we judged it to be the outlet of Lake Vernon … On Monday Con had a chill, but recovered sufficiently to travel a few miles in the afternoon. We camped on the Big Oak Flat Road on the Second Stream beyond the South Fork … On Tuesday we stumbled on our first Sequoia in the Tuolomne grove. It looked much like a cedar, was two hundred feet high and about eighteen feet thick at the butt. We gazed long in admiration of this forest giant.

Another journal entry detailed the beauties of Yosemite:

Aug 23, 1911

Here I am at Mother Bishop's all set for the journey home. Sunday Con and I came into town, dirty, hungry and decidedly tired of walking expeditions. It was a hard, hard tramp but still we think the game was worth the candle. I lost fifteen pounds. We averaged 20 miles a day and on one day went more than 30. The Yosemite is a wonderful valley; first it is a very steep canyon, the deepest I ever saw. In the bottom are fine meadows. But the waterfalls are what make Yosemite unique.

The Bridal Veil is a cloud mist at the foot of its 940 foot drop, blown hither and thither by the breeze and lightened into flashing rainbows by the sunshine. Yosemite is the highest falls, coming from the top of the canyon in two levels. The Illilouette and Vernal are not to be compared with the giant Nevada Falls. The latter, I think, are the finest sight in the whole region, the most wonderful phenomenon I ever did see. The Merced River drops 605 feet. The water is so shining white, the volume so majestic and the roar so deafening that one gazes in awe and wonder and delight …

In early September 1911 after bidding goodbye to Mr. Joyce, George Kennedy, and his friends at West Side, Edmund began his homeward journey. After a brief visit with his brother Will in Portland, he went on to Vancouver and travelled eastward on the Canadian Pacific Railway, passing across the wide-open western Canadian provinces. Edmund's train travels westward the year before had revealed to him the enormous size of the American West—it took him thirty-three hours to go from Ashland to Denver, and then it took another sixty-six hours to travel from Denver to Portland.

A variety of jobs during the past year had given him experience and confidence as well. He found he could handle a ten-hour-long day of tedious work and support himself on a paltry wage, with only an occasional bit of help from William. He learned to get along with a variety of co-workers, the likeable ones as well as the misfits, drifters, and chronic alcoholics. He had been down to his last nickel more than once. Nowhere in his journal are there traces of a "poor me" attitude.

During those summer months of 1911, Edmund had slept in a tent near the sublime setting of Yosemite National Park. Often the surveyors caught fish in nearby streams and cooked them over a fire for supper. Dr. Murphy would have approved of the outdoor arrangement.

In the course of carrying out his surveying assignments, Edmund had also hiked an untold number of miles. By then his cough was gone, his face was sunburned and his hands callused. He had gained weight, muscle, and self-confidence. And on September 20, after the long journey across Canada, when his train finally pulled into the Ashland station, Edmund could see William, Catherine, and Isabel from the window, standing together on the platform waving and smiling. He was overjoyed to reach home at last, and grateful to possess what he had gone to such great lengths to seek—the inestimable gift of good health.

After visiting with his family, Edmund returned to his studies at the University of Wisconsin. Two years later, in June 1913, he graduated with high honors and a Phi Beta Kappa key.

Unfolding the Letters: Edmund to Dorothy
July–December 1916

It is the pen that dreams …

—Gaston Bachelard, *The Poetics of Reverie*

After graduating from law school in June 1916, Edmund lived at home for the remainder of the year while he worked in William's office, learning from an experienced mentor how to practice law in a small town.

One of his chief delights was exchanging letters with Dorothy every other week or so. But since they had been in each other's company only a few brief times, he knew it would have been out of order for him to express sentiments of affection.

In September, feeling blue when his recollection of their conversations suddenly took on a dream-like quality, he wrote that he wondered if their meeting had actually taken place: "Sometimes I think you are unreal, only a poetic fancy, that I never saw you in the flesh and that I will never see you again." To "scatter the goblins," as he put it, he asked for a picture.

But even if Dorothy responded to his request and sent a photograph, Edmund's dilemma would continue. How would she know that he cared for her if he was not free to mention his feelings?

He continued on, reporting bits and pieces of his daily life in Ashland, and often made references to his visit in Montgomery, to Marion Rushton, and to the brief times he and Dorothy had spent together.

William F. Shea
Attorney of Law
August 14, 1916
Ashland, Wisconsin

Dear Dorothy:

This is but a line from the front to assure you that all is well and to inquire as to yourself. Your last letter came while I was away in the woods. Four of the boys including my older brother and two friends of the family, and my young Wellesley sister whom I told you of spent several days canoeing and fishing up the shore of the lake. We loafed and fished a good deal and paddled about sixty miles, doing our own cooking and sleeping under the sky, only using the tent when the weather threatened. Do you like camping? You ought to, I should think. At least you would if you gave it a fair trial. Someday I hope to see you in these parts.

How are you liking *Tom Jones*? It is a brisk sort of intellectual diet, I am told, but no doubt your physician prescribed it with knowledge of his case and his skill in such matters is well known.

I have been reading *The Virginians*. Thackeray is my favorite. You must like him too, and you will sooner or later.

What has the Corporation been doing? That man Rushton doesn't write to me and that leaves a double burden on you.

And about that fortune-teller. That is what I am most curious about. Please give me a full and faithful description.

Tomorrow I argue my first case.

Please don't wait very long.

Yours,
Edmund

Ashland
October 12, 1916

Dear Dorothy:

Your letter was the very breath of your personality, and I enjoyed it accordingly. Why in the world have I waited a whole week to beg you for another? Please do not adopt a week as the standard waiting period. It would be perfectly conventional and although I have no equity to ask you to cut it down this time, I pray that you will.

Does it ever strike you as extraordinary that such random persons as you and I are acquainted — that our paths ever crossed? Are you a fatalist or do you think that events are haphazard? I never have devoted much time to the problem but it does seem strange that things worked out in the way they did. Those days — and nights — and afternoons in Montgomery were so brief and sometimes I think you are unreal — only a poetic fancy, that I never saw you in the flesh and that I never will see you again. At such times your letters are a potent argument to scatter these little Christian Science goblins. Your picture will be a great help too in keeping you on the earth. It is very kind of you to promise me one and I hope that its arrival is not far distant.

Please write.

Yours,
Edmund

Ashland Wisconsin
October 14, 1916

Dear Dorothy:

This is in the nature of a codicil to what I wrote a few days ago. I may have overstated the point about being skeptical at times of your reality but there is no fault in my memory. I can see you exactly as you were on every occasion I saw you from the first time when it was necessary to peer under that broad diaphanous hat and the time next when you had on something of pale orange and a little halo to match with a streamer attached, to the last time when you had on white shoes and all. And really your existence is as real as anything in the world. But of course there have always been people who say that the world isn't real and perhaps they are right, but I think they are wrong especially when I see your eyes — and I often do.

I forgot to tell you about a certain little message from your sister Elisabeth sent me by Mary Rushton.[5] I am sure you will appreciate it. Miss Elisabeth requested that I please not write things to Dorothy that she could not understand! It takes me back to the years when I used to keep right up to date on all of my older brother's pink letter correspondence, when he was a safe distance away from the private depository. But who would think it of that angelic child?

I haven't been within range of a photographer for a long time. But if Dorothy wants pictures they shall be had — i.e., one. You are not being threatened with a plurality.

This seems to be the end of the codicil, but there is no assurance that it is the last.

Goodnight Soul of the Corporation,
Edmund

By the time Edmund wrote to Dorothy in late December 1916, he had finally found a way to begin to express what he longed to say. He would lead into the subject of his feelings indirectly by telling a story. In fact, he used materials from two different source narratives and wove them into a new tale in which he was the protagonist in disguise. In each story he chose, a young man falls in love instantly with a young woman. Edmund had already mentioned one source in the first letter he wrote to Dorothy. He told her then about reading "The Agony Column" in the copy of the *Saturday Evening Post* he found on the train when he left Montgomery in July.

To refresh: In that story, Geoffrey West, a young American playwright, sees a young woman walk into the hotel breakfast room where he is sitting and falls fast in love with her. Unable to introduce himself directly, he writes her a note asking if they can meet. She replies by inviting him to write seven letters, one each day. Then she will decide if he is worthy to make her acquaintance.

Geoffrey dreams up a number of cliff-hanging episodes and fits them into six letters. By the time he sends the seventh, the young woman with violet eyes has fallen in love with the dashing youth in the letters.

Through reference to a second story in his letter of December 1916, what Edmund hopes to communicate indirectly is his commitment to inner values. *Men of Iron*, the novel he was gripped by at fourteen, continued to inspire him. He found a lifelong role model in its main character, the young knight Myles Falworthy. In 1916, eleven years after reading the book, Edmund still aspires to be like Myles and live as an inner-directed, single-hearted knight. But it is not just knightly virtues Edmund desires to emulate. In the novel, Myles falls in love

---

[5] Mary, Marion Rushton's youngest sister, was fourteen years old in 1916, the same age as Dorothy's younger sister Elisabeth Thigpen. Mary and Elisabeth were friends and classmates and sometimes yielded to an uncontrollable desire to read personal correspondence written to their older siblings. From now on Elisabeth will be referred to in Dorothy's and Edmund's letters as the Angelic Child.

with Lady Alice, a young woman he meets by chance. After enduring a long separation, Myles and Lady Alice reconnect and marry at the end of the book.

The story Edmund tells Dorothy weaves the two narratives into one, bringing the tale of the medieval knight together with the story of the smitten playwright:

A young knight desires to make the acquaintance of a lady who lives in a distant land. She invites him to complete several tasks and then she directs him to write seven letters. Edmund continues, with astonishing confidence:

> . . . the knight never fails to fulfill the test to the letter, and generally throws in a dragon or two for good measure. And when the beautiful lady said, "Seven letters shalt thou write," the youth was given power to write such letters as never he writ before with results satisfactory to all concerned.

At the close of his late December 1916 letter, Edmund wishes Dorothy "all blessings at this season and during the coming year." His mood is upbeat and confident. As long as Dorothy continues to answer his letters, he believes there is hope. If the words in the story can touch the heart of the lady he is writing to, he believes, she will perceive his real identity and fall in love.

"It is the pen that dreams."

14

Edmund in Ashland
Winter 1917

My goodly pen has got lost and I am using a miserable scratcher
of my sister's. Imagine going through life with such a pen!
—Edmund Shea, letter, February 1, 1917

Heavy snow fell in Ashland the last week of 1916 and on Christmas
morning when Edmund looked out of his bedroom window,
the beauty of every branch coated with fresh white evoked a vivid
memory.

He was ten years old on that long ago day in 1902 when he raced
downstairs and caught sight of his heart's desire. On the far side
of the balsam fir stood his own shiny Flexible Flyer. Never again
would he borrow his sisters' dilapidated sleds with rusty runners;
the thought of flying down the snow-packed hills on his own Pegasus
filled his heart with joy.

He was home for Christmas for the first time in three years, and
enjoying the company of the three sisters who returned home for
the holiday made the celebration a splendid one. But by New Year's
Day, Louise, Catherine, and Edith had departed, and the house on
Front Street settled back into its quiet rhythm.

On the bitter cold evenings of January, after Isabel had gone upstairs to finish her high school homework, Edmund and his parents
gathered around the warmth of the living room fireplace. Nora picked

up her knitting and Edmund and William opened another long conversation, often exchanging opinions about the latest war news.

In recent months, German U-boats had sunk a number of British merchant ships in attempts by the German navy to prevent food supplies from reaching England. On February 1 the situation worsened when Germany announced the beginning of a new policy of unrestricted submarine warfare. President Woodrow Wilson responded quickly by severing diplomatic relations with Germany.

Wilson had favored a position of American neutrality. But by the winter of 1917, he realized he was powerless to prevent the inevitable. The United States was moving progressively closer to the destructive horror of war.

~ ~ ~

One evening in early February, Edmund asked William about his grandparents, Patrick and Eliza Shea, and why they left their homeland in Ireland.

They had no choice, William said. The devastating potato blight that ruined crops in the mid-1840s led to the deaths of over one million Irish farmers and their families. Another million fled to America or Canada. His father and mother were among the fortunate ones.

The blight, caused by an airborne fungus called *Phytopthora infestans*, had a terrifying power to reduce potatoes to inedible mush, both the harvested crops and the potatoes still growing in the ground. The mid-1840s were terrible years.

The Irish had also been suffering for almost two centuries under English oppression. Under the harsh Penal Code laws that went into effect in the late 1600s, Irish farmers were not allowed to own land, establish schools, or worship in Catholic churches. Former Irish landowners were obligated to become tenant farmers to British landlords, many of whom lived in England and had little concern either for the welfare of their tenants, or for the appalling fact that many Irish families, trying to subsist on a diet of milk and potatoes, simply starved to death. In Edmund Burke's scathing words, the Penal Laws were "a machine of wise and elaborate contrivance, as well-fitted for the oppression, impoverishment and degradation of a people, and the debasement in them of human nature itself, as ever proceeded from the perverted ingenuity of man."

Patrick Shea and Eliza Meagher, both from County Tipperary, were among the lucky emigrants who survived a six-week voyage across the Atlantic. The crowded, masted boats were called "coffin ships" because so many passengers died of typhus or cholera or dysentery before they reached their port of destination.

Patrick, born in 1820, and Eliza, born eight years later, met in Barnardston, Massachusetts, in 1849. They married there in January 1850.

Attracted by news that unskilled workers were needed to build new sections of the Vermont Railway, the newlyweds moved across the Massachusetts border into southern Vermont. Patrick found a job in Brattleboro as an unskilled railroad laborer, and he and Eliza moved into the Irish settlement nearby, a collection of cabins hastily put together in the 1840s to accommodate the rapid influx of Irish immigrant families. The dwellings were flimsy and carefully set apart from the town of Brattleboro by proud Yankee settlers, determined to preserve the Protestant character of their community.

In October 1850, Eliza gave birth to her first child, a daughter named Mary. A year and a half later, in early April 1852, William Francis Shea came into the world. By the late 1850s, Patrick and Eliza had four children. Encouraged by favorable reports from Patrick and Bridget McGowan, friends who had recently left the Brattleboro Irish community, the Sheas moved westward to Brookfield, Wisconsin, where they lived next door to the McGowans. Two years later both families moved north to Kewaunee, a little fishing and lumber town on the shore of Lake Michigan, one hundred miles north of Milwaukee.

In the 1860s, Kewaunee was still frontier country. Large stands of white pine and spruce as well as tall oaks and maples stood untouched and wildlife flourished — bear, deer, beaver, fox, badger, as well as pheasant, ducks, geese, and songbirds. Flocks of migrating passenger pigeons filled the sky each spring and fall.

Many of the settlers of Kewaunee were immigrants from Ireland, Bohemia, and Germany. They were grateful to own a piece of land and they worked together to build a new community on the edge of civilization.

By 1863 William, his older sister Mary, and his younger brother Richard were old enough to walk to the one-room school in the center of town. A potbellied stove provided warmth in the winter while one energetic young schoolteacher worked hard to keep the attention of children whose ages ranged from six to thirteen. She also relied on the well-designed McGuffey Readers, excellent textbooks to stimulate learning. Children read stories aloud and then formed their own responses to her spontaneous questions. In addition to learning the fundamentals of math and spelling, children memorized the proverbs of Ben Franklin and internalized their practical wisdom. In the process, they learned to become optimistic and resourceful young pioneers themselves.

William turned eleven in April 1863. He loved school and enjoyed the exhilaration that comes from learning through the written word. But that was when his career as a schoolboy came to an abrupt halt.

Patrick and Eliza had six children, and without enough money to feed and clothe them, they were obliged to send William to work in the local shingle mill. Three years later, at age fourteen, William said goodbye to his family and began a job at a nearby sawmill. In Suamico, Wisconsin, he moved into a boarding house with twenty other mill workers.

Lumber mill laborers in rural Wisconsin in the 1860s and 1870s endured an exhausting six-day week of twelve-hour days. Often their jobs required them to stand in close proximity to fast-moving blades or sharp saws. No child labor laws existed. Nor was there any workman's compensation for gruesome accidents that sometimes involved the loss of fingers or a hand, or even worse, caused sudden death.

William spent seven years working in lumber mills under conditions burdensome enough to dull the curiosity and imagination of a young boy. Yet when he emerged in 1870, what burned within him was a desire to read and learn. He was eighteen then, when he found a part-time job teaching in a high school near Kewaunee. Soon he combined teaching responsibilities with taking sporadic courses at the State Normal School.

A few years later, a chance conversation with young Kewaunee attorney William Timlin had far-reaching consequences. When Mr. Timlin learned of William's aspiration to become a lawyer, he offered encouragement and gave William access to his own private library — law books as well as classics in Greek and Roman philosophy, and English and American history and literature. With the gift of this astonishing resource, William devoted all of his spare time during the next several years to reading and assimilating all the knowledge he could. In 1878 he passed the Wisconsin bar exams.[6]

A few years prior to taking the bar exams, William's life changed in a dramatic way. He met Nora Madden, a girl of seventeen who lived in a log cabin in the nearby town of Clay Banks, Wisconsin. Nora's father was a farmer, and William and Nora met at a husking bee, an annual autumn festival held in many American farm communities to

---

[6] While I was writing this chapter, I called the Wisconsin Historical Society, hoping to learn more about William Timlin. The archivist I spoke to sent me a detailed obituary, adding that Judge Timlin served as a Wisconsin Supreme Court Justice from 1907 to 1916. After finding his portrait online, I studied his face, taking in his white hair and mustache and his expression of calm benevolence. I regretted having no way to thank him for his act of kindness, which changed the entire course of my grandfather's life.

celebrate the harvesting of crops. Husking bees had ancient roots in many European countries, including Ireland, England, and Scotland. They often took place in September, on an evening when the moon was full, and in Clay Banks, fiddle music, dancing, and a potluck dinner followed the communal effort to husk large quantities of corn.

After corresponding with Nora for two years, William put on his best suit and high-topped shoes and walked to Clay Banks, twenty miles north of Kewaunee. Though written evidence has vanished, his letters were clearly persuasive, for Nora accepted William's proposal on the spot.

~ ~ ~

Almost forty years later, William's son also relied on letters to keep the woman he courted up to date on matters in his life. As the new year of 1917 began, Edmund wrote to Dorothy from Ashland.

January 2, 1917
Ashland, Wisconsin

Dear S.C.:[7]

... It was so good of you to write me from Montgomery. Your letter made Christmas and the days following brighter. I didn't dream of getting any such consideration. Your going home seemed to mean the eclipse of your dealings with remote corners of the planet, and although I wished you all the happiness possible, I couldn't take a friendly view of what was snatching you away — that is the social whirl and particularly the masculine elements thereof. Having decided on ten days of oblivion without in the least being resigned to the fate, you may imagine the effect of your letter. And your later one, which just came, makes me ashamed of not having told you before and thanked you ...

---

[7] Soul of the Corporation.

... Christmas at home seemed mighty good after three years away. Most of the family was here and that means a small sized regiment and it seemed like old times to have the house full of company and ourselves with the fragrant *Weihnachtsbaum* radiating its Christmas atmosphere. A few of my friends are here but only a few, for the rest are married and scattered far and wide — it is amazing how fast Father Time brings around his changes.

There is abundant snow & cold weather, below zero some nights and skating on the bay is good. So one manages to enjoy life and his fellow beings even in Ashland, but many a time have I wished that the directors could get together and further corporate interests. Six months since the last session and the Great Seal will be as forlorn as the musket & drum of little boy blue ...

In the Corporation,
Edmund

Your Christmas greeting stands out distinctively from the mass of others in which it rests. It makes me think of you.

EBS

~ ~ ~

While the days of February 1917 continued to pass, and President Wilson anguished over the threatening prospect of the United States' involvement in the war, Edmund was caught in the midst of his own private torment.

For the last eight months he and Dorothy had been exchanging letters on a pen-pal basis every week or two. But in early February her letters, often bearing the return address of "Box 12, Inman Hall, Agnes Scott College, Decatur, Georgia," suddenly stopped arriving. Nothing Dorothy had said indicated that anything was amiss, and Edmund was left in the dark, perplexed and worried about the silence.

When he thought back to the four times they had been together, and the one in-depth conversation they had the evening they met, he still recalled the extraordinary rapport he felt with her, a closeness he hoped she felt, too. That was what had led him to give her his Phi Beta Kappa key to keep for his remaining week in Montgomery — to remind her to live up to the ideals she believed in. The key was also a way to formalize her membership in the Corporation.

Though the philosophic questions the Corporation examined — such as "how does one lead a good life?" — didn't come up directly in the letters, they were questions he cared about and he sensed she did, too. And even if the daunting distance standing between Wisconsin and Alabama made a meeting impossible anytime soon, he still relished the chance to stay in touch with Dorothy, for he already hoped their conversations would never come to an end.

In the last week of February, Edmund gathered his nerve and wrote her a letter, expressing his concern. He wondered if she had taken ill, or if she had decided to bring an end to their correspondence. Then he signed the letter and took it to the Ashland post office, bracing himself for the possibility that he might never hear from her again.

Ashland, Wisconsin
February 26, 1917

Dear Dorothy:

I ought not to write to you tonight. The weather is gloomy and gets into one's bones. I have been on the verge of some kind of ailment for the past few days, spending many pleasant moments speculating on just what kind of a visitation is at hand. Everybody has gone off to bed leaving the war news and the fire to my undisputed possession. It makes me savage to read of the harvest gathered by these miserable German sea-monsters.[8] So you see how unfavorable are the circumstances for a decent letter. Then why don't I wait for an apple pie mood?

Because I am anxious to find out what in the world is wrong. It is at least a month since you have written me a word. I have done more watchful waiting for mail than in my whole life together. Of course it is quite true that there is no law obliging you to cast away letters on a stray from another world who wandered across your path. Probably it is presumption that makes me complain of your silence when I ought to feel flattered and grateful for the notice you paid me. Perhaps so, but I don't feel very humble. If you are done with me, it is simply up to me to live down the disappointment. I don't change the impression of you that I got in the beginning. You have a spark of something that is rare, just what it is I can't tell, but you are capable of things that ordinary humans don't dream of. It is not discreet to talk to you that way, but it is the very thing uppermost in my mind.

I thought you were a little bit interested in me and the idea of knowing you was very appealing but you must have changed during the last half year. I am sorry. There is one ray of hope that I see. After all, my imagination may possibly have created the situation and you may have been sick or preternaturally busy. That is possible, and mail has been known to go astray. Think of the vast comfort in this last reflection! The simple truth is that you have me at sea, out of sight of land, and I pray you to break the spell. That is not much to ask. If you say so I will never write to you again, but please don't leave me groping about in uncertainty.

Yours,
Edmund

---

[8] Edmund refers to the increasing number of torpedo attacks German submarines made on American and British ships while they crossed the Atlantic in the winter months of 1917.

In early March, several days after sending his letter, Edmund was overjoyed to receive a reply. He found a letter waiting on the table near the front door when he came home from William's office. He carried it upstairs to his third floor bedroom and sat down on his bed. Then he took a deep breath, opened the envelope, and began reading. To his immense relief, nothing Dorothy said indicated that anything was amiss, and their correspondence resumed its usual form and content—sharing bits and pieces of their daily lives.

March 13, 1917

Dear Dorothy:

This is as wild a night as you could wish for. If you remember how the rain fell in Alabama last July and if you imagine that rain is snow driven by a gale from the north that keeps sweeping up the snow already fallen and driving it along in clouds that make the street lights dim blurs in the mist, you will have a picture of this country as it now looks. When you plough through the drifts and consider the snowplow of the traction company laboriously creeping along the streetcar tracks, the works of man seem puny indeed. The feeling you have in a blizzard is like that you have on the top of a deep canyon when you look gingerly at the bottom of the pit.

However this isn't a Burton Holmes travelogue. I want your sage advice on a weighty question. Perhaps the war will come and the question will not need to be decided, but perhaps, too, the British fleet will fight our fight for us and it is well to be ready for either event. The weighty question is where shall a person practice law? My contract in this office is for a year ending next July. Of course I can stay and inherit the business with perhaps some prestige because it is by far the best practice in town or in any of the neighboring counties and lawyers never starve in small towns. There are fifteen thousand white people here and one Negro. The prospect is one of somewhat congenial surroundings, a fair income and certain — and that is all. It is not hard to get to the top, but the top isn't far from the bottom. On the other hand the place for good lawyers is the city — fame and fortune are there but poor lawyers are bound to starve there all their lives and even many a good man gets under the wheel. It amounts to this: in the small place the odds are small and the stakes small, in the city the odds and stakes are large. There is the gamble and the question is which game to sit in. I have been thinking about it all winter without reaching any conclusion. Sometimes the first place in the Iberian village seems enough and at other times the hand beckons towards Rome. Please take a few moments from the hours dedicated to the *Agonistic*[9] and tell me your ideas. Perhaps it wouldn't be a dead loss to the estimable weekly. You might publish something under some such title as "Letters from a Lay Lady to the Bar" or "Talks to Young Lawyers on Timely Topics."

Please don't succumb to the measles.

Yours,
Edmund

---

[9] The *Agonistic* was the Agnes Scott student newspaper. Dorothy was one of its editors.

Easter Holidays in Montgomery
April 1917

How you get there is where
you'll arrive.
—Philip Booth, "Heading Out"

E aster fell on April 8 in 1917, and when the college holiday began
the Wednesday before, Dorothy packed a suitcase and took
the train from Atlanta to Montgomery. In early April, the flowering
beauty of wild pear and redbud still lingered in Alabama, a gift
Dorothy looked forward to appreciating during her week at home,
along with a respite from studies, time to visit with friends, and
the peace and quiet of her own bedroom.

What greeted her when she walked into the pillared house was
a profusion of Easter flowers. Pots of white narcissus, tall Easter
lilies, bright tulips, and lavender hyacinths were banked together
in front of the white marble fireplace, all of them gifts from Dr.
Charlie's grateful patients. And through the wide door into the
dining room she could see a collection of delectable looking cakes —
yellow sponge sprinkled with powdered sugar and several frosted
chocolate layer cakes standing on a table in the far corner, more
Easter presents for Dr. Charlie.

That evening after dinner, when Elisabeth and young Charles
had gone upstairs, Dorothy and her parents gathered in the library.

Charles lit a fire and Daisy related details about the recent engagement party given for Maude and Bethune, friends of Dorothy's since childhood.

Then Daisy handed Dorothy a section of the *Montgomery Advertiser* she had saved, and when Dorothy unfolded it, her eye fell on Tom Owen's name in a headline. It was on the society page, and she read on, learning details about his marriage to Mabel Hays. The wedding had taken place in a church in San Antonio, Texas, on March 17 — a little over two weeks earlier. Lieutenant Owen was currently stationed near San Antonio with General Pershing's army unit.

As the news sank in, Dorothy felt nothing but shock followed by anger and hurt that Tom had not even cared enough to send her a note about his wedding plans. Daisy murmured and Charles was silent and Dorothy had no desire to say anything.

She had been aware of their doubts about him from the beginning, back to the time of her high school days when Tom was a freshman at the University of Alabama. Daisy was careful not to criticize him though she once commented that he was entirely too brash and presuming. And Dorothy knew, without being told, how her father detested the smell of tobacco that lingered in the parlor after she and Tom left to go out for the evening. Of course she herself had reservations about him, about his lack of integrity. That was what led her to break up with him during the Christmas holidays last winter.

But last June when Tom had reappeared, looking splendid in his military uniform, she consented to see him again. Everyone in Montgomery agreed that he looked as handsome as a hero, and that she and Tom made a beautiful pair.

That was the trouble, she thought, caring too much about what other people thought. She had been swept off her feet by his charm and then influenced by her vain desire to listen to him tell her that she was more beautiful and glamorous than anyone else. But the truth was she never could be happy if she couldn't trust him. After Tom had shown her a letter from his new girlfriend Dell and she told him she could no longer see him, Tom insisted on having the last word. He said he would come back when Dell no longer loved him.

While Dorothy sat on the green sofa in the library absorbed in thought, still holding the newspaper in her hand, with her parents nearby, and while the clock ticked on the mantel and no one said a word, she began to feel an overwhelming sense of relief that Tom was out of her life for good.

Later that evening when she went upstairs to her room, Dorothy propped pillows against the headboard and made herself comfortable. How many nights she had slept in this room, as far back as her memory went. And how often she had sat here, writing down glimpses of her life in memory books, or composing letters to Tom, or more recently, making entries in her diary last summer.

She remembered the afternoon last July when she and Virginia went to see Leota, the fortune-teller, in her gypsy wagon. Leota had told Dorothy then that she would fall in love and marry someone her parents disapproved of. But Tom was already married to Mabel, so now their worries were over, she thought, feeling a wave of relief all over again.

While Tom's new life with Mabel had already begun, she had trouble imagining what her own future looked like. Parental discussions on the subject had not taken place, yet she knew expectations existed. The assumption was that like other young women in her circle, she would fall in love, marry, and settle down in a nearby town, or even better, continue to live in Montgomery. Then her parents could easily participate in the lives of their grandchildren.

Based on the examples already set by young women she knew in Montgomery, an eligible suitor would be a Protestant who came from "good people," forebears who possessed character and respectability.

Preferably, he would come from old money and would manage financial matters capably.

But what was the use of such speculation? She got up and unpacked her suitcase and put away her clothes. Then she slipped into bed, grateful to be home again in a place where she felt secure.

Edmund Joins the Army
April 1917

It is exactly a year ago that I was in Montgomery!
— Edmund Shea, letter, July 2, 1917

On Friday, April 6, 1917, morning headlines shouted across the front pages of the Ashland paper:

UNITED STATES DECLARES WAR ON GERMANY!!

Americans who favored a position of neutrality greeted the news with reluctance. But reading about the declaration had an immediate, galvanizing effect on Edmund.

That evening after dinner, he and William set out for their customary walk along Front Street, a route that paralleled the shore of Lake Superior. Edmund told his father that he had already decided to enlist in the Officers' Reserve.

William gave a laconic response: "It is right," he said, confirming their shared conviction that when action is called for, one steps forward to do one's duty without hesitation or complaint.

William was sixty-five. And though a forty-year age difference stood between them, they enjoyed a closeness more often found between congenial brothers. Still, one wonders what ambivalent feelings ran through the heart of the white-haired parent. Neither spoke during the remainder of their walk.

On Monday, the day after Easter, Edmund boarded the train for Chicago. After finding his way to Fort Sheridan, he passed the physical and signed up for a training program beginning in early May.

Edmund's letters relate details about his adjustment to a Spartan life in the military. Marching drills, vigorous exercises, and instruction classes about the tactics of field artillery took up the majority of the day. He also took his turn cleaning the barracks and became adept at taking apart and reassembling his rifle.

In the spring of 1917, the United States was unprepared to wage a war. Individual states had working National Guard units, but the number of full-time soldiers stood at approximately a hundred thousand men. The need to quickly train many more thousands of officers and men confronted military leaders with daunting, urgent challenges.

When Dorothy learned from Edmund that he had enlisted, she wrote to ask what would befall the Corporation. By then, she had heard that both Marion Rushton and Tommy Sanders were considering enlisting in the reserves.

April 26, 1917
Auditorium Hotel
Chicago

Dear Dorothy:

… Your inquiry about what will happen to the Corporation when you are its sole survivor in civil life is easy to answer. The law is familiar with what is termed a "one-man corporation," which you will be presently. All of the various interests and duties will be transferred to you and over the corporate listing you will reign supreme, until the dove of peace returns. Then let us hope that the meeting on the porch at Grandview, which you dreamed of, will be convened with a full membership so that obituary notices can be dispensed with.

I hate to think of giving it up this summer for Fort Sheridan, but there is no choice. The camp here opens the eighth of May and *Deo volente* I shall be an "attendant" as the circular describes the would-be officers. Of course my eyes may be defective or they may discover beriberi or some other little thing to keep me out, but I think I am fit and I expect to be examined today.

Yours,

Edmund

(This will be continued)

1st Battery, 10th Reg.
Fort Sheridan, Ill.
Thursday, June 1917

Dear Dorothy:

Please forgive this long, long pause. This is about the first break in a two-week round of unending activity. I am squad room orderly and my sweeping is done for the morning, so that I can dash off a few of the things waiting to be said to you. It is rainy outside and a bit dismal and your society is a refuge from the unfavorable circumstances of camp.

Your last letter from the mountains certainly breathed the air of the heights.[10] Why should I have suggested Wordsworthian tastes? I didn't appreciate the actual conditions and besides I believe that you belong rather in the Byronic school of outdoor enthusiasts. Mountains are also a delight to me and I know how you felt. There is much to be said for the sunset in the hills but do you think it is in the same class with a sunrise that

---

[10] Dorothy was spending a week in the Blue Ridge Mountains where Agnes Scott's YWCA chapter owned a cabin. A small group of ASC students were chosen each June to travel to North Carolina with a faculty member. They enjoyed the peace and beauty of the mountains and then, before leaving, they reaffirmed their intention to live lives of Christian service.

gradually spreads upwards from the ridges and down into the blue canyons driving away the mists and filling the world with pink? You probably stayed up so late discussing weighty problems and otherwise with the other girls that the sunrises escaped observation, but please let me recommend them.

I am highly impressed by your suggestion of a Corporation party in those hills when the war is over and we all come marching home from Berlin and Munich. It will be something to spur us on to fight hard and end it quickly.

Isn't it strange how one's ideas on war change and grow as time passes. Two months ago I had no enthusiasm for going across the Atlantic to kill Huns. I felt much like the little band that used to sail off to Crete each spring to provide nourishment for the Minotaur, and couldn't help a certain feeling of lingering regret for the peaceful associations and prospects of my civil existence. Perhaps it is the over-confidence of the amateur, perhaps a reversion to barbaric tendencies and perhaps a certain perspective of the noble object in view, but I have cut loose from the past and embarked on the crusade for good and all. This morning's paper told of our soldiers landing in France. It is a bit thrilling, don't you think so? Winter seems a long time for the rest of us to wait, but it will probably take that long to get us into form. I wish we could sail tomorrow.

I am glad Marion had a good word to say for his ex-roommate. He certainly knows enough of the facts to make or ruin me.

There is a stack of letters here to be answered so I must break off and continue later.

Please don't discipline me for not being more prompt. I am wonderfully responsive to good treatment.

Yours,

Edmund

1st Battery, 10th Reg.
Fort Sheridan, Ill.
July 2, 1917

Dear S.C.:

Your excellent letter is hereby acknowledged. It crossed one I had sent. Otherwise my conscience, corporately and otherwise, would be smitten more sorely than it is. As for my devotion to the worthy society of which you are the center, doubt me not. I am a most staunch director. And if you give any credence to the lord's opinion regarding his reception when he comes to Ashland twenty years hence — if you do, then please believe that the corporation will be my first thought when the war is over. There will be considerable business to be taken up.

This ought to be the time for our annual meeting. How things have changed. Do you know that it is exactly a year ago that I was in Montgomery! And how it rained, even on the night that your little fête was carried out. Do you remember how you persecuted me at dinner and, which I believe is extraordinary, my arsenal seemed to contain no weapon to turn aside the attack. Doubtless you have forgotten what I am talking about so I won't continue on that tack.

We have a holiday on the fourth and I may have time to add something to this, but this must be said right now: Do you remember any previous discussion about your sending me a picture? Of course you remember. Please do. I have no place to put it up but at least I can see you in my trunk. It would be a great comfort. If your bargaining instinct is overpowering I will contribute one of some my mother had done of me just before I left home.

Goodnight,
Edmund

Edmund had passed the halfway mark in the training program at Fort Sheridan, and remained as full of thoughts of Dorothy as ever. His teasing reference to their misunderstanding at the dinner in Montgomery a year earlier and his renewed request for a photograph show that whether he cast his mind back to reminisce or forward to dream, she was there.

Summer in Montgomery
1917

Who looks outside dreams; who looks inside awakes.

—Carl Gustav Jung

E dmund's early July letter reached Dorothy in Montgomery where she was spending the summer at home. The morning it arrived, she carried it upstairs to her favorite reading place, on her bed with the pillows propped against the headboard.

The discretion of his request for a photograph made her smile. It was not his first, she realized, and she fully intended to send one. The trouble was, she had nothing on hand that was recent. He was five and a half years older, and the only photos she had were ancient, like the ones she gave Wilmer and Billy, chums who were smitten with her years ago when they were all in high school. She'd given one of those to Tom, too.

The thought of Tom triggered memories of a year ago last summer, the only time in her life she could remember feeling tormented. And for months after their goodbye in August, when he left with his army unit for the Texas-Mexico border, she continued to blame him for her lingering unhappiness. He had been disloyal, and she hated him for it, especially when he had the nerve to tell her he loved her more than his new girlfriend Dell.

But hearing the news of Tom's marriage when she was home for Easter in April shocked her into deeper soul-searching. By then she could look back and admit what an infatuated little schoolgirl she had been, postponing a final goodbye to him even after she knew about Dell. Yet her feelings were still unresolved when she returned to college.

Then, late one night toward the end of May, without warning, her thinking shifted. She was lying in her iron cot on the second floor of Inman Hall and a breeze was coming in through the open window. Her roommate, Lucy, was fast asleep. It was while she was staring up at the ceiling that a recognition of the person she longed to become came into focus.

She understood then how misguided her wish had been for Tom to put her on a pedestal and worship her beauty in some moonlit place. She could see that in her heart being Tom's glamor girl was not what she wanted. Staring into the dark, she saw that her own inner torment arose from listening to Tom's shallow version of love when she did not truly love him.

This humbling realization of the vanity of her desires helped her understand on a deeper level something Dr. Gaines had broached the day before. In his weekly chapel talk to the sophomore class, he had brought up the subject of the mysterious relationship that exists between the outer and inner selves — between the public self we reveal to others and the private one that lives hidden in the psyche. It was essential for each of us to become conscious of the way we envision ourselves in our imagination, he said. The thoughts and feelings we entertain and the convictions we hold in our heart actually create the person we become, both the inner and the outer person. "So pay very close attention to the thoughts and feelings you cultivate," he said, "and take responsibility for becoming the kind of person you can look up to. Aim to be a person of goodness. By endeavoring to do so, you will not only find happiness, you will understand your true calling."

Dorothy was thinking about the way his words confirmed her desire to live up to what she believed in. When she closed her eyes and fell asleep, the silence around her felt like a benediction.

~ ~ ~

When the second semester ended at Agnes Scott in early June, Dorothy said goodbye to her friends and returned to Montgomery for the summer.

The afternoon she arrived home, she ran upstairs, eager to reclaim the peace and quiet of her own bedroom after the cramped quarters in the dorm. While unpacking her suitcase and putting away her clothes, she happened to glance over toward her desk and realized they were still there — Tom's letters. She walked across the room, took the packet out of the left drawer, and sat down on the pink chaise.

Untying the ribbon took her back to the way she had once felt, enthralled each time another envelope arrived from the University of Alabama. She was so certain then that she had found her heart's desire while she poured over his breathy sentences with their underlined words and exclamation points that made whatever he said sound effusive. Effusive and false, she thought, as she tore up each letter without reading it.

~ ~ ~

It was Daisy who unwittingly solved her daughter's need for an updated photograph. When August arrived, Dorothy's birthday month, she suddenly realized that ten years had passed since Dorothy's last formal portrait. She was ten years old then, when she sat on a chair wearing a high-necked Victorian dress. It was high time for a new picture, Daisy said, and offered to schedule an appointment with the same photographer on Dexter Avenue.

On August 23, 1917, the day Dorothy turned twenty years old, Daisy and Charles presented her with a platinum diamond and pearl brooch that had belonged to Sarah Bissell, Dorothy's grandmother.

Daisy also passed on another gift, a grey squirrel stole. Graduating from one's teenage years called for a memorable celebration, they reminded her, conscious also of their own genuine relief, which they kept to themselves, that the stormy chapter with Tom had come to an end.

On the evening of the birthday dinner, with Elisabeth and little Charles to round out the family circle, Dorothy was the guest of honor in the candlelit dining room. Patsy served maple mousse on a silver platter for dessert.

~ ~ ~

In early September, on the morning of the appointment with the photographer, Dorothy put on the clothes she had laid out the evening before. First, she fastened the diamond and pearl brooch to a strip of ivory lace on the front of her best dress — ankle-length azure silk with long sleeves. She had always taken creative delight in the realm of clothes, in the variety of styles and colors and the subtle way they communicated something intangible about the person wearing them.

Studying her reflection for a moment in the mirror above the marble-topped bureau, she adjusted her favorite hat, tilting it to the desired angle, enjoying the combination of texture and color — a royal blue velvet crown set off by cream colored ostrich feathers circling its wide brim.

Then, wrapping the fur stole around her shoulders, Dorothy turned to the mirror again to catch a final glimpse, hoping she resembled the mature young woman she was beginning to believe she was becoming.

Edmund's Unexpected Transfer

I did want to see you before going to France ...
— Edmund Shea, letter, September 24, 1917

When Edmund's ROTC program at Fort Sheridan ended in late August 1917, he received a commission as second lieutenant along with a ten-day leave. After visiting his family in Ashland, he travelled to Battle Creek, Michigan, to begin a new training assignment at Camp Custer.

Custer, in the autumn of 1917, was a place teeming with noise and chaos brought on by its enormous expansion. When all the unfinished buildings were ready for use, the base would be home to forty thousand soldiers.

Camp Custer
Battle Creek, Michigan
August 31, 1917

Dear Dorothy:

... We had a good ten days at home. Five of my sisters were home and also various other friends and relatives so that the average at the table — the only place I was able to take count — was ten or twelve. The great drawback was that they all insisted on putting me in the center of the ring, a place I never have cared for. Millions of questions, about everything, some of them intelligent, most of them not. War has no terrors any more. I disposed of my civilian effects, hung up my clothes, destroyed a few tons of papers whose importance has become a thing of the past and put the balance of my worldly property in a steamer trunk and duffel bag and came hither.

I wish you could see the miles of debris, lumber piles, ditches and half completed frame buildings that is known to the world as Camp Custer. There will be forty thousand troops here. At present the human element consists of a few thousand work-men, a regiment of militia and Filipinos on guard duty and a thousand or more of officers. A camp of officers is a curious thing — simply a case of too much familiarity removing the illusions. And what would the world be without illusions.

Many of the boys have their cars, which are extremely conve-nient in a camp that is eight miles from Battle Creek and eigh-teen from Kalamazoo. And many have their wives — recently achieved. I think the spirit of a girl willing to marry a person in such circumstances is splendid. The whole sacrifice is hers if the gamble loses.

September 4, or 4 Sept., as one says in the army, draws on apace. I am all expectation for the daily arrival of the long promised picture.

Be sure to put Lieut. in my address. I am not jealous of the rank, but it makes a great difference in the matter of receiving mail. I might not get it otherwise.

Yours,
Edmund

Though on his arrival Edmund had expected to stay at Custer for three months, before the end of September he had packed his foot-locker and was on a train headed southeast toward North Carolina.

As he explained to Dorothy, when an opportunity to transfer arose out of the blue, he leapt at the chance. Camp Greene, situated on the outskirts of Charlotte, was a mere 250 miles from Atlanta. And Atlanta, he knew, was only a few miles away from the Agnes Scott campus. The very thought of seeing Dorothy again before he sailed for France took precedence over everything else going through his mind.

Charlotte, NC
September 24, 1917

Dear Dorothy:

You see what has happened. I hardly dared hope for such good luck and actually held my breath until the whole thing was run through. It all came about as follows: on Thursday evening last at supper the sergeant major came with orders from the war department for nine lieutenants of the 328th F.A. The order was simply to report here at Camp Greene for service with the least practicable delay. Accordingly we congregated our effects and at 8 the next morning Hunter, of whom you will hear and see more hereafter, and I drove out of Camp Custer with the aforesaid effects piled on the top, back and sides of his roadster. We got here this morning, but we didn't come in the roadster. So did a hundred and seventy other lieutenants from Custer ordered to infantry and machine gun organizations.

Don't you think I am lucky? Of course I had many good friends at Custer and hated to leave the 328th, which I saw emerge from nothingness to six batteries of six or eight hundred men. But I did want to see you before going to France and this seemed the golden opportunity. Hence I waved aside the boys who wanted to transfer here in my place.

As soon as I get my luggage and get squared around I am going to see about the chance of getting to Atlanta — if you approve.

Edmund

Charlotte, NC
Sept 29, 1917
Saturday night

Dear SOC:

The letter that you sent sailing up to Battle Creek just sailed into camp this afternoon. I was then on my way into town and have enjoyed the luxury of a warm bath at the YMCA. It is about time for mess — to be technical — but there is always time to answer an SOS. I suppose our radio communication will be in the Kindred Spirit Code, regarding which I shall need some further instruction. I accept your very kind invitation to join. I hope it is the *rara avis* of a society without dues. When was it formed and what are its articles? As to the other members I do not particularly care, for I am very democratic.

I am going to descend on you at the first opportunity, next weekend if the train schedules will permit. I look forward to it as much as to the journey to France and that is a strong statement. Think how long it is since we organized the corporation, and of the events that the year has brought forth! There is nothing to speed up the blood like a war. Don't you think that in such times as these people live more intensely than in the spacious reign of peace? And I also marvel, to resume the story, that with all of the distractions that have come across your path you still honor me with occasional attention, of the SOS variety and otherwise. It has been different with me, isolated in a small community where I had only a few friends.

The fortune-teller story is most interesting.[11]

I know we will get only fairly started when it will be time to rush back here. We might prepare a list of interrogatories beforehand, and then again we might not. At any rate I will have a good look at you and that is the important thing. If you have changed any I will have this theoretical picture to warn me. I am afraid that picture has been an old man of the sea about your neck. It is your conscience not the Keeper that is the cause.[12]

This evening the 148th is invited to a cabaret-reception and dance given by the Stonewall Jackson chapter of the United Daughters of the Confederacy, if you please. I doubt not that it will be a magnificent spectacle of southern hospitality.

I will consult you again in a few days about coming down there.

Yours,
The Keeper

---

[11] Dorothy has at last told Edmund of Leota's prediction in the summer of 1916 that she would marry a young man her parents would not approve of.

[12] The recent photograph Dorothy had taken in Montgomery had not yet been sent to Edmund, or, the Keeper, a name Dorothy had recently given him.

19

The Failed Rendezvous

Esse Quam Videri
(Be, and do not pretend to be)
— Cicero, "On Friendship"

I n mid-September 1917, the day classes began at Agnes Scott, Dorothy and Lucy were sitting together near the front of the chapel when Dr. Gaines walked in.

How swiftly time passes, he commented, realizing that the young women gathered before him were not freshmen nor even sophomores. Instead, he was addressing students who were about to begin their third year of college. He praised them for developing disciplined habits of study and encouraged them to explore new fields of learning in both the arts and sciences. He also commended them for already completing four out of the eight mandatory courses in Bible study.

Then he encouraged them to look ahead to their remaining time, and to be attentive to the chief reason each of them had come to college: to find her individual vocation, her calling in life. Last, to send them off with inspiring thoughts, he made some remarks about Cicero's essay on friendship, *De Amicitia*.

Most humans like to assume they are virtuous, Cicero said. But don't be misled by flashy first impressions. Someone who merely pretends to be virtuous is a *videri* person. A true friend is one who is authentic and trustworthy, and who does not dissimulate. Such a friend is an *esse* person, Dr. Gaines said, adding that, while observing others one should be especially aware of the person one wants to become oneself. Be genuine! Endeavoring to become an *esse* person is what each human being is called to do with the God-given gift of life, Dr. Gaines said.

~ ~ ~

One afternoon in late September when Dorothy walked down the Inman Hall corridor to the mail cubbies, she found several pieces of mail awaiting her, including a letter with Lieutenant Shea's familiar handwriting on the envelope. But how odd, she thought, noticing the unfamiliar return address. Instead of Battle Creek, Michigan, he had written "Camp Greene, Charlotte, North Carolina."

She opened the letter and read it, and then reread it, trying to assimilate the news. Edmund had transferred to Camp Greene. Not only that, he was also talking about his hope to arrange for an overnight pass so he could come to Atlanta some weekend soon. He wanted to have a brief visit with Dorothy and Marion Rushton.

What he said was not only unexpected, it verged on the impossible. For well over a year since their goodbye in July 1916, she assumed that their paths would never again cross. Geographical distance ruled out the chance, and she accepted it as fact. If that was the way it was, why should she think of Edmund except as a person she enjoyed corresponding with, a friend whom she wouldn't see again?

For months after they began exchanging letters, "Mr. Shea" seemed the appropriate appellation. But the past summer, somehow, she felt she had come to know him better. He had been at Camp Sheridan, and she had begun calling him Edmund, for she considered him a good friend. Then more recently, in the last few weeks, the closeness she felt to him led her to begin calling him "Keeper."

Marion bestowed the name because Edmund's golden key was

the Great Seal in their virtual seventeenth-century corporation. When the King's Great Seal was affixed to a document, signed by the King in the days of the first corporation in England, it guaranteed the authenticity of a document. By extension, a keeper of the Great Seal was a person who embodied genuine virtues. Edmund seemed to qualify as an *esse* person, Dorothy was beginning to realize then, thinking back to Dr. Gaines's remarks. But still, the thought of seeing him face-to-face was something she hadn't adjusted to. He inhabited her imagination rather than her day-to-day life.

That evening she sat down at her desk and replied to his letter, endorsing the idea of planning a rendezvous in Atlanta sometime soon. She said she would be able to get permission to leave campus on a Saturday noon as long as she was back before the ten o'clock curfew that evening.

During the next few weeks, Edmund and Marion exchanged letters, finally agreeing that Saturday, October 20, would be the best day to meet in Atlanta. Marion, who was working in his father's law office in Montgomery, offered to reserve a room at the Piedmont for Edmund and himself.

~ ~ ~

Well ahead of time, Dorothy arranged to get permission from the Dean to get the trolley from Decatur to Atlanta on the twentieth after her Saturday class ended. Marion arrived by train, and he and Dorothy met as planned at Union Station, with time to spare before Edmund's scheduled arrival in the early afternoon.

When the train from Charlotte pulled to a stop, their eyes focused on each passenger that alighted from the passenger cars. But after several minutes of anxious waiting and watching, they heard the Porter call "all aboard." The train cars closed and the engine began to move forward. Still, there was no sign of Edmund. Marion went inside the station to learn what he could — was another train expected from Charlotte later, sometime in the evening?

No, there was not. The next train would arrive midafternoon the next day. Marion and Dorothy looked at one another, aware that something had kept Edmund from coming. But why hadn't he sent a message? The uncertainty was unnerving. They felt worried as well as tremendously let down.

Dorothy kept her crushed feelings to herself, not realizing until then how keenly she had been looking forward to seeing Edmund again, especially once she had learned that his field artillery unit would likely leave for France in the near future.

She thought about her recent inspiration to call him "keeper," because the voice she heard in his letters convinced her he was trustworthy. That was why his failure to show up as promised was such a blow. All she felt that afternoon was keen letdown and disappointment.

Marion's younger sister Rachel was a sophomore at Agnes Scott, and before he and Dorothy left the station, Marion telephoned the Dean's office to explain the situation and request that Rachel come to Atlanta and join them for dinner. Before long Rachel walked into the lobby of the Piedmont, and the three of them kept up their spirits during their time together in the hotel dining room. A bit of pleasure was salvaged from the failed rendezvous.

20

Crossing the Atlantic
Christmas 1917

The separation in space between you and France
is considerable, but theoretically space *non est* when
"kindred spirits" are concerned.

—Edmund Shea, letter, November 3, 1917

E dmund's next letter provided Dorothy with an explanation for what had happened at Camp Greene. On the Saturday morning he expected to leave for Atlanta, all train passes were canceled without explanation. No outgoing telephone calls or telegrams were permitted. The colonel in command of the brigade had received word that orders to proceed to a port of embarkation were imminent.

The orders arrived Monday, October 23, and the next morning Edmund left by train for Camp Mills, New York. What greeted him on Long Island was an unusually early winter, complete with snow. Instead of finding the expected comfort of heated living quarters, officers and men slept in tents on dirt floors. There was no escape from the cold.

~ ~ ~

In Dorothy's reply of October 29, 1917, the reader will hear her speak to Edmund for the first time. By openly expressing her disappointment over the failed meeting in Atlanta, she disregards guidelines handed down to her by postbellum elders. Young women in the

Deep South in Dorothy's day were advised when corresponding with a young man to keep him in the dark concerning her affections. It was one small way for them to assert independence in a male-dominated culture.

But Dorothy shows no interest in keeping Edmund in the dark. She tells him he is a kindred spirit, someone she trusts, feels close to, and cares for. And though the word "love" is not used, it hovers in the air.

By the time she wrote to Edmund in late October, Dorothy was beginning to perceive him in a new light. Though in his most recent letter he did not dwell on his own disappointment over their failure to meet, she sensed that what he regretted most about not coming was his inability to keep his promise. It was true, he had not shown up in Atlanta for their rendezvous. But he hadn't let her down, and she realized then that he never would.

From Dorothy to Edmund

October 29, 1917

Dear Keeper —

... I really cannot tell you how disappointed I was over not seeing you. If you had not been so near it would not have been so perfectly exasperating — which confession brings me to one of the four things which I think I should like to tell you now. It isn't very much except that I like you so. You know the kind of life I had at home and you know the sort of people I'm thrown with. Since I have been in college, I have almost hated it sometimes. Don't think that I am not frivolous and that I don't like good times because I do but when I have only that, it seems so terribly superficial at times and I have missed so not knowing more real people. The men who are my friends for the most part merely like me because I entertain them a little. And so you have stood out against most of the people I know.

Do you know that when I go home in the summers I have to hide everything I've learned in college the winter before! To say the least it does not look like a principle of compensation and it might make me cynical but I don't let it. You see, I seem to have got to know you so very well during the time I have been writing to you and have found out incidentally how worthwhile you are and how much I really like you. I hope you don't mind this; probably I shouldn't be telling you at all considering the fact that I only saw you for such a short time, but you see I have made of you a Kindred Spirit, and therefore you will understand what I mean.

I am wondering seriously if you are smiling through the whole of this. Please don't think I am taking a very tragic view of my existence because I really love it but I hate to think of your going. I may never see you again and in case I don't, I should like you to know how very thankful I am for having known you.

Please write to me often and don't be a ship which passes in the night and only speaks in passing. And you will come back I know, only I wish most positively that you weren't going.

Please remember all the maternal formula stressed corporatively with the added injunction of not developing enough "mad stuff" to get wounded or disabled. The picture will be sent immediately. I do not like it and I do not belong to the iconoclastic party in the case of my own pictures, for I take most terrible ones and I would much prefer your retaining your "fair" impression of me as you call it, but I shall mail it in the morning.

Have you any idea of when you will sail? I'm reading an account of a monastic order in the 9th century and found the most encouraging material: "But the corporation never died." I shall accordingly await you at an early meeting after the war is over.

Remember how the corporate thoughts of a soul are following you so please do not forget her.

Always in the Corporation,
Dorothy

P.S. I am making you a sweater. I suppose you have one already but this one will come in well when you have worn out your present one. I am very deliberate in knitting. D.

From Edmund to Dorothy

Camp Mills, New York
Nov. 3, 1917

Dear Dorothy:

Your letter carried a vast amount of relief and comfort. I had been worrying about the state of the corporation and had considered various means for rehabilitating it as a going concern. The corporate message came just as I was rushing off to the city to procure various and expensive accouterments that even second lieutenants must have for the Hun campaign. After the stores closed I was for settling down at the Yale Club for a quiet evening of telling you about things in general but the man with me, Bates Hunter, one of the best in the world, insisted on histrionic diversion, so we went to see Laurette Taylor in *Out There*: Did you see it here last summer? All evening I kept thinking about you and of the things you said as well as the way you say them and finally I told Bates what manner of person you are and promised him the opportunity of meeting you sometime, after the war!

Here it is Saturday morning. There is no fire in the tent, the dirt floor is wet and frozen and my fingers are a bit stiff from the cold, but otherwise all is well. Nothing happens in camp Saturday morning except inspection, which is finished, and officer's school, which has not yet commenced. The only activity in the vicinity is flying. I can hear their great motors rumbling through the sky and see the flashes of sunlight on the planes far off in the blue. It is very fascinating.

It is hard to write down in black and white, or rather in Waterman's blue, what I think about you. I thought to tell you viva voce just two weeks ago. As you say we may not meet again on earth. That was what I referred to in the wire about changing the place of meeting, although I must admit the reference was somewhat blind. I care for you a great deal, so much that seeing you is the chief thing I look towards. This is the adventure of my life, and beyond it everything is distant and vague, everything except your fair image.

If the God of battles sees fit to let me slip through with the survivors, you may count on having to reckon with me after the Hun is chastised. To know that you really like me a little bit will be a constant comfort. It will make the rigors of a winter campaign easy. Please, please don't change you ideas before I come back. The separation in space between you and France is considerable but theoretically space *non est* when "kindred spirits" are concerned. If writing will do any good, as you incline to think, I will write, write, write. Altho that will be something of a boomerang in furnishing so much evidence for the court. But I will gamble on the chance.

As for leaving here I cannot ethically tell what little I know. They move out constantly and even more silently and unostentatiously than the Arab because they leave their tents standing, and often the lights burning. The passage takes much longer than you would suppose. After we leave, my address will be 146th F.A., 41st Div., American Expeditionary Forces, France. You will be able to tell we have left when the stream of letters stops. Goodbye. I am looking for the picture in today's mail.

The Keeper

The Great Seal is in Ashland with all other civilian properties of the corp.

From Edmund to Dorothy

Camp Mills
17 Nov 1917

Fairest:

I feel like apologizing for being on this side of ocean's stream after heralding my departure so industriously. You must be good enough to call it the fault of the war department. Even my sister Catherine who is taking some work at Columbia and whom I called on each weekend I hesitate to inform that I am still present. However the end is near.

Your picture came in the same mail with your letter and greeted my return from a tour of M.P. duty. I like it. One of the three lieutenants with whom I was then quartered said, "She has a serious look, just as my wife has." (They are all married.) You were not exactly in a mood for climbing apple trees when it was taken, but it was a good mood — an excellent mood.[13]

---

[13] Dorothy told Edmund in an earlier letter about her fondness for climbing a certain tree that stood on the campus of Agnes Scott.

Our colonel once told us to judge a soldier by his eyes. "His uniform is that of every other man in the battery. The eye tells the kind of man he is." And the colonel was quite right. It is the window of the soul. And as one of your friends once told you in a burst of analysis, you have a soul, and a very strong and high soul it is. You have changed a little during the last year. (Please let me use this pencil. My pen is parched and everybody in the regiment is abed.) You have grown up somewhat. Here there must be a certain reservation as I think of your arboreal proclivities. That question must be taken up at another time. The subject under discussion is your picture and incidentally your character. I am very glad to have it on my travels — and my thanks.

… This is a perfectly black night and overhead there is a wild aeroplane sailing around among the stars above camp. It must be wonderful sport. I never thought about night speeding before now.

There are so many things to tell you, and it is long, long after taps and it is freezing cold in the tent. My bunkie, as the Plattsburg Manual prescribes as army slang to describe one's tent mate, is still out someplace and the candle is getting low. Moreover my fingers are stiff.

As for the picture I will do as you say, provided there is an opportunity. One never knows.

Your letters are a delight. May you continue in the cause of Athens. There will be one more letter from here.

Pax Vobiscum —
Edmund

From Edmund to Dorothy

New York
Dec. 1, 1917

Dear Dorothy:

… I wonder every day how much you like me. Some days I am fairly optimistic and some days decidedly not. It is almost too much to ask. And I worry constantly about the myriad of O.R.C. brethren in and about Atlanta.[14] Among them you are bound to meet some splendid men. The one who peregrinated with you as far as Hogansville who couldn't be stirred by the sunset may not have made much headway, though you were not explicit in this respect, but he is only one from a large group. He is Lieut. A and I see the procession behind him, B & C and the ominous crowd of Xs. I hope they all may be speedily sent somewhere else. They are close by you while I shall be thousands of miles thence — living in a ditch and wearing a tin hat: How I envy them!

Dear Dorothy, please tell me that I have a chance of standing first among the men you know, and of winning your heart. It comes hard to write these things. They are poorly expressed, but I am truly in earnest and what I say comes from my soul.

Where your answer will reach me is hard to say. Nor do I care particularly, if only you will say what I pray is true. If only I could talk to you and see your eyes and hear the sound of your voice! This seems so feeble and expressionless — mere paper and ink. Only your kindness can make it mean what I am so anxious to say.

Goodnight, dearest,
Edmund

---

[14] ORC=Officers' Reserve Corps.

Chapter 20

From Dorothy to Edmund

Sunday Afternoon
December 2, 1917

Dear K.S.[15]

Last Sunday I wrote you a very poor excuse for a letter on
the train going home for another wedding which occurred
last Tuesday, but I am afraid you never received it. I gave it
to a questionable looking man to mail for me at a little station
where we stopped for water so that you would get it before
sailing, but I have my doubts about his having done it. It was
a very wild affair so that it made no difference; I wrote it with
the train lurching frantically, and as I told you therein, I hated
to spoil your good disposition.

I had such a gay time at home. I only returned Thursday
or rather Friday at 4 A.M. The wedding was beautiful and I
cannot get the rhythm of a poem by Keats into my head after
the wedding march. All the bridesmaids wore white dresses
trimmed with silver and silver slippers and carried gorgeous
bouquets of pink roses. You may remember meeting the girl
who was married: Lucie Wood. I am sure you met her.

I stayed over Thanksgiving and went to parties and dances
the whole time and consequently am a wreck after losing so
much sleep. Wednesday night there was a dinner and a dance
and I was simply perishing to stay over Thanksgiving night
for the Country Club but my boring conscience wouldn't let
me, so I took the train back at 6 P.M.

... I shall write again soon. I know the long-suffering censor
will come to dread my handwriting if he has as much trouble

---

[15] Kindred Spirit.

reading it as most people do. My roommate who has a brother in France has advised me to cut this short as censors cut all letters out when they are too long. I cannot imagine one without a sense of humor!

Marion Black is here on a visit & sends you her love—

Please write—

For the Corporation,
Dorothy

From Edmund to Dorothy

Camp Merritt
Tenafly, New Jersey
December 12, 1917

Dear Dorothy:

… The other night, when I sent you my confession of faith, it seemed that the 146th was upon the eve of its march towards the center of activities. The order was given to prepare our freight and baggage for shipment. The task of attending to this work for C battery devolved on me and kept me rushing about until our three hundred odd pieces had been properly marked and loaded. We thought it was for ocean shipment. This order to get the impedimenta ready came at noon. By night everything was on the cars except the stoves and breakfast. Reveille was at 4 the next morning, and shortly after daylight we marched out of Camp Mills.

It would impress you to see a regiment, or two or three, in heavy marching order. At the head comes the colonel and staff, the flag carried in its case, then the batteries, the men wearing overcoats and carrying blankets and saddle bags on their backs. The officers all have on their overcoats too and this adds to the going away effect. Nobody says a word and the column tramps along without a sound except the beat of thousands of shoes. When you stop to think of the distance they are going it reminds you of a crusaders army winding across the plain in some old imaginative drawing. We entrained, went to the other end of Long Island, got on a ferry and were taken around Manhattan to Jersey City. Everybody thought we were going to get on the boat, even then. The *Vaterland* was there, painted dull grey, and waiting for troops. It carries thirteen thousand. But instead we got on the train again and came here.

This is nothing more nor less than a permanent embarkation camp — consisting of wooden cantonments, arranged like the national army camp. The barracks are heated by huge coal stoves, and lighted with electricity. These are the height of luxury to those who have been wintering in the summer resort known as Camp Mills. It has been zero weather ever since we left there and one day we had a young blizzard. Perhaps it was the weather that led the War Dept. to move us. They tell us that no regiment stays here less than three nor more than ten days. I have seen several go since we came. This is our sixth day. It looked as though we were going yesterday, but no.

It isn't right to thrust statistics and dry-as-dust facts upon you and I am sorry for having given you so many. The trouble is that I am surrounded by them and live with freight, invoices and embarkation orders. The other evening my good friend Hunter came over to my tent and read Browning until the candles were all burned up. My only contribution was "Ulysses" which I think breathes the spirit of the soldier better than anything I know of. It was a vast relief to hear the poetry. The only book I am carrying besides a tiny *Meditations of Marcus Aurelius* is an old *British Poets of the 19th Century*. Perhaps you have used it as a text. Did you ever see so much concentrated in so small a compass? That is why it is with me. There isn't much time to indulge one's poetic fancy or taste but a few minutes occasionally help to keep one from relapsing too rapidly. Your influence has much the same effect. To read your letters — which I have missed for a long time — and to think of you takes me to a different world — a different plane of civilization from the one I exist in. So you see that you are doing a great deal to keep a fraction of the expeditionary forces in the proper moral state.

Please do not regard me as having gone to another planet and out of your reckoning. France is only across the Atlantic and the war won't last more than a year or two. And time and space are such relative terms. Let's imagine that as far as time and space are concerned you are in college and I in Charlotte and that a weekend descent is about to occur! Possibly that is a poor illustration for my point. But I am so afraid of being considered a past chapter in your life instead of a present one with ascending interest. That is asking for more than ordinary people are capable of. The greatest encouragement I have is the miraculous way that our affairs have reached the pass they now are in. Your memory, your imagination, your confidence in Rushton's opinions are all that I depend on in addition to my feeble efforts with a fountain pen. And when our work is done I will fly back here and plead my cause *ore tenus, coram judice*.[16] Please tell me what you think about the cause.

Good night, fair one. It will be a long time before your letters will catch up with me. It is good to know that you think of the K.S. sometimes. He does a great deal of thinking too and is a great believer in telepathy. God be with you.

Edmund

---

[16] *Ore tenus* — by word of mouth; evidence given orally. *Coram judice* — in the presence of the judge.

Chapter 20

From Edmund to Dorothy

Dec 16, 1917

Dear S o C:

You have so many titles and appellations, some of which you know and some of which you do not, that I hesitate to choose among them. This morning from the time I first awoke I have been thinking about you so hard that you must have known it. This radio system of ours opens up wide possibilities that may bridge over the troublous times that have befallen the Corporation. Hunter with whom I spent the night said he believes in telepathy and his opinion is a great weight in its favor.

I am about to dash off to Columbia to see my sister Catherine and thence back to Tenafly, so this must needs be short.

Did I thank you for making me the excellent sweater?[17] It came in the confusion of getting out of Camp Mills and I may have neglected to tell you how touched I was to be favored by so untold an amount of your handiwork. As a garment it is above criticism and it keeps me warm, but that is the least of its merits. It makes me think of you, and then I consider your goodness in doing the thing for no greater a person than myself, and it encourages me to believe that you care for me to a certain extent, at least. Then I decide to become more worthy of your confidence. So you see the O.D. sweater is filling an important mission as a Corporation symbol ...

---

[17] By December 16, Dorothy's hand-knit wool sweater had reached Edmund. Except for a collection of her letters and the long-awaited photograph, this gift was the only tangible reminder he had of her. He wore the olive drab sweater under his army shirt where it generated warmth and allowed him to envision her as deliciously close.

... I got your Christmas greeting! — the very first to come. The postmaster was too quick for you. The thought impresses me much. For saying those words, "and may we be together," I thank you and add a deep and prolonged "Amen." If God is willing it shall be so.

The embarkation regulations have been changed as to addressing mail abroad. The division is not to appear, nor "France." Just "146th F.A., A.E.F. via New York."

Goodbye dear one,
Edmund

From Dorothy to Edmund

December 17, 1917

Dear Keeper —

The same ironical Fate which did not let you come from Charlotte will see that you have embarked just as this sails into Camp Merritt, but I will take a chance though something tells me that the same Fate could not be so kind as to let me tell you what I want to before it whisks you off to the other side.

Last Sunday I sent you a letter to France, it being the second one to go across in addition to a Christmas message which I sent some weeks ago. I hope this particular letter written last Sunday did not go to the bottom, not because it was a good letter at all but because I told you everything and it took me such ages to tell you. It was written in answer to your confessional one. Mine was also in the nature of a confession — going into great detail, part of which was unnecessary but I wanted you to know everything — how I felt about you and about everything else connected with you. I told you that I cared more than I imagined I could, more than I imagined I could ever care and that I didn't understand it at all—and I told you how I hoped with all my heart that you would come back safely. It was a very long letter but I felt as if I must tell you everything and I tried to be absolutely honest with you and with myself as well as rational and clear-headed about the whole affair. As you say, there is something miraculous about it. I do not understand why you should remember me and care except that I remember you and care and I do want you to come back so. The reason I am scribbling this off in such hot haste tonight when I have such worlds of classes to get up for tomorrow is to let you know, if the Fates are charitable before you sail. I told you in my letter that I know I did not care lightly or quickly and that I did not understand anything about myself and the way I feel about you except that you are very fine—

Good-night, K.S.

Dorothy

P.S. I like for correspondences to be regular. I shall write you Sundays if you like.

2nd P.S. I have been praying for those on the deep the last 10 days or so. It is very disturbing not to know whether you are on land or sea, but I suppose if I pray with all my heart that you be safe, it makes no difference. D.

From Edmund to Dorothy

Camp Merritt, Tenafly N.J.
22 December 1917

Dear Dorothy,

I hope that this will reach you Christmas morning to tell you that I wish you every blessing—on Christmas and on the days that shall follow Christmas.

Tonight came another stroke of evil fortune. One of the battery buglers, a little chap named John Kern, came down with scarlet fever. The consequence is that the battery is quarantined — for two weeks at least and instead of spending Christmas en route to France we shall be confined here. It made all of us feel pretty sick. This boy you would be sorry for. He is so young — about eighteen with pink cheeks and the brightest eyes. At Saturday inspection he never could keep his face straight when the scowling procession of officers came by to look him over, and he generally caused the lieutenants to bite their lips and hurry on. I never dared look at his cherubic face. He is very sick. I wish his mother were here.

The trouble is that these weeks which should be spent training in France are being lost and we shall likely be pushed into the thick of it without any decent preparation — out of pure necessity. They say this is slated as a sacrifice division. Our horses went straight to Newport News when we left Charlotte and since then we have had no artillery drill worth mentioning.[18] Perhaps our luck will change. Could you include the division in your prayers?

Goodnight, my dear,
Edmund

---

[18] In the American field artillery camps where Edmund trained, the large guns were pulled by horses. As he would discover when he reached the French Camp de Souge, when a French field artillery unit moved, the large guns were towed by tractor trucks. Because the Sixty-sixth Field Artillery Brigade in France used French guns, there was no need for horses.

From Dorothy to Edmund

Montgomery
December 22, 1917

Dear Edmund —

I came home Thursday night for the holidays having remained over a day later at college to finish a paper from which much time had been taken by returning home for two weddings. It is so good to be here again although the people who are nice to me are in the army — those of them who aren't married and flying around the country according to the fancy of a whimsical War Dept. So everything is unusually quiet. I don't mind, for it is really the first chance I've had to see my family well since summer.

I have just returned from a hunt with Father and the small brother who is no longer small but tall and sparrow-like in appearance.[19] I am always most flattered when they ask me to accompany them for they are K.S.'s to each other and usually desire no others.[20]

It was such a wonderful afternoon to be in the woods. The fields and grass were all brown and there were burrs and soft whirry things which stuck to you everywhere and nothing green except clumps of pines here and there and a few lovely red bushes which had not given up their leaves yet. We tramped about all afternoon and the dogs got four trails but we only got one rabbit and several birds. The one rabbit was certainly an inhabitant of the proverbial "briar patch." Never have I felt such briars. We have only just returned and it is almost suppertime now.

---

[19] Young Charles was thirteen years old.
[20] K.S.'s=Kindred Spirits.

I thought of you during the ride home just before dusk. There were long sweeping lines of pines which lay black against the burning beauty of the sunset, which became fainter and fainter as the first stars came out. Father and Charles are such silent companions that I was free to think about you and wonder what you were doing, with the wind blowing cold in my face and the dogs lying close about me to keep warm. I always think of you when I get out of doors and in the free air. I do not know why except that you like it too. Nobody knows how I love it. It is such a passion with me that sometimes I think I will die if I do not get free somewhere in the woods with the wind in my face ...

Christmas Afternoon – 1917 –

... This was interrupted the other day and I have not had a chance to continue until now. I take back what I said in the beginning about this being a quiet Christmas. There is a dance every night beginning tomorrow night and I go on a weekend camp Saturday in the woods. Tomorrow night when I go to the Country Club I shall be thinking of you and working our radio-system, so be looking out for a message.

The roses you sent are so lovely. They came this morning before I was up and the Angelic Child who was roaming about at an early hour found them at the door and put them in my room so that they were the first things I saw when I awoke this morning. They are so fresh and cool and beautiful that I love them and I thank you for your Christmas thought of me. I wore some of them to church this morning and to dinner.

In spite of the festivities of the day and the other people about me I have been thinking of you very constantly. My one regret for the day was that I could not see you for I do want to so much. I am just wondering why it is, when there are often men in my life, that I remember you and care so even when I am with them. I do not know why it is. I only know that I would give anything to see you now and that because it is Christmas day I wish for you every happiness now and in the year to come. I do not even know where you are tonight, but I repeat what I said in my message to you — may we be together next Christmas —

Dorothy

From Edmund to Dorothy

S.S. *Lapland*
Christmas 1917

Dearest:

My father, of whom you are likely to hear more and more as time goes on, always discourages the abuse of superlatives, on the theory that if one is continually sounding off "wolf, wolf" he will be discounted and his words will fall on deaf ears. And having been educated by my father, I use superlatives quite guardedly and sparingly always. There is no one else in the world or in my philosophy with the title of dearest. I hope that it does not bring your disapproval?

Christmas on the ocean is a new experience. It looked as though we were to stay on dry land but at the last moment the quarantine was lifted and an hour later we were on the road to the pier. When I wrote last Saturday our trunks and all of the men's baggage had left camp. It wasn't proper to tell you just what the plans were, much as I wanted to. Sunday night when I wrote you again the quarantine was still in effect but the decision to move Monday morning was made. That letter I intended to mail at the gangplank and it was unsealed in accordance with instructions from the censor. It had to be innocent of military information but I mailed it at a village outside of camp and probably forgot to seal it. You must have gathered that we were moving. We boarded the ship about noon and shortly afterward slipped down the harbor past the symbol of liberty and thence to Sandy Hook and the blue Atlantic.

So here we are, out of sight of everything but water and sky in a dull grey ship beneath a dull grey sky and trying to remember it is Christmas.

We are likely to be on the water two weeks or more and I expect to add to this every now and then and mail the net results to you from somewhere in France. Think of the size this letter will have assumed! If the censors throw away long letters it would doubtless be better policy to send it in several envelopes. I don't trust them much.

You are probably about to have dinner. I remember your dining room perfectly — the long table, the door at one end where the servants passed and re-passed — and don't the windows face the back of the house? And the other doors leading to the front of the house. Probably there are candles and evergreens and company. I was there but once but you impressed the occasion on my memory. Doctor Wilkerson — I think that was his name — sat on my left and I barely knew that he was present. The only thing he said was that he had been at the Harvard-Yale game the fall previous and from that time on, I saw nothing and nobody but the person at my right who was worrying me considerably. And notwithstanding your conduct and your unreasonableness I liked you immensely. That brings us to a large subject, doesn't it! At any rate I hope you are having as joyful a Christmas as you deserve.

… There is a little chapter in my family history that might strike you as it did me. I had forgotten about it until my sister spoke of it the other day. My father first met my mother when she was only about seventeen, at a husking bee or some rustic merrymaking. He rode away and didn't see her again for two years. About that time he commenced writing a series [of letters] that is still tied up in a blue ribbon in an old bookcase at home. And he went to see her again and asked her to marry him — which she did. That was forty years ago. Of course things don't happen that way anymore. It is merely a romantic incident of times that are gone.

The ship has several bronze tablets in the upper stairways commemorating voyages with other troops, the first of which was in September 1914, a month after the war began. The Canadians who made that trip have long since been exterminated. It has made a number of trips with American troops but there are no tablets.

Yours,
Edmund

After Edmund finished his Christmas Day letter to Dorothy, he walked along the ship's darkened hall and went downstairs to the officers' sleeping quarters below decks. While lying in his bunk, feeling the rhythmic pitch and roll of the ship, he wondered what Dorothy would think about the family story he had included in the letter — a third time he had given her a brief description of a young man falling in love at first sight.

Edmund hoped that the sense of mutual closeness and affection he and Dorothy had begun to express in their letters would increase and intensify. Yet destiny had placed him where he was, on a troopship crammed full of Yanks heading toward England, and from there, all of them would go into a war raging in France. His future—his life—would soon be plunged into uncertainty, into jeopardy. And with each passing hour, the *Lapland* was carrying him farther away from the young woman he loved.

Edmund Shea, 1917

Dorothy Thigpen, 1917

1200 South Perry Street,
Dorothy's childhood home

Touring car, 1916

Above: Daisy Lee Bissell Thigpen
and Dorothy, 1899;
Top right: Dr. Charles Thigpen;
Right: Dorothy, 1907

Dorothy and Daisy, 1932

Top: Dorothy's wedding
portrait, 1920; Above:
1200 South Perry parlor,
decorated for the
wedding; Right: 1200
South Perry staircase

From top left: Shea family portrait, 1916: (back row) Will, Eugenie, William, Nora, Isabel; (front row) Louise, Edmund, Edith, Catherine; William Francis Shea, 1852–1928; Lieutenant Edmund Shea, July 1918 ("I haven't taken off my shoes in a week.")

Shea family home in Ashland, Wisconsin.

Top: White Woods in winter; Above left: Living room at White Woods, 1932; Right: Shea children: Charlie, Betsy, Sheila, Wendy, Christmas 1932

Dearest Aunt Kitty —
This is a message of loving thought & Christmas affection from all of us at White Woods. You are very close in our minds & hearts this year of all years.
Always devotedly
Dorothy

Edmund Burke Shea, 1947

Dorothy Thigpen Shea, 1947

White Woods in autumn

Dorothy and Edmund, 40th anniversary of their meeting, 1956

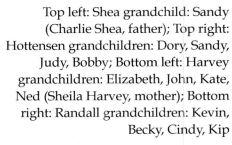

Top left: Shea grandchild: Sandy (Charlie Shea, father); Top right: Hottensen grandchildren: Dory, Sandy, Judy, Bobby; Bottom left: Harvey grandchildren: Elizabeth, John, Kate, Ned (Sheila Harvey, mother); Bottom right: Randall grandchildren: Kevin, Becky, Cindy, Kip

Dorothy Shea, walking on the path, White Woods, 1950

Edmund Shea, walking on the path, Italy, 1969

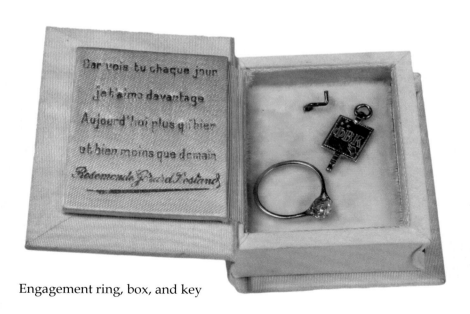

Engagement ring, box, and key

21

Ludendorff Goes on the Offensive

The Soul thinks of you with all her power and prays
while the Germans hammer at the line.
— Dorothy Thigpen, letter, April 14, 1918

After a two-week journey across the Atlantic, the *Lapland* landed in Liverpool on January 8, 1918. Edmund then travelled by train to spend a few days in a British army camp located on the outskirts of Winchester.

From Edmund to Dorothy

Winchester, England
January 9, 1918, Wednesday

Dear Dorothy:

… This has been a good day. I wish you were here to see the quaint town of Winchester. Preston and I walked in this morning and did the sights and the shops. A most courteous clerical gentleman discovered us in the cathedral and took an hour or more to show us about. You know I am more or less conservative and have respect for tradition, and in that old Norman monument one is truly bathed in antiquity. Think of seeing the chests that contain the bones of the Saxon kings, including Edmund, who I find was also a saint, duly canonized.

The remains of Cardinal Beaufort, Izaak Walton and various other celebrated persons are there. There were the marks in the floors made by Cromwell's soldiers' horses when they were stabled in the cathedral. And did you know that the wretch had some of the stained-glass windows smashed? I have always hated Cromwell and I like to find evidence against him. The stonework of the Normans is most impressive.

In France — Friday, January 11, 1918

Fairest, this is becoming a diary rather than a letter. The orders to move came while I was scribbling the above at my hut in the camp at Winnall Down, Winchester. I rather like the name don't you? And we have been on the move ever since. The passage across the English Channel was made at night in a very fast boat. It is only a question of time and gambling chances before the submarines pick off a troopship or two.[21]

And at last we are on the soil of poor old France. There wasn't much ceremony connected with our arrival, it was merely a case of coming off a crowded ship and marching through the town in the rain and mud. But seeing so many different kinds of soldiers — Frenchmen with their lengthy bayonets, Englishmen and Highlanders, Australians and Algerians, not to mention the German prisoners — is a reminder that one is near the center of

---

[21] *A History of the Sixty-sixth Field Artillery Brigade* includes an account of the tragic fate of the *Tuscania*, a troopship that left New York on January 18, 1918, less than a month after Edmund's departure. The *Tuscania*, with over two thousand AEF soldiers aboard, was struck by a German torpedo and sank off the coast of Scotland. The writer of the *History* adds: "The running away and leaving Americans to drown went against the grain of every man on the *Baltic*, but under the rules of the submarine fighting game, nothing could be gained by staying, and the *Baltic* would have been endangered." The *Baltic*, the ship in the convoy travelling a few hundred yards behind the *Tuscania*, carried soldiers belonging to the 148th Field Artillery Brigade, a unit that was also training at Camp Greene when Edmund was there in 1917.

the war stage. One of the most noticeable things is the youth of the American soldier compared with the maturity of the other nationalities. He may not have so much sense, but ought to be a better fighter for it.

I think I will send you a cable before dinner, just to dispose of any uncertainty regarding my whereabouts, if you have bothered to think of it—as I know you have. Somewhere in this country I hope to find some mail from you. It is such a long time. And please dear Dorothy, say that you care for me and that I haven't gone out of your life.

Yours devotedly,
Edmund

~ ~ ~

After reaching Le Havre in an early morning rain, members of the brigade marched to the railroad station and began a long ride southward, passing through Normandy and Brittany before reaching their destination near Bordeaux.

From Edmund to Dorothy

France
Thursday, January 17, 1918

The men rode in miniature boxcars with never a bench or cushion to relieve the bareness. The cars are marked "Hommes 40-Chevaux 8" but with twenty-five men in a car it was so crowded that there wasn't room to stretch out at night. You can imagine this train of fifty little cars with soldiers filling the doorways winding through a country of gardens, woods, vineyards and towns. Wherever we passed the people waved and cheered and seemed delighted at our being here. There were two ordinary passenger carriages for the officers, but no blankets and no rations, so that in comforts we hardly exceeded the men. One morning I washed at a water tank beside the track and the next morning did not have a chance to wash at all. We subsisted on rye bread, Camembert, and vin rouge purchased at the station lunch counters. One slept sitting up. But it was a pleasant and interesting trip not soon to be forgotten. At all events, dearest Dorothy, your humble keeper cares for you above all the women in the world.

Yours devotedly,
Edmund

On January 17, Edmund reached Camp de Souge, a French Artillery Camp near Bordeaux where he would live and attend classes for the next two months. Officers of the Sixty-sixth had come to de Souge to learn from French bilingual instructors how to use the GPF, the Grande Puissance Filloux, a large artillery gun considered the acme of perfection in its realm. The 155-mm canon, mounted on rubber tires, weighed 25,740 pounds and had a range of almost ten miles.

From Edmund to Dorothy

20 January 1918

Fairest:

This is Sunday night—a mild, dark evening with the breath of spring in the air. How I wish you were here, to walk down the road beyond the camp gate, between the rows of pine trees, past the little cluster of one-story shops that cater to soldiers' needs and weaknesses and where they are gathered tonight— Americans, Frenchmen and Chinamen all somewhat warm with vin rouge, jabbering and fraternizing with the utmost amiability. They would interest you, and you would like the walk. Wouldn't you?

It is a month since your last letter came. So many things can happen in thirty-one days. I never realized so keenly the separation of these continents. The only thought that gives me any comfort is that you cared for me a month ago and then my faith says that you do still and that you will persevere. But my reason tells me I have only a precarium at best.[22] Dorothy, I beg you to wait to hear what I shall tell you as soon as the war is over, if I am alive — and if I am presentable. I have seen some sorry cripples. But there are not any or at least many ex-artillery cripples, and please excuse me for mentioning such things.

I have some letters I wrote on the boat and put in my trunk, thinking we would go right through England to France. The trunk didn't come until we had arrived here, so the letters are a bit ancient. They really are your property so I will shoot them along.

> Goodnight SOC. God be with you.
> *Edmund*

On Sunday, January 27, 1918, Edmund attended Mass in Bordeaux at the Cathedral of St. André.

From Edmund to Dorothy

Dimanche 27 Janvier 1918

Fairest:

… I went to church this morning, for the first time since leaving Camp Merritt. And I wished that you were there.

The two towers loomed up at the end of a long street and when we got nearer the bells began to chime. They were the

---

[22] Edmund uses the legal term *precarium*, meaning a contract in which the grantor can revoke what was lent at any time, as in a tenancy at will.

most wonderful bells. Then came a view of the building itself, a tremendous Gothic monument of grey stone, crumbling and green with age, flanked with enormous flying buttresses.

To describe the interior of the cathedral is quite beyond me, but you know how they look. This was built in the 14th century and what impressed me most were the richly colored stained-glass windows and the stonework — course after course of it — piled in great masses, grouped into fluted columns that soared and soared until they reached the stone ceiling which was lit up by the sunlight through the upper windows. Generations of men must have worked on it.

Being the seat of a cardinal, the choral work was especially good. I love the chanting of those ancient Latin prayers. And the organ was so tremendous that it fairly shook the walls. There was the procession of priests and clergy garbed in all the pomp of Rome — and led by an individual clothed in a frock coat, an Admiral's hat of the Geo. Wash. Model, a great red girdle and a drum-major's staff. How proud of him must be his family and relatives! The people were mixed — civilians and soldiers. I saw an extraordinary number of women in mourning (and not only at church). Near us were two black soldiers in the Alice blue uniform of France. They looked like good soldiers. All of which made me feel quite religious, and made me think of you. I wonder how you would have been impressed.

The thought came, how much do you care for the fair Dorothy? Suppose she were translated or otherwise taken out of your existence, how then? I never considered such a contingency before and I was appalled by the emptiness that loomed up. You have become a part of all that I do and think of doing. That is as plainly as I can express it, and if only you will let me worship and—no that is a great deal but not enough. I want you to care for me more than for any man in the world.

I always thought I would never commit to paper these private matters. I shrink from it even now. But there is no choice. I must sometimes bubble over and just tell you how I feel. Perhaps I won't do it again for some time.

We have a marvelous climate. My overcoat has hung unused ever since we came. The sun is warm and even the nights are hardly cold enough for a fire or a wrap. It seems like summer. In town there are cafes with tables set on the sidewalk, an arrangement that I never saw elsewhere and there in the afternoon and evening they sip their wine and chat. There is little music anywhere—this is a luxury eliminated by war. Everywhere there are soldiers in the unceasing variety of French uniform. They lay more stress on decorations than do we. There is the war Cross, the Cross of the Legion of Honor, the chevron for wounds, the cord for Mention in the dispatches, which varies with the number of mentions. I daresay Americans will take slight interest in those external marks of distinction. And if they receive decorations I doubt if they will wear them. Doing his utmost is part of the day's work, simply his duty. That is the Roman and I think the correct way of looking at it.

> Goodnight dear Dorothy.
> *Edmund*

Edmund's Christmas Day letter finally reached Dorothy's Agnes Scott mail cubby six weeks later …

From Dorothy to Edmund

February 2, 1918

Dear One —

Your first letters came to me yesterday and I cannot tell you how glad I was to find two in my box — the one written Christmas day and the one the day after — was more than I hoped for ...

This morning I was at a church where a man spoke of those who would not come back. I try not to think about it, and yet I never seem to get away from the idea. It came to me this morning as he was talking, that if you do not, I shall have always the memory of something rare in having known you. And you must come back. I have said it to you so much that your father would call it "wolf, wolf" but I think about it all the time and want it more than anything ...

There is just one other thing before I stop. I like your father's and your mother's romance.[23] You do not think things like that happen now? I do. If only people care enough and believe strongly enough in each other and in the everlasting spirit of romance and if they pray much.

Goodnight,
The Soul

P.S. I hate that Tommy Sanders man. He has never sent me the pictures of you. If I knew how to reach him, he should be put out of the Corporation this minute. In fact he is. — D.

---

[23] Dorothy's comment refers to the story Edmund told in his Christmas Day 1917 letter of his parents' correspondence, which led to their engagement and marriage.

Chapter 21

From Edmund to Dorothy

February 15, 1918

Dear SOC:

Three letters from you came in the mail today, for which I thank you from the bottom of my heart. The other evening forty-two sacks of mail came to the regiment, one sack for about each twenty-five men, and I stepped lightly up to the battery to look for a word from you, only to be disappointed. You have said that it is always well to be braced against adversity from any quarter, but I had neglected the prudential props and dragged my feet homeward with my spirit drooping. Tonight it is quite the reverse. Serials IV, V and the blessed little inter-chapter will keep me content for several days.

... As for my superfluity of sweaters, I fear that you have been misinformed. Though three were in fact presented to me last fall only one has survived and that is your handiwork. It has sheltered me almost every day this winter and is valued least of all for its caloric properties. It has some holes in it and has stretched the least little bit but honestly, Dorothy, it is the last shred of personal property I would part with. You won't ever suggest that I give it away to a bugler or an orderly, will you?

You were on the point of asking me something at the end of that letter. It was like the mid-air suspense that comes before "to be continued in the next number." Please ask me before the next world commences. And let the wisdom of the inquiry go. Just say — this is question X.

I like the inter-chapter. Things done on impulse have an atmosphere that more deliberate acts lack. I don't mean to philosophize: One of my great delights is watching your varying moods, as far as I can from the record of your pen. Really I know a great deal about you, your tastes, dislikes and virtues, but only a fraction of what I want to know. A dashed off inter-chapter is virtually a small part of yourself, and is of course apt to be quite a faithful index. The idea is simply another statement of the truth that underlies "veritas in vino."

Now you know the reception given to your letter of the 27th January, written after the war talk at the Y.M.C.A. When you say the things that come from down deep and rarely get said at all I fairly hold my breath. And then I say "God bless her." As you say the war has melted away so many little conventions. People don't camouflage their feelings as we have always been accustomed to do. And as for cheerfulness that you don't happen to feel, please don't plague yourself and me with it. The YMCA doesn't correctly state the case of the soldier. When his turn comes he will be picked off—not sooner, and there is a fair chance of seeing the thing through. Whatever the risk, it is incidental to the game and quite a subordinate matter. I don't know any other theory that will keep a man a soldier and keep his nerves together.

... I enclose a Valentine that our friend Tuesley left here last night. As you see he is somewhat versatile.

To be continued Sunday.

Goodnight, fairest,
The Keeper

Chapter 21

From Dorothy to Edmund

Sunday Morning
Feb. 17, 1918

Dear Keeper —

This has been the most joyful corporate week of my life, I think. First came a letter the early part of the week begun in England and ended when you landed in France, then the cable which did me a world of good and then yesterday <u>six</u> letters, two in the morning and four last night. I really do not know when I have been so foolishly happy. You should have seen the radiant smiles I passed around the supper table just after the mail came and how suddenly philosophical I became over the existence of a restless day yesterday. I cannot tell you how glad I was. If you only knew how much your letters mean to me you would write perpetually and stop being the censor. I humbly beg his pardon for my uncomplimentary remarks as to his disposition, appearance and general makeup.[24]

I was thinking this morning when I came back from church and as I often think, that you really do not know how much I care for you. I am not quite sure myself but I only know that it is <u>very</u> deeply.

… Last night when I was looking through a box of old letters I came across a diary I began the summer I met you.[25] I suppose everybody has been so benighted once or twice as to keep one, and I have spasmodic fits of it every now and then. This one was kept at a time in my life when I had need of analyzing my feelings on a certain subject pretty thoroughly — at a time

---

[24] Dorothy now realizes that Edmund is the censor for his battery. Hence, he has the privilege of stamping his own letters as "censored."

[25] Dorothy refers to the diary she kept for six weeks in the summer of 1916.

153

when I was, or thought myself, in love with the soldier youth whom you may remember. My family objected to him quite strenuously, and I was forbidden to see him just at the time I met you. It came hard at the time, though I knew they were quite right, considering the sort of person he was. No one was more thoroughly aware of his limitations than I, but as I say, I had to get my thoughts and my feelings clearly in line, and the diary seemed to answer the need.

My first impression of you might amuse you as set therein. I shall enclose a portion. The whole seems to be a succession of "verys" and even at the time, you can see that you impressed me rather profoundly:

July 1916

"Mr. Shea, the Harvard man (Marion's friend), is very, very, very, nice. I have not said very much about him but we have gotten to be very good friends in the four times I have seen him. His eyes are also nice. He is very quiet. Well, to go on with the dinner. It was lovely ..."

And as I look back over the time which almost approaches two years, I realize how my feeling for you has grown in proportion as I learned to know you and to know the kind of person you are. Now it means more to me than anything else in the world that you come back. I know that I should not be writing like this but in the face of everything I really couldn't help it. When I think that you may be terribly near danger it makes me throw discretion out of the front window and put every selfish thought that I have about whether I should be writing like this out of my head. I am so afraid of appearing insincere to you that I try to keep my feelings about you out of my letters though I do not succeed at all. Sometimes it seems so strange that the way I care should have been built up out of a chance acquaintance and a correspondence which has not ended, as most correspondences usually do. If there were no other people in my life I could understand it in a measure, but you know there are, and at home I am constantly meeting new men.

I wish when you have a chance you would write that unreliable Tommy Sanders and <u>order</u> him to send me those pictures of you. If I knew where to get him he would hear what I think of him. Please tell him for me and tell him that he is out of the Corporation so far as the Soul is concerned. Of course he would take it in a good-natured way and merely laugh but even that does not mitigate the hard feelings I have toward him ...

Wednesday Night
March 6, 1918
In the Library

Dearest —

... Tonight as I was walking over here from a meeting in the Cabinet Room I stopped for a full minute by a very tall pine tree in which you can nearly always hear the wind and I looked up at the everlasting stars and thought of you so that you must have known. The things you said in your letters mean so much. You really do not know.

I was thinking too of what a very high opinion you have of my virtues and how short I fall. But I know Edmund, that my capability for caring is probably the best thing about me and is deeper and finer than anyone guesses and I trust to that to make up for the other things which I lack.

You say that I do not know whether I care for you or not. I am quite sure now, as sure as I am of anything else in the world, that I do. And please know it because it means much to me that you should believe me when you may have to go at anytime. Please promise me that you will.

You can see that this is an interchapter from my heart and that it is an index to my feelings. If I waited till morning I would never send it but I hate my reason and my miserable share of discretion and I like to beat them.

It took several minutes for me to decide to begin this the way I did. I have never said that to any man before though it may seem strange for me to have arrived at the age of twenty and not have said it. I am very glad that I have not.

Goodnight dearest —
The Soul

From Dorothy to Edmund

Sunday Afternoon
March 24, 1918
On the fire escape

Dear Keeper,

… A letter came last night containing two notes — one dated the 24th Feb. — and the small picture. You do not know how thankful I was. It was the first time I had heard in two weeks and each day I looked in my box only to be disappointed. There is another girl in my wing who has been hearing from France regularly also and she received no mail either, which was a comfort to me and I could lay the blame on the boats and forget for a time the things I imagined as having happened to you. But I was so thankful to hear last night. And the picture is exceedingly good. I have looked at it a dozen times already and I feel almost as if I am looking at you really and I love the way the eyes squint and the set to the shoulder. Make the good Lieut. Tuesley snap some more and send them. Thank you for seeing to Tommy, though I am sorry he has not responded. I hate to seem persistent about the matter but pictures mean much when I have not seen you for almost two years and when no immediate opportunity is in view. So continue to stir Tommy whose dependability I do not trust in.

… I liked your (imagined) trip to Montgomery to my house on Perry Street only there was a mistake. You said the lady would be upstairs and would wonder which Lieutenant was there. She will know because she has been waiting a very long time for the soldier to come and she will come down and will wear a blue dress or a yellow one or a white one or whatever kind the soldier likes best, and after he has given the countersign she will ask him if he is disappointed in her as a Soul and if he says he is not, the lady will look into his eyes and tell him what she has been waiting so long to tell him if he wishes to hear it. It may be long but it is not uncertain, for the lady wills with all her soul that he come back.

… The hair is quite dry and I must dress for supper. There is one more thing before I stop. I must ask you not to write letters to me and then not send them. You can't imagine how exasperating it is. You have no right to do it because they belong to me. Friday I am going home for Easter and shall come back the following Wednesday so you will hear from me at home. I shall try to write you again before I go though. I am rather rushed for time.

> Goodbye until then — Optimus —
> *Dorothy*

From Dorothy to Edmund

Wednesday Morning
April 3, 1918
Somewhere between
Montgomery & Atlanta

Dear one –

This is not the day for my regular message but I did not tell you half I had to say Sunday night and so much has happened since then. This is a very bumpy train and you will perhaps have a hard time making anything out of my rambling, but I must talk to you and tell you that I feel as if I had had a glimpse of you last night, because I talked about you to someone who knows you for a full twenty or thirty minutes at a dance last night—Miss Olive McDonald.[26] You really do not know how satisfying it was! She is on a visit here. She used to live here you know, and the first thing she spoke about was the Corporation.

And how we did talk about you! We agreed perfectly in our opinion of you and she admires you exceedingly—nearly as much as the Soul does. It was nearly as good as seeing you for we spoke of everything from your sense of humor to your eyes and she told me how everyone liked you in Boston and how lovely your sister Edith is and that you used to wear a moustache—I am glad you do not anymore. She said you were the realest person she knew and I told her I thought so too and that was perhaps the reason I had never forgotten you even for a space in the two years since we parted. I made her promise to write to you and tell you whether she approved of me. There

---

[26] Miss Olive was one of Dorothy's teachers at the Montgomery School for Girls. She was also Marion Rushton's aunt. Miss Olive later moved to Boston where she met Edmund during the time that he and Marion shared an apartment in Cambridge, from 1914 to 1916.

were dozens of other things to ask her about, but someone insisted on my dancing and she left before I got a chance to see her again. It was so good to talk about you to somebody.

... You know last night Miss Olive spoke several times of how strange it was that we should remember each other vividly. She asked me if I really cared for you and she told me to be sure before I told you because she says you are not the kind of person to be trifled with. I know that of course, and I beg you to believe me Edmund when I say that I care. I know it seems strange and I can't understand why some of the numerous Lieutenants and Captains about Montgomery shouldn't appeal to me, but they don't and unconsciously I make comparisons and then contrasts and I am thankful that you crossed my path. I think always of the time when you will come back.

> Goodbye dearest until Sunday —
> *Dorothy*

From Dorothy to Edmund

April 1918

... You know when I get your letters, I forget that nearly a month has passed since they were written and you seem so near. I have not forgotten anything about you and sometimes I can see you so very plainly. I wonder if you remember the very last thing you said that Sunday afternoon at home when you were going back to Wisconsin. I have never forgotten it. You said you would see me again someday, and I have thought of it so much and of the gambler's chance that you have, and I have wondered and I have prayed. ...

From Dorothy to Edmund

Agnes Scott
Sunday Afternoon
April 14, 1918

Dear Keeper —

Last night ended a strenuous week with every minute filled by lessons and lectures and meetings and it was only redeemed by two letters from you — one which came Friday night, and another Saturday morning. I had just about given up when the first one came for I had not heard in sixteen days. I do not ever attempt to generalize about the peculiarities of the mail boats for your letters come in at the strangest times and Friday I got one written March 23rd and yesterday one written March 15th! I was so glad to hear, though, that a small thing like that made no difference. Isn't it hopeless when you think you are going to get a letter and don't? You should see me go twice a day to the faithful and long-suffering Box 12 and look hopefully within, only to be disappointed and then slam unoffending member shut with such force that it is almost demolished.

You asked me what I liked in a man. There are many things — a certain combination of strength and gentleness which makes the will balance evenly with the emotions, a sense of values which puts honesty and fair dealing along with clean living and a hatred of things which one could not do openly, and besides that a certain spirit of generosity and charitableness which pardons much where other people condemn. And then more than almost anything, I want him with an understanding soul and a love of certain things which I count highly — of human things and of beautiful things and of humorous things and of adventure. And I want him to hate wrongdoing as he loves other things and I would want him in this war today. It all sounds rather vague and I think I have included almost everything but nevertheless it is what I want and it is not impossible. Because you come nearer to it than any man I know, I care for you — and I think I am coming to care more as I learn to know you better and to see how fine you are. You have helped me to form my ideal of a man in part and it is bigger and broader for my having known you. Will you tell me what you like in a woman?

Please write me as often as you can. I have been trying every now and then to send you an extra message during the week but it is hard in these days when everything is in a rush. I believe I forgot to tell you that much of my time is taken up with learning how to hurl the discus as I am cast in the role of a Greek youth in the Blackfriars spring play which is always given in the open. I do not think I was intended for the Golden Age of Greece or at whatever period they held the races and games, for the stage directions have the four of us who are so cast "prance in like horses" and it is the most miserable failure! And I do not get the swing of the discus hurling at all so I practice hurling it in my odd moments so as not to disgrace the Corporation when the event comes off. No more am I cut out for acting than for the Greek state. I wonder how I ever got in the Blackfriars and passed the judges when I view myself as the Greek youth.

Goodbye, dearest. The Soul thinks of you with all her power and prays while the Germans hammer at the line.

The Soul

Tractor Training School, St. Maur
Spring 1918

It was not so much what you talked of
as your point of view that impressed me.
—Edmund Shea, letter, April 21, 1918

I n the spring of 1918 Edmund and a group of brigade soldiers went for two months to live in St. Maur, a small town on the outskirts of Paris. As students in the French Tractor Artillery School, they gained competence in the use and maintenance of large tractor trucks that pulled GPF guns when the brigade was on the move.

During his stay in St. Maur, Dorothy's letters continued to arrive, bringing assurance that her fondness for him was deepening.

From Edmund to Dorothy

Grand Hotel-Paris
12 Boulevard des Capucines
Paris, le 21 April 1918

Dearest Dorothy:

It is ten days since a letter from you has come. This being the fourth I have written during the meantime. I would write to you every day if I had the remotest idea that it would make you like me better. When these long intervals come I am always disturbed about what may have happened. Then I think of the optimistic Micawber! and my faith tells me that you are well and have not forgotten me.[27] When we were in Winchester Tuesley bought a little brass image of Mr. Micawber in one of the shops. Sometime I must bribe him to part with it and I will present it to our Corporate museum.

You must not think I am up where the war is until we really get there. When the papers talk of General Pershing's army marching beside the French and British, they refer only to the portion of the forces that have finished training and are ready for the technical sort of warfare that is now in vogue. Really I feel rather foolish when you speak of my being up there. It is reaping undeserved laurels. Before leaving camp I told you we would be in it by the time you got the letter. That was the best information available. The regiment has completed its training and is ready to move at any moment. I still think that what I said will be borne out by the course of events. But in the meantime I am a student in the French school near Paris and lead a life that is anything but heroic. It is quite as safe as New York or Atlanta.

… Do you think I have an exaggerated idea of your virtues? You are extremely modest. Really I have not. Possibly my judgment was not exactly cold and judicial, because I liked you so much from the first, but it was no more than just. Do you remember that first night at the Country Club when we went outside to discuss things in some obliging person's touring

---

[27] Mr. Micawber, a perennial optimist, is a character in Charles Dickens's novel *David Copperfield*.

car—and you told me about the soldier youth and his desire to be killed by Mexicans?[28] Surely a dire fate.

It was not so much what you talked of as your point of view that impressed me. From that time forth I had quite a good idea of your qualities. Your letters were corroborating testimony. Now I do not presume to know you like a book—that would take even so astute a person as our friend Mr. Rushton a hundred years or two hundred perhaps, and I am not astute but I do know something of your tastes, your capabilities, your devotion, your sincerity and your extreme unselfishness. You sum up the things that I value most, and that is why I care for you so much.

When I was young and growing my father kept rather a careful eye on my reading and in accordance with his theories supplied many volumes of brave adventure. The *Odyssey* and *Iliad*, the tales from Herodotus, the *Lays of Ancient Rome*, the sagas of Siegfried and the *Chanson of Roland* and the Arthurian legends I knew almost by heart. And somehow the cycle of Nick Carter and the Tip Top weekly did not displace the first favorites though the latter were pursued quite assiduously for a time. I have never got over the spirit of those old stories nor ceased to admire the heroes. And as a small boy might feel, I often fancy that I am a novice in arms, wearing in my helm your own colors and starting out, not in quest of adventure, but into an adventure that is ready and waiting for all comers.

---

[28] Edmund refers to what Dorothy had told him she had just learned from Tom: that he had a new girlfriend, that he still loved her, and that he was leaving soon with his army unit for the Texas-Mexico border and wished to die. Dorothy had confided to Edmund that she knew she must break up with Tom, since he did not share her ideals, yet she was conflicted because she was still attracted to him. Edmund had encouraged her then to hold fast to her ideals.

And the best that is in me must be used not only for the sake of the cause, but also for your own dear sake. Otherwise how could I go back to you afterward and report that the errand was accomplished? You are an inspiration always, behind the front as well as at the front and *per omnia saecula saeculorum.*[29]

> Goodbye dear one,
> *The Keeper*

~ ~ ~

Not long after Edmund mailed his April 21 letter, while walking along a street in Paris he passed by a shop and noticed in the window a display of women's compacts. One of them caught his fancy, and he stepped inside to take a closer look. After Edmund pointed to the one covered with robin's egg blue enamel, the shopkeeper handed it to him and he looked at it carefully. Yes, it was what he had in mind, he said, and after settling the bill, he left instructions to have it packed and mailed to Dorothy Thigpen at Agnes Scott College.

From Edmund to Dorothy

Late April, 1918

I have been promoted and now wear the silver bar of a first lieutenant. It is some evidence that I have done my duty and for that reason I know you will be glad to hear of it. Only two second lieutenants have been promoted since we left the states — in the 146th.

Yesterday I found a little trinket that I hope you will like, although its chance of reaching you is somewhat precarious. When I go by the shop windows I always wonder which of the

---

[29] *Per omnia saecula saeculorum* — for ever and ever, for ages of ages.

things might appeal to you and it is so hard to decide. I know a captain who bought a hat for his wife and sent it to her. Can't you see the expression on her face when she brought it into the light of the Idaho day? Someday perhaps I will get a brown and blue hat for you to present to our buried friends the Micawbers. That was a funny letter, fair one. I read it over the other evening, for when no new letters come I go back over the old ones, and was highly entertained. You have a graceful touch.

You would be charmed with Paris at this season; the flowers and trees are at their best and the boulevards are an unending delight. When I am rich, dearest, you shall see them. Possibly long before then.

Goodbye,
Edmund

~ ~ ~

In late May Edmund completed the training in St. Maur and returned to the regiment. By then his unit had moved from Camp de Souge to St. Amande, a small town near Puy-de-Dôme. A stable served as an orderly room and when mail arrived for the battery, it was placed in a large manger for horses.

From Edmund to Dorothy

May 22, 1918

Fairest:

Last evening I reached the regiment and in the manger of the orderly room was my mail—five letters from you. There were sixteen others of less consequence, but for yours the journey up and down France, including two nights in crowded railway carriages—not sleeping cars—was the merest trifle. When I had consumed them I was speechless, with the same feeling that I had when first I entered Notre Dame. It is always hard for me to articulate my feelings. Words seem so inadequate. The messages that I send you through the ether must reach you because you seem to understand so well.

The letters were written on divers occasions between the first of April and the second of May. It was midnight when they all were finished and I tumbled into the ancient and vast bed of which this billet boasts to dream of you. Today in between drills my mind has come back constantly to your latest words. That you could and actually do care so fairly overwhelms me. It makes me hold my breath to think of the reality. And strangely it makes the war with its incidental circumstances dwindle into insignificance. I fear that is a bit unpatriotic, but in fact it is more scorning the Boches and his devices than forgetting my duty to chastise him.

But Dorothy, I feel as though I had practiced fraud upon your believing nature. You thought me on the brink of the adventure. Perhaps the vision of these peaceful billets would have made you feel differently. At any rate I am sorry to have told you what events did not justify. It is perfectly true that we were to take our place up yonder the first week of this month and that we were equipped and ready to go. Why we did not go and still linger here is because of one circumstance, ulterior to the regiment, that I cannot disclose. Hereafter I shall not prophesy. And dearest, I am ashamed of having caused you so much unnecessary worry. I am so sorry. Please forgive me, won't you?

Your picture is on the mantel above the fireplace. The billets all are profusely decorated with statuary and pictures dealing with religious persons. I have not meditated on my host's favorites but your picture makes me worship the fair being whom it represents. I think of you as something more than mortal, somewhat in the way I think of my mother, and yet so differently. Only to see you, to hear your voice, to be with you for a little while, I would give anything in the world. It is such a boon that I fear it may slip away into eternity as a blessing that was withheld because too great, and I unworthy. The longer I live the more worthy of you I shall be, that is certain, so it would seem to be a race against time and old man Probability. It is a fair contest.

The candle is burning low and I must study so as not to disgrace us both tomorrow before the battery.

Goodnight beloved,
The Keeper

From Edmund to Dorothy

May 1918

Dimanche.

The quondam occupation of censoring mail has been resumed, and as formerly I turn from eavesdropping to telling you about it. It is such a comfort to imagine that I am talking to you as the pen moves along. For you see that I am likely to tell you just what I am thinking of and with almost everyone else I resort to camouflage of a more or less passive variety. You are the "understanding soul" and I a worshipful communicant.

The letters are better than they used to be.[30] Practice seems to have cultivated a certain facility and even grace of diction that is quite new in the Idaho soldiery. There is a good deal of humor, good-natured humor in their point of view. Jokes about the girls' wooden shoes never end. Bad spelling always

---

[30] Edmund refers to his role as censor for the battery.

amuses me, though you well know that my house, particularly my French house, is made of a thin variety of glass. One of the warriors confided in his brother that he was now saving his francs for a certain French girl who had promised to marry him and go to America after the war. Unfortunately for Lochinvar, "her old man wants to come with her." His solution was an alternative, either to "steel her and make a hurry-up trip across" or "bring along the old man and put him to work on the ranch." Can't you see the transplanted father and daughter on the Idaho ranch!

… The idea you sketched of a lieutenant in action is dashing but hardly accurate for artillery. The doughboys do have a hard time of it because there is so much of climbing in and out of trenches, hand-grenading, sniping, raiding in the night and bayonet combat. This in addition to shell and gas. We get none of the first things, though we carry rifles and pistols, and only gas and an extra quantity of shell. The light artillery and smaller howitzers are within say a mile of the front. Farther back is the corps artillery, ordinarily, and except when it is doing counter battery work. The heaviest howitzers and railroad guns are farther in the rear. The lieutenants simply see to it that the guns are fired properly, emplaced properly and withdrawn properly — and censor letters. The ordinary routine is nothing to worry about.

A French officer said that one morning in his dugout at the battery, six meters underground, while the earth was quivering under the shock of German shell, an officer immaculately attired stepped in with a notebook to inquire how many men in the organization needed dental work done.

Unworthy! That you could think such a thing is only evidence of a most rare sense of honor. It is the modesty of a very lofty point of view. That seems a bit vague but I mean, dearest Dorothy, that your goodness exceeds any standard I have seen. Probably you have imperfections. Everybody does. You often love your friends for their faults, do you not? At any rate, I know that seeing you will only make me care more, if that were possible. You are half of my life now and you never can be less. It is I that should worry about measuring up to the man that my zealous friends have pictured. Do not expect the superman whom you deserve but only one whose numerous shortcomings are partly bridged over by a most deep devotion to you. For I love you Dorothy far more than ever I could commit to this heartless sheet of paper. You believe me, and you care enough to wait for me. That is enough to fill my cup. The length of the war is not so important. The vision of you will blur the passage of time.

Moreover, there is an order providing that after eighteen months overseas an officer will serve a month at home and have a short leave. Could you believe that within a month we all get our first gold service stripe for six months abroad! So that a year from now the eighteen months will be up and I will be putting on all sail for America, with three service stripes and many interesting little fireside anecdotes about the war. Only we won't talk much about the war. You will be almost through college and perhaps I can give you some suggestions about the momentous question of the future that you meditate on when the air is balmy. The way in which you can best use your gifts is surely a question of vital corporate importance. It calls for a meeting and deliberation.

There is also an order permitting us to tell the people at home just where in France we are. This applies to all troops not in the zone of the advance. It has not been officially received here, but probably next time I write you will know.

I do not know when we will be ordered into action. I hope it may be soon in order that we may justify our existence and finish up the Hun.

This is about the longest letter I ever wrote. I fear it stands for quantity not quality. Am I "steeling" your time, please?

> Farewell
> *The Keeper*

From Edmund to Dorothy

June 6, 1918

Dear SOC:

Two letters came from you in the heavy mail of last evening. I surely appreciate your taking time for the midweek messages, for well do I know the endless and insistent demands upon every minute of your time. It is that kind of generosity that makes you different from other people ...

What do you think of suicides? And what would you think of a soldier, a member of C Battery 146th F.A., who cut his throat from ear to ear? I do not know whether he should be condemned or not.

Just before supper a man ran up out of breath saying that one of the men in his billet was bleeding to death. We got the battalion doctor and hastened to the billet where the poor wretch lay on the floor in a pool of crimson blood, a razor near his hand. He was white as a ghost. The doctor bound up his wound and took him to town in the ambulance. The boy was a good soldier but lately has been under the weather and apparently depressed and brooding.

That point of view I cannot understand and that is why I hesitate to condemn him. Who knows what he has gone through? There is a grim humor connected with the affair—a man trained to fight for his country, equipped with rifle, gas mask and helmet and supposed to be on the point of combat with the Hun—stultifying his weapons and depriving the army of a soldier. He must have felt as did another of our fighting men who in condoling with his sister over the loss of their father observed "this world isn't such a hell of a swell place to want to be in, after all." (I ran across that in a letter I was censoring.)

While the doctor was at the boy's head and the orderlies alongside to hold his body still during the wait for the ambulance, I looked out of the little window in the upper story of this stone barn. The soft sunlight of evening was lighting up the hillsides and the world was so peaceful and smiling that I wondered how anyone could wish to leave it. And I thought of you, dear Dorothy, and of the bright plans that I have woven about you, which seemed more bright by contrast with the vanishing outlook of the boy who lay there dying ...

Sunday, June 9, 1918

Dear Lady:

It seems a misnomer to call one a knight who does not cross weapons with the heathen. Better call him a squire, a novice, or something of the sort that is not too warlike in tone. Really I don't have the hardihood to assume the service chevron that we are legally entitled to put on when the 24th of June is here. True it is that our mission will be a weighty one when the hour strikes, but to wait here on the verge is worse than waiting in the states. I have almost got to the stage of being ashamed to write to anybody except my family and you, fairest. You understand and there is nothing that I do not tell you freely. There is nothing of mine that is not yours too, if you care for it. I often feel as though I should like to lay before you the world and all that it contains. Which is an extravagant aspiration and really not sensible. After that was done it would seem not enough. And besides you would not want such a white elephant.

So instead of material things, I give you my heart and the devotion of my soul. It is not much, for how insignificant a mite is one squire on the edge of a field where millions of brave men are struggling, but it is all that I have to give. Nor have I those gifts now, for they have long since been given. If only you will keep them — I ask no more. This is not the way that I intended to write, Dorothy. I have assailed your reason again, and I feel as Catiline must have felt. The hour is late. So goodnight.

Yours devotedly,
Edmund

From Dorothy to Edmund

Montgomery
Sunday A.M.
June 16, 1918

Dearest —

Last night I came home after a weary trip of a day and a half and I found when I walked into the house two letters from you along with my family and I felt as if you were actually here to greet me. I cannot quite tell you the feeling it gave me: as if I were coming home to you as well as to them and that somehow you were even gladder to see me than they. I did not even stop to get off my hat and gloves before I read them and just as I finished a first rapid reading, the man from Camp Sheridan whom I had promised to see for a few minutes arrived and I could not take in everything you said until he left. He was a selfish brute, or rather he isn't because he couldn't be expected to know how infinitely weary I was after that trip nor how I longed to get back to my letters. He stayed two hours instead of the few minutes I promised him so I did not really get to your letters until I went upstairs to go to bed.

I wanted to scribble you a line last night and at least say good night but I was so tired. The railroads you know are in a hopeless tangle as far as decent travelling is concerned and I had to come all the way from North Carolina on day-coaches of various kinds, except a brief period from 1:30 A.M. to 5:30 A.M. of yesterday and there were such long periods of waiting in various places that the trip took me a day and a half ...

I wish I could tell you what I think of these letters which I found waiting for me last night. Edmund dearest, when you say that you think of me as something more than mortal in the way you think of your mother there is something which catches in my throat and for a moment I can not see for the tears which are there for happiness I think. If I can only grow to be the person you think I am and if I can be worthy of your love, it is all that I can ask, because I think that is my ideal for myself. Because I love you with all my strength I am trying to be as fine and good as you think I am. And if you should not come back I shall be trying all the more because I shall be trying to give other people a little of the strength and forgiveness and the tenderness which I glimpsed in you.

The possibility of seeing you when the eighteen months is up made me so happy that I have scarcely thought of anything else all day. I have planned everything. What I will wear and what you will say and how your eyes will look and how many,

many things we shall have to tell each other. A year from now you may be with me — and a year is nothing when one is waiting for a Keeper. You are right about the length of the war not mattering. I have promised to wait for you — I care not how long. The vital thing is that some day I shall have you and that the dear God will let you come back to me.

I hope that you and General Pershing do not mind the fact that I have decided to write you corporatively twice a week instead of once a week. My decision has nothing to do with the matter for I have been doing it regularly since college closed. I have decided on Wednesdays and Sundays in order that you may get it at regular intervals.

Do not feel that you have to do likewise. You know what your letters mean to me and know how I want them but I realize how rushed you are for time and how you must struggle for moments in which to write letters so the fact that I shall write more letters than you matters not at all.

I think I am "stealing" a great deal of your time and also some sleep from myself. I must go to bed. Do you know beloved, what I say every night, the last thing in my prayers and a dozen times a day besides?

"Dear God, keep him very safe and make him know that I care for him more than for anything else in the world."

Goodnight,
Dorothy

June 19, 1918

P.S. I am almost forgetting to tell you that the "trinket" you sent from Paris came the other day and that I love it. The work and design on it I like and it was most thoughtful of you to send it. I do not know what French mademoiselles would use it for, but I shall carry it in my mesh purse to contain powder. Thank you very much, dear one.

23

The Second Battle of the Marne
July 1918

I haven't taken off my shoes in a week.
—Edmund Shea, letter, July 1918

I n the winter of 1918, a time when Edmund and Dorothy's letters radiated joy over their deepening love, German General Erich Ludendorff's mind focused on one desire: to crush French, British, and American armies and win a glorious victory for Germany.

Aware that thousands of new American soldiers were arriving each month in France, Ludendorff knew he must act quickly, and by March, he was ready. Operation Michael, named for the patron saint of Germany, began on the early foggy morning of March 21, 1918. Seven hundred thousand German troops advanced rapidly across the French border, almost as far north as Arras and nearly as far south as Saint-Quentin. German shells released large quantities of mustard and tear gas, blinding or asphyxiating thousands of Allied soldiers, most of them British troops serving in an army that numbered about three hundred thousand men. Operation Michael ended on April 5, leaving a large salient that bulged to the west as far as Cantigny and Montdidier.

In another Ludendorff offensive from May 27 to June 5, German troops moved west and took the city of Soissons, an important rail center. They also reached Château-Thierry on the Marne River and from there, large German artillery guns lobbed shells as far as Paris, striking terror into the hearts of its inhabitants. A million French families fled.

By June 1918, the Allied leaders, Generals Foch, Haig, and Pershing were nearly ready to launch their own counteroffensive. Having learned from German prisoners that Ludendorff was preparing a new attack on Château-Thierry at midnight on July 15, General Foch ordered Allied armies to begin firing at 11:30 P.M. on the fourteenth of July, a major French holiday. The Allies caught the Germans off-guard, and for the next three days the Second Battle of the Marne raged.

The Sixty-sixth Field Artillery Brigade was on the line with other American units, providing important support for French troops. Edmund's battery was positioned in Dormans, on the south side of the Marne, embedded with the French sixth army, under the leadership of Colonel Charlier. The Allied armies quickly pushed the Germans back across the Marne. Three days later the new Allied offensive, known as the Aisne-Marne campaign began, a decisive battle that turned the tide of the war.

~~~

By July 21, according to a letter Edmund wrote to Dorothy, he was in Bézu-St.-Germain when "an aeroplane dropped a bomb near the kitchen stove but did no damage. It woke me up and showered me with debris. This was our first experience with bombs ..."

On July 22, Edmund's journal reported that he went

> into camp at Belleau Wood where the New England troops had been fighting. There were great quantities of equipment and many unburied Americans and Boches strewn through the woods and grain fields. It was the closest we had come to infantry fighting, and the men began to appreciate that there is a great deal of grief in going over the top. Near Bouresches there was a captain with his lieutenant and thirty or forty of his

men in a row on a railroad fill where they were mowed down while advancing against Hun machine guns.

The significance of the Allied victory in the Battle of Aisne-Marne was quickly recognized by leaders on both sides. German Chancellor Georg von Herteling described the way his mind suddenly changed in July, 1918:

> At the beginning of July, 1918, I was convinced, I confess it, that before the first of September our adversaries would send us peace proposals ... We expected grave events in Paris for the end of July. That was on the 15th. On the 18th, even the most optimistic of us knew that all was lost. The history of the world was played out in three days.[31]

John Eisenhower, in his book *Yanks*, quotes General George Marshall on the dramatic role the Aisne-Marne Battle played:

> The entire aspect of the war had changed. The great counteroffensive on July 18 at Soissons had swung the tide of the battle in favor of the Allies, and the profound depression which had been accumulating since March 21 was in a day dissipated and replaced by a wild enthusiasm throughout France, and especially directed toward American troops who had so unexpectedly assumed the leading role in the Marne operation. Only one who has witnessed the despair and experienced the desperate resolution when defeat is anticipated, can fully realize the reversal of feeling flowing from the sudden vision of a not too distant victory.[32]

~~~

In July 1918, while Edmund was caught up in the exhausting schedule of a soldier at the front, Dorothy was spending the summer at home with her family.

---

[31] Byron Farwell, *Over There: The United States in the Great War, 1917–1918*, p. 184.

[32] John Eisenhower, *Yanks: The Epic Story of the American Army in World War I*, p. 173.

Reports about the war in the *Montgomery Advertiser* kept readers informed in a general way. And surely the news of the Aisne-Marne campaign was encouraging and even inspiring. At the same time, for Dorothy, the statistics that revealed increased numbers of injuries and deaths among Allied soldiers were also distressing. Edmund's letters usually took at least two weeks to arrive, and recently, some had taken a month to reach Montgomery. Knowing that in all likelihood he was on the line in the Aisne-Marne battle left her worried about his well-being, about his very life.

Meanwhile, Dorothy's father's desire to be of direct help to AEF soldiers with eye injuries led him to volunteer his services as an experienced eye surgeon to the U.S. Army. In late July he said goodbye to his family and left for the base hospital in Fort Monroe, Virginia.

Dorothy continued to write to Edmund twice a week. On August 4, 1918, without having any recent information about his whereabouts, and aware that she might never see him again, she wrote an eloquent letter that summed up the way she felt about him, about herself, and about her faith in the unseen verities:

From Dorothy to Edmund

August 4, 1918

… I wish I could make you know what your faith in me means. To know that you trust me and that you will never doubt me until you hear it from my lips means more than anything else in the world to me except that you care for me. And I trust you in the same way. I promise that you will never regret putting your faith in me. You will probably be disappointed countless times because I do not possess the extraordinary virtue which you fondly imagine I have, but you shall never be disappointed in the sincerity of my devotion to you. And I know too, that my belief in you is something that steadies me through all things. I have ceased trying to explain it. It is the same way about my religion. After a year in college I was at sea about many things. So much that I had believed seemed doubtful. I suppose everyone goes through the experience, and consciousness of the reality of unseen things comes very slowly, and with it comes the conviction that there is something which is far stronger and far mightier than all the laws of logic. And that is faith — as I have in the existence and in the eternal goodness of God ...

Edmund Returns to the United States
September 1918

And I know that our castles are going to be built ...
— Edmund Shea, letter, September 27, 1918

W hen the Aisne-Marne campaign ended the second week in August 1918, Edmund's brigade and other units in the U.S. First Army Corps came out of the line. As the Sixty-sixth began to leave the Marne Valley, Edmund looked back toward the place where the city his battalion had helped to liberate had once stood. A few days after the liberation, the buildings and bridges of Château-Thierry were blown up and reduced to rubble by retreating German soldiers.

The long convoy, with its large guns pulled by tractor trucks, headed southeast toward Lorraine and crept along slowly, filling the French roads from edge to edge. At times, the procession detoured across newly-mown grain fields, and finding a good place to stop in the late afternoon was always a relief. Often they spent the night in an open, quiet field, at other times near a river bank.

By August twenty-third, the convoy reached the town of Dom-martin-le-Saint-Père. Edmund noted in his journal that "tents were pitched in rows. American troops had never before been in the village, and the people were greatly pleased."

A week later Edmund's unit arrived in Rupt-en-Woëvre, a town on the Meuse River, perched on the border between France and Germany, a little south of Verdun. By then it was no secret that the U.S. First Corps would participate in the Battle of St. Mihiel. The battle that began in the second week of September was the first offensive led by an American general, using U.S. troops without support from French or British military leaders.

But on August 30, Edmund received an unexpected letter from regimental headquarters that changed the direction of his life. U.S. Army orders directed him and eleven other brigade officers to return immediately to the United States. They would serve as instructors in a three-month program to train new field artillery troops for combat. Allied leaders put out an urgent call for more soldiers, firmly believing the war would go on for at least another year, perhaps two. Edmund and the other officers expected to rejoin the brigade in France in January 1919.

After saying goodbye to Captain Pettit and his friends in the battery, Edmund went to Clermont-Ferrand to have his orders stamped. Then he got on another train bound for Paris. This one, he reported, was "packed with French pensionnaires from the front, thousands of them it seemed. When the train reached Gare d'Est, a river of blue uniforms flowed over the platform through the station ..."

The next day, September 3, after experiencing the rare luxury of a bath and a good night's sleep at the Grand Hotel, he had breakfast and set out, walking along the nearby rue du Quatre-Septembre toward his destination. His journal entry about that morning is exceedingly brief—"I bought a ring at Tiffany's for Dorothy"—but it still allows one to imagine the scene in detail:

A young American officer opens the door and steps inside the store. A clerk, smiling as he approaches, waits for him to speak. In halting French he explains his reason for being there. He has come to look for ... a ring ... *une bague.*

"Ah, mais bien sûr, mon lieutenant, nous avons vraiment beaucoup de très belle bagues. Voyons ... let me show you some for your consideration." She steps behind the glass display case and selects a dozen or more possibilities, placing them on a tray covered with black velvet. He bends over the counter to look, taking time to study a variety of rings. Some are set in gold, others in platinum, several are elaborate, others less so.

He picks one up to look at it more carefully.

"Ah, vous voyez. C'est une très belle bague, celle-là. Vraiment."

The solitaire he is holding is an old European cut diamond. There are fifty-seven facets cut onto its surface, all done by hand. Each facet must be cut with the utmost care and precision, she tells him. If the work is done well, the maximum brilliance shines through. *"Vous voyez?"* She holds the ring up toward the light of the store window.

Yes, he tells her, it is just what he had in mind.

Then she reaches under the display case and brings forth a box, asking him if he would like it for the ring. It would be a safe way to carry it, she says.

"Vous voyez?" She wants him to look carefully. It is small, about the size of a portly matchbox, and covered in white grosgrain silk. Its lid opens from right to left, like the cover of a book. After opening the box, she points to some gold lettering stamped on the inside of the white silk cover. The interior of the box is lined with cream velvet.

"Allow me to read the inscription," she says. "It is a very beautiful thought, words of Rosemonde Rostand, wife of Edmond Rostand. Perhaps you have read his play, *Cyrano de Bergerac*?" Madame Rostand says:

> *Car, vois-tu, chaque jour je t'aime davantage,*
> *Aujourd'hui plus qu'hier et biens moins que demain.*[33]

---

[33] "For, you see, each day I will love you more than I did yesterday but less than I will tomorrow."

He smiles. Taking some French francs out of his wallet, he settles the bill, thanks her, and puts the box and ring in the left pocket of his uniform jacket.

After saying goodbye, he opens the door of the store, steps out into the air of a mellow September morning, and retraces his steps, heading back toward the hotel, aware that this is his last day in Paris. He feels happy.

~~~

The next morning, with his footlocker and duffle bag squeezed into the trunk of a taxi, Edmund went to the Gare Montparnasse and boarded a train headed for Brest, his port of embarkation. This time the train was less crowded. He wrote to Dorothy: "We flew westward all day. It was a pleasant ride ... the country was good to gaze upon ... especially the latter part of the ride through Brittany and Normandy. The roads are good and the villages so picturesque, someday I hope to return and motor through."

On September 11, Edmund boarded the naval transport ship, the USS *Leviathan*. In a letter to Dorothy, he mentioned that among the passengers aboard were Assistant Secretary of the Navy, Franklin D. Roosevelt, and the Prince of Denmark. Edmund continued: "This evening after supper I bumped into his majesty himself. I recognized him by 1) his accent 2) his uniform 3) the rank of the ship officer escorting him and 4) finally and most convincingly, by the ever-present orderly who silently shadowed the royal footsteps ..."

After a long day of waiting in the Brest harbor, the *Leviathan* finally sailed on Thursday, September 12. That afternoon, he said in his letter to Dorothy:

a convoy of seven ships arrived in the harbor from the States with troops, and in leaving we passed slowly by some of them. This ship is still a curiosity and on all the transports the soldiers and sailors both watched us in passing. Not a voice was heard nor a wave of a hand given … We just gazed at one another. I wondered what the new soldiers were thinking, and how the wounded on this ship felt. On the upper deck, on the sunny side, is a long row of cots occupied by boys with tuberculosis caused by gas. Your heart would be touched by their thin wan faces. And they are so young. What can they be looking forward to?

~~~

On September 19 the *Leviathan* eased up New York Harbor past the Statue of Liberty and docked at Hoboken. At the port of embarkation, Edmund received his orders to report to Camp Meade near Baltimore, "after seven days of leave enroute being allowed." Later that afternoon he got a ticket for the Wolverine, a train to Chicago. Soldiers travelled for one penny per mile, he was happy to note in his diary.

The next afternoon he stepped off the train in Ashland, greeted by William, Edith, and Isabel, and the day after that he spent surrounded by doting family members, all of them grateful for his safe return. Mindful of the clock, Edmund left Ashland after a two-day visit and got back on the train, this time headed for Atlanta.

On the evening of Wednesday, September 24, his train arrived at Union Station. Eleven months had passed since his failed rendezvous with Dorothy and Marion Rushton in October 1917. This time he did show up and Dorothy was there waiting for him in the dim light of the platform, overjoyed when she saw him step off the train. Their long separation had finally come to an end.

Edmund and Dorothy walked together to nearby Piedmont Park and found a bench where they sat together and began their first conversation in twenty-six months.

Would they ever be able to describe it afterward, the wonderment they felt while sitting next to each other on a green park bench? They discussed whether their joy was best described as a miraculous reality or the reality of a miracle, and decided it was both.

He told her about finding the ring at Tiffany's in Paris, and that he had it in the pocket of his uniform. But mindful of the unconventional nature of their courtship, he said he wanted to give her time to reflect on the tremendously important subject he hoped to bring up when he returned to Atlanta in a month's time.

The next day he took the trolley to Decatur and waited at Agnes Scott College until Dorothy's classes ended at noon. They spent the afternoon there together until they returned to Atlanta, had supper, and then walked to Union Station, talking until Edmund's train arrived. Dorothy waited until the train was out of sight before she left the platform.

~~~

Letters between Edmund and Dorothy travelled back and forth between Agnes Scott and Washington, D.C. Edmund was spending nights with his sister Louise and her husband Paul while a flu epidemic at Camp Meade was still acute.

Though Edmund had not yet formally proposed, and Dorothy had not given her acceptance, their hearts raced ahead. After their brief meeting in Atlanta, new subjects began to come up in their letters, questions that had never entered their minds before, such as what kind of house they wanted to live in after their marriage. For two people who hadn't laid eyes on one another for over two years, these were questions that engaged their imaginations in dazzling ways.

From Dorothy to Edmund

Thursday night
September 26, 1918
In the Library

Dearest —

This is just by way of a good-night before I go to a Pan-Hellenic meeting & to tell you how I have missed you since last night. I should be refreshing my memory for English class to-morrow but instead I sit here at a table telling you how I have thought of you constantly since I watched you go down the steps of the station last night. You did not know that I watched you clear out of sight from the gate just above the one which led to "track 6" and when I went back inside the waiting room I felt as if everything had gone — for a space. I pray it may be a little space ...

I got through all my classes all right except German when I had to hand in some poorly written prose but what difference does that make? My mind was constantly wandering to you during all my lectures today and I have seen nothing but your eyes when information about Thales and other early Greek philosophers should have been before me.

It really is impossible to tell you all that seeing you meant. All that I can think of now is the great wash of thankfulness which comes over me at the knowledge that I have seen you and felt the touch of your hands and looked into your eyes and that I care and that you care. Nothing else seems to matter at all — except that I miss you so. Now it is 8:05 pm, just about the time last evening we were finishing supper and starting for the station and it seems like such a minute ago and yet like such ages.

And you are quite, quite, quite sure that I was all that you wanted and expected? Quite? A startling thought came to me today: that you saw me at my best — I am not always as nice looking as I was then — sometimes. And remember about the hair being skimmed back and my disposition and everything. And remember too how infinitely more you with your twenty-six years know than do I and how much more you have seen of the world and how hopelessly ignorant I am about some things. Your superior knowledge frightens me sometimes. I do not know very much but I have a passionate desire and love for all knowledge and beauty which is truth and perhaps you can instruct me. And we can study together can't we, and you can direct my education. Yours is like a well-regulated flower garden, neatly divided off — mine a mixture of ragged hollyhocks and larkspur and weeds ...

From Edmund to Dorothy

Copley Court,
Washington, D.C.
September 27, 1918

Dearest:

I sincerely hope that you achieved more sleep than I did Wednesday night, for you had many cares and I was merely travelling away from Mecca. What you said kept coursing through my brain and your fair image was before me every time I closed my eyes.

Dorothy, before seeing you this week I was not sure that I was not cherishing a vision of what could not be real. But now it is confirmed as positively as anything can be in this world. And I know that our castles are going to be built and our dreams realized in the golden age about to be reinstated. Incidentally, I have decided to save a hundred dollars each month commencing this month that will eke out the returns from a slender practice when the Hun has been chastised and the army mustered out.

Please write to me here (101 Copley Court).

Goodnight, precious child.
Edmund

From Edmund to Dorothy

Sunday September 29

Have you considered today's news?[34] It is the most important in many a long month. So many consequences are possible that it is fascinating — though futile, to speculate. I believe Foch hardly dared to hope for such success. The few days between now and winter will settle the location of the lines until spring.

I never was so concerned over my lack of pecuniary resources. In fact I never thought much about wealth. And now I do because it must be the means to so many objectives in our plans. It is the bridge across the Marne. And it shall be forthcoming, but not from the chest of the war quartermaster. My clients are not in the immediate foreground to be sure, but things will work out all right. If only you are with me, anything is possible.

Please write and tell me what you are doing and thinking and that you care for me.

Toujours,
Edmund

---

[34] Edmund refers to a new Allied campaign that began on September 26. The Meuse-Argonne Offensive ended the war on Armistice Day, November 11, 1918. It was the longest and most costly battle of World War I in terms of American deaths and casualties.

From Dorothy to Edmund

October 2, 1918

… I said this was to be a letter on houses, today, didn't I? I haven't any very definite convictions on the subject except that I like small ones best. If we live in a wild place I should like a cabin with nothing but fireplaces inside. And if the place is civilized I want mostly a white house although I'm not sure. It depends on the setting and the number of trees etc. And the library I want in green or brown with a few good pictures and many books and a fireplace and a lampshade of either rose or gold silk and a few brass things sitting around and andirons. I just want the house small because I think you can make its homelikeness more strongly concentrated if you don't have so much space. And every square inch of it must be home to both of us.

I never thought before how absurdly much houses must cost. It just seems hopeless to think of our ever having enough money to build one with. The thought of skillets and boilers and pans haunts me. I suppose they must cost a good deal. I think I shall spend next summer finding out about things like that. I'm not strongly domestic, you know, when it comes down to rock-bottom and to skillets. I think I have domestic instincts to a certain extent … and I think that people can learn anything if they put their minds on it … I am very glad that I don't have to have expensive surroundings to make me happy. Any kind of house will do until we can satisfy our tastes in constructing a real castle.

Always devotedly,
Dorothy

From Edmund to Dorothy

Washington
10 October 1918

Dearest:

Your "confessional" note came yesterday and it stirred me up a good deal, so much so that I spent two hours and more last night telling you about our affairs but today the whole thing seemed not to deserve so much space in our annuals, so the remarks were censored and withheld from the mails. I cursed the C.G. from the bottom of my heart.[35] It still makes me angry to think of your being subjected to his impudence but there is some satisfaction in knowing that he was suitably answered. Please tell me his name for someday we shall meet and I have something to tell him that is not romantic in any sense of the word. Enough of him.

Good luck to you and the *Aurora!*[36] I know the anxieties and pains of the editor of a sheet that purports to be "literary." There are some rewards too but not very notable ones. However the whole experience is bound to be very much worthwhile and may God speed your undertaking! Please send me a copy.

And Dorothy, anybody who really thinks you are a romantic schoolgirl is very shallow. I have seen a great many people during the last ten or fifteen years and my judgment is rather

---

[35] The "Cambridge Gentleman," the most opinionated and persistent of Dorothy's former suitors, visited her at Agnes Scott in October 1918. His refusal to take her attachment to Edmund seriously led Edmund to warn Dorothy in a subsequent letter that if the C.G. tried to kiss her, he "would cut his heart out." Beneath a serene demeanor lived a man of passionate intensity, one ready to take immediate action if necessary to defend the honor of his beloved.

[36] The *Aurora* was the Agnes Scott monthly magazine. Dorothy was one of its editors.

good. Your devotion to the things of the mind is one of the things that lifts you above the throng of worldly wise. May you always remain as you are and God bless you.

Yours always,
Edmund

From Edmund to Dorothy

Copley Court
Washington, D.C.
October 10, 1918

... Am I sure? And sure that I am sure? As time goes on I am more certain that you are the woman I have idealized since the time my beard began to appear. It was an odd stroke of fate that we ever came to see or hear of each other. The rest is not so strange. I love you because you are as you are—for your gifts, your heart, your honor and your unspoiled soul. You see this is independent of the way in which you comb your hair. We have seen little of each other and not because of that as in the movie drama, but in spite of it I have glimpsed enough in you to know that there is no mistake. I believe you when you say that you care for me—because you say so. I cannot reason out what the cause is for I am so plain and undistinguished in every respect. I accept it as one of the many mysteries of the world. And Dorothy dearest, your caring means more than anything else in my life. I ask only to spend it with you, protecting you, caring for you, making you happy. I can look forward to nothing else. Of course, it is a momentous thing to work out one's destiny with another mortal and that is why I wanted you to consider well. There is everything at stake. As far as I am concerned everything that I have said I abide by. I am quite certain—and that should answer your inquiry.

And so goodnight. Love shield thee well,

Yours worshipfully,
The Keeper

Edmund sent a telegram that reached Dorothy on October 14. True to his promise, he was making another trip to Atlanta to see her. Edmund planned to ask her to marry him.

From Dorothy to Edmund

Monday night
Oct. 14, 1918
(In great haste)

Dearest —

Your telegram came this morning and I can't tell you how glad I am that there is a possibility of seeing you so soon. I have not been able to think of anything else since I heard.

I answered it this afternoon and I hope you could understand it. I have no faculty for composing crisp concise telegrams (nor cables) and I do not know whether you could read between the disjointed words or not. This note now is in the nature of an explanation and must be brief for I have a world of things to do between now and the time I retire (10:30 as a result of the health talks).

We are quarantined and while it isn't strict at all I had to use all my arts on the mighty Dean to get her permission to go into town if you should arrive Saturday. She wasn't very hard to manage and she said I might. At any rate wire me exactly when you are coming. If it is after two I can be at the station (provided it is not night). If before, meet me in the lobby of the Piedmont at 2.

I must get to German. I can hardly wait to see you again and I do hope, hope, hope you can come Saturday.

Good-night dearest demon,
The Soul

From Edmund to Dorothy

Camp Meade
13 October 1918

Chere:

… Herein is an old letter of Isabel's — and her picture. She is the baby of the family. But do not bother with reading it unless you are especially interested in doing so. If you reach any opinions I will tell you more about her another time. I am anxious to have you know my family and to care for them as I do. They will appreciate you and love you I am sure …

From Isabel to Edmund

Monday May 27, 1918

Dearest Edmund,

Oh, Edmund you don't know how I appreciate you sending me that $100. Why absolutely it was perfectly wonderful of you. I was so surprised when I got it that I thought it was a mistake. As yet I haven't had it cashed but I shall soon. On the money order it says personal identification is required but no doubt I can work some sort of camouflage. Well, Ed, thank you just millions of times.

I wrote you a great many letters which apparently you never received. Papa was so worried and he wrote to me several times telling me to be sure to write you. The truth of the matter is I had written to you every week for some time. It rather took the wind out of my sails when you didn't receive them. So that is why I haven't written to you in some time. However I'm with you in spirit always—don't forget that will you?

… Thank you again, Ed, just millions for that $100. Believe me, I won't waste it.

With a great deal of love to you.

Your devoted sister,
Isabel

~ ~ ~

Edmund wrote to his mother to tell her about his intention to marry Dorothy.

From Edmund to Nora

October 18, 1918
YMCA Officer's Club, Camp Meade, MD

Dear Mother:

Would you be surprised if I told you that I have found the girl whom I wish to marry? And would you think I was hasty in my judgment if you knew that for almost a year my mind has been made up about her? Her name is Dorothy Thigpen and you must have heard me speak of her. We are not engaged. She has not even said that she will marry me. And if she does consent there will be no wedding bells for a long time—not until I can support her by the practice of law. But nevertheless if I am not killed in the war it is fairly certain that we will be married sometime.[37] And because it is more or less of a certainty I want you to know my plans.

---

[37] Edmund expected to return to France in January 1919.

Now, mother, Dorothy is an Episcopalian not a Catholic. I wish she were of our own faith but the fact is that she is not, and that I want to marry her in spite of that fact. When you know her you will understand how I feel about it. I know that you wanted me to acquire some sweet, good Catholic girl who would take good care of me and of the house. I can see the type you would select—in accordance with the offer you have so often repeated. In these things each person must rely on his judgment—on the instincts that God gave him. I have done only that and I have been very deliberate, mother.

I have always thought to choose a wife who would care for you and the rest of our family and who would also be admired and loved by all of you. That is a test I have always used on all of my friends. And did I ever bring anybody home that you did not like? So trust your son's taste and his good sense and believe that Dorothy is the kind of a daughter that you would be proud of. I should like to have her come to Ashland next summer. That is still a long way off. Please write to me what you think about my plans and keep the whole thing under a rigid censorship. I hate to entertain the Ashland gossips.

> With much love,
> *Edmund*

~ ~ ~

Edmund arrived at Union Station in Atlanta on Tuesday evening, October 20, 1918. Did he and Dorothy walk to Piedmont Park again and sit on the same green bench? No one can say. But when Dorothy accepted his proposal, he took the ring out of the little white box and put it on her finger.

The next evening, after they had supper together in Atlanta, Edmund said goodbye to Dorothy, got on the train, and returned to Camp Meade.

From Edmund to Dorothy

Camp Meade
24 October 1918

Fairest:

Once there was a knight who loved a lady. She was a paragon of womanly excellence, a creature of fire and gentleness, but his ardent desire to be a "parfit gentil knyght" fell far short of the ideals of his order and it seemed to him almost a hopeless aspiration that he might win her. The wars came on and thinking to gain some merit in fighting the heathen and purify his heart by courageous deeds, the knight went beyond the seas where the wars were. Always he cherished the hope that if he survived he might return a worthier knight, and so with some confidence, seek out the woman of his heart and offer himself to her. For she had been strangely gracious towards him in spite of his deficiencies and seemed to read his heart.

The wars went merrily on and it seemed well possible that some work of noble note might be accomplished by the eager champion, but his dreams of success were shattered by an order from his commander to return across the seas and teach the arts of destruction to the new legions that were flocking to the standard. There glimmering went the plans of knightly achievement, though true it is that his heart rejoiced at the near prospect of the dear lady. Across the sea he went and straightway sought her out to make his suit, unworthy and unproven though he was. The lady was still kind and gracious and by a miracle of faith and goodness accepted the knight as her lord, not as the gentle reader must know, for any merit that he had demonstrated, nor as Heaven knows, for his external beauty, for this knight had been but poorly favored by nature, but it must needs have been because in his soul her intuition found the seeds of manly worth, however slight the promise of fulfillment.

The camp wherein were gathering the new armies was far from the abode of the knight's lady and rarely could he see her. When it was possible to journey thither he eagerly set forth and spent with the lady the most joyful hours of his life. Returning his heart sank with the thought of how far deficient had been his power to express what he felt and how far short he fell from that which he fain would be for the lady's sweet sake. And so he longed for opportunities to do deeds worthy of a valiant man and chafed in the camp routine. After much reflection he saw the folly of waiting for battles with the heathen for proving himself, and the knight resolved to perform all things whatsoever that it befell his lot to do with the knightliest spirit, to be brave and magnanimous and truthful in common things and so develop the springs of virtue divined by the lady. And this resolution founded in him new courage and faith that in time he might so improve and develop his nature as to deserve the companionship of the fairest one, which he desired above all else in the world.

And which he desires as much as the salvation of his soul.

Edmund

From Edmund to Dorothy

Washington 27 October 1918

… What kind of a house do you dream of when you lie on the balcony under the stars with the wind blowing across you face? There are some white ones near Boston that I am anxious for you to see before we build our castle. I often think of the fire, our books and now also the piano. Think how much company we will get from those three things! And in how many homes are they wanting. And I imagine you there and see the light in your dear eyes and the fulfillment of all that I desire most. It is only a week ago tonight and it seems like seven years …

Yours devotedly
Edmund

From Edmund to Dorothy

Officer's Club, Camp Meade, MD
November 6, 1918

Dearest child:

I should like to wait calmly to the very last paragraph but lest I burst in the meantime know that I was today appointed "captain, field artillery, United States Army, with rank from July 30, 1918." It is not deserved if one judges by antebellum standards of experience and learning, but of necessity the age limit has been lowered and even now artillery officers are hard to get. I know that I can turn out a battery that can shoot with the best which is the most important thing! And the honor, if there be any in the appointment, I lay at your feet. For as I told you that first night, all that I acquire and all that I am or shall be belongs to you …

Dorothy dear, I knew that this matter of religion was troubling you. It has troubled me, too, and I have tried and tried to solve the riddle only to be baffled and come always back to the starting point. That is why I have never written a word about it. You are quite right in saying that we must look the question square in the face. But because it is about the only thing of any consequence that we differ upon I have hesitated to say anything without being sure of the ground on which I was treading.

First, it must not stand in the way of our being married. I know that Mr. Britling knew whereof he spoke, and my own mother's words are ringing in my ears, but I care for you too strongly to be restrained by any such prudential consideration. Surely Dorothy we agree upon this.

Then the matter becomes one of regulation and adjustment. If our house is to be small there must be much peace in the atmosphere! There can not and there must not be any "widening gulf."

You see how natural it is for me to believe in the teachings that have been held by my mystical Celtic ancestors for fifteen hundred years. I respect them greatly. I have never had any very serious doubts. Which may betoken a shallow understanding, for I know the fearful struggles that some men have — Carlyle for example. I might as well confess to you that I have not pondered the matter deeply and I know little of theology. You might be surprised in the simplicity of my religious philosophy. Most of the time I have been associated with people more or less resembling the Lord and Tommy, never with Catholics to any extent. This has been merely the way things happened. The Church certainly would not endorse me either as qualified to expound her teaching or as an example of piety. And yet I cling to this institution because it offers a rational explanation of the meaning and purpose of life. Of course there are details of doctrine that offend my nostrils, and there are practices in the church, both in the past and now, that I frown upon. But practices and rules are temporary, ephemeral and depend upon the people in the church and are not a part of the philosophy upon which the church is built. And so I blink at some things rather than repudiate the whole. I always test other systems of religion by the comparison with that which I believe in both as to reasonableness and results and then inquire: which on the whole is preferable? The choice has always been plain.

I know the popular prejudice against the Church. And I partly understand the reasons, which are complex and sometime fugitive. This is no time to discuss them, but I do know that the common feeling against Catholicism does not at all go to the merits.

Suppose I were a trapper and that we lived together in the depths of the wilderness. Our ideas on the question of religion would not disturb much the calm of our household, would they? Then, why, the difference that is produced is due to other people — tertium quids — and is traceable to human respect. Is the opinion of other people or of all mankind together enough to affect the way we feel towards each other? I believe that nine tenths of American religious opinion is a matter of social expedience and not of any conviction, or at least the convictions grow out of and are fostered by social pressure and human respect.

And finally, Dorothy, I am bold enough to believe that I can persuade you to see things as I do, not by dint of scholastic syllogisms, but by a moderate amount of explanations of things you misunderstand. Of course if you wanted to resist it would be impossible to make any headway but I only ask you to be fair and listen. I promise not to bore you.

So in the glad days after we have embarked on the adventure what I see instead of a "widening gulf"—that frightened you a little and I do not wonder that it did—is an ever narrowing field of disagreement between us on the religious issue. I do not know how set your ideas are, though I appreciate your saying that they will never change. I know the force of your will and your character. I know also that you are fair and honest in everything and that you love, and I rely on those points. And I have firm faith that the time will come when we will agree as perfectly in our religion as in other things.

With all my love,
Edmund

Charles and Daisy Learn the News

I do not believe happiness will result from a union of
Catholicism and Protestantism.

—Major Charles Thigpen, letter, November 29, 1918

When Dorothy's letter announcing her engagement to Edmund reached her parents in the second week of November, her father and mother looked at one another dumbstruck.

Stationed since late July at the base hospital at Fort Monroe, Virginia, Major Charles Thigpen was in charge of American soldiers with eye injuries sustained in recent AEF campaigns in France. Daisy had just arrived from Montgomery with young Charles to visit him, and when the envelope bearing their daughter's handwriting arrived that morning, Daisy opened it and began reading aloud. That was when the startling news tumbled out that Dorothy had accepted Edmund Shea's proposal of marriage.

Charles's anger erupted and he jumped to his feet, storming back and forth across the sitting room of his quarters in the Chamberlin Hotel. Certainly not! He had no intention of giving his consent! Never! And the rhetoric of his God-fearing Southern Baptist upbringing burst forth: Catholics were anathema, all of them! The Church was the Whore of Babylon, a satanic institution, and he went on to rail against the arrogant priests he'd dealt with in New Orleans when he was in medical school at Tulane.

To make matters worse, Charles knew that Edmund came from a forsaken corner of northern Wisconsin, and the thought of becoming the father-in-law of a full-blooded Yankee pushed him beyond the limit. He pulled a chair over to the desk and reached for pen and paper.

Daisy, the peacemaker in the family, brooded over the news of her firstborn child, whose loveliness endeared her to everyone she met. Dorothy's future had seemed so promising up to this moment.

Brought up in the Episcopal Church in Charleston, South Carolina, Daisy was a Colonial Dame and a loyal Daughter of the Confederacy, and like other mothers in her Montgomery circle of friends, she took it for granted that her daughter would marry and settle down nearby with an eligible young Southerner. What Daisy had in mind was a man with character and background, someone who would provide financial security.

Daisy was aware that Dorothy had been corresponding with Edmund, but they hadn't laid eyes on one another for over two years. The idea of falling in love with someone's letters was utterly preposterous, especially when Dorothy had always had plenty of beaus, and still did!

But Daisy was caught up short then, realizing the luxury of daydreaming about an ideal husband for her daughter had ended. The thought of welcoming a son-in-law so different from the one she had in mind — so unsuitable, it felt like — caused a wave of despair to sweep through her, and she went to find writing paper and a pen. She needed to tell Dorothy what she feared most: that a marriage between a Protestant and a Catholic was bound to end in bitter unhappiness.

The next morning Charles and Daisy awakened, plagued with second thoughts. Their strong-minded daughter had already made her decision and unless they amended their messages, they were in danger of losing her. Each of them sat down and composed another letter. Charles managed to withdraw his refusal of consent, though not without expressing his conviction that Dorothy was "making the biggest mistake of her life." Daisy attempted to smooth troubled waters by offering maternal reassurance and, despite her own misgivings, suggested waiting until they could have a family discussion in Montgomery at Christmastime.

Considering the hidebound traditions and constraints that governed the way Southerners thought about themselves in 1918, it is no wonder Charles and Daisy were distraught. By choosing to marry a Roman Catholic Yankee, Dorothy had stepped beyond the permissible limit not once but twice, on subjects Southerners felt passionate about. Yet Charles and Daisy's soul-searching discussions in the Chamberlin Hotel had also led them to acknowledge that Dorothy's life belonged to her, and the freedom to choose the man she wanted to marry was also hers. In spite of their fears, they respected her inner freedom and allowed the lines of communication to remain open.

Meanwhile, Edmund's family in the little town of Ashland, Wisconsin, was taken aback by the news of his engagement. His father William, a non-practicing Catholic with a tolerant slant on life, was surprised but not scandalized by his son's decision. But Edmund's mother Nora, a devout Catholic, was deeply offended. The Vatican I church of the time took a unilateral stand against mixed marriages, and warned its young men and women that such a choice automatically placed the soul of the Catholic party in mortal danger. Nora's younger brother was a priest, which led her to take the Church's disapproval especially seriously.

From Dorothy to Edmund

Monday A.M. November 18, 1918
In the Library

Dearest —

I am supposed to be reading "Adonais" this hour and weeping for him according to the command of the poet but such a disturbing epistle came from the Major at Fortress Monroe this morning that I am hastening to transmit the news to you.[38] After I got over being completely stunned by the contents I wept a little and stormed for a moment or so until the full humor of the situation burst upon me. I would send you the letter except that it sounds the least bit brutal to anyone who does not understand him as well as I do.

He says in hard and decided English that I shall never marry a Catholic. It is not as hard as it is decided in tone and he goes on to inform me that he is considering my happiness in the matter and advising me for my own good. When it had completely soaked in I tried to review it calmly and collectedly and I cannot help but be struck by the humor of the whole thing in spite of its undoubted seriousness. It is the eternal triangle except with an unusual man playing an unemotional part in affairs. My father at the apex quite decided in his own mind over this question and who will remain so, I believe. And you are at one end, quite, quite decided as to your religious faith and immovable. And I am at the other, as decided as either of you that I shall marry you and that nothing can come between us. Voilà. And we are all three rather decided creatures. That is the humor of it.

I cannot see the solution at the present moment because I do not think he will change, nor would I have you give up your faith even if you would, nor could I oppose him in a matter of this kind — and yet I fully intend to marry you. I do not see exactly how it is going to be accomplished and yet it simply has to be. It is all so utterly preposterous that right now I can see nothing but the absurdity of it. His words continue to echo

---

[38] Dr. Charlie's first letter to Dorothy has not survived, but from Dorothy's comments, her father's disapproval was decided and vehement.

in my mind: "He will have to give up either you or his religion. You will never marry one of his faith with my consent or approval." You shall not give up either and I shall marry you with his consent and approval — somehow. I do not flatter myself that I can move him, for being older, he cannot see the things as you and I do and he has one of the strongest wills I have ever come in contact with.

Please don't think I am writing this with the idea of even faintly suggesting that you choose between me and your faith. I think — I am almost sure that you would choose the latter and such a choice would not make me think that your love for me were any the less powerful or strong than it is. I would understand it perfectly and the point of view from which the choice were made. I will not have you make any such absurd choice. I merely tell you this because it is very serious and I think you should know how my father feels. Probably your own family is just as opposed to me. It is simply a difference of viewpoint.

Isn't it absurd? We are being treated like children and I am twenty-one years old! I do not of course resent anything he said because I can see his attitude. He is looking out for my happiness, he thinks, and I love him all the more for it but it is nevertheless perfectly absurd and very disturbing.

And write me at once and promise me not to worry. I am not — that is, not much. And I shall pray that his heart may be softened as Moses prayed for Pharaoh's. Do not think I am flippant but I see no other way to regard it except as humorous.

And do not worry because something just <u>has</u> to happen because we love each other.

Devotedly yours,
Dorothy

Chapter 25

From Edmund to Dorothy

Wednesday, Nov 20, 1918

My dearest Dorothy:

Your letter telling of the major's ideas and prohibition came today. And I have not a thing to say nor a thought that is not dreary. What he says cuts. I had not expected it and I am utterly at a loss to understand what he is thinking of. His point of view is one that I am not familiar with. But it is not his opinion of me that discourages me but his proposing to prevent you from marrying me. That simply takes the wind out of my sails — and they flap. His wishes weigh heavily with you. It is right that they should. I hate to work at cross purposes with your father. The idea of opposing the very man who loves you most, outside the Corporation, and with you as the center of contention is maddening. The trouble is in the choice that he forces upon you. For your father is wrong when he says I must choose — I have chosen, and my beloved, I want you far more than life or anything temporal — and life always has been exhilarating and sweet. Never will my heart change, never, never.

If you take either alternative you wound one of us. To simply disregard his earnest wishes is unfilial. Were he a tyrant, the tactics of Lochinvar might be justifiable, but he is not — merely very unreasonable, and entirely mistaken in his ideas in this instance. I know that if you married me against your father's direct order, you would have to pay the price. And it would be a bitter sacrifice. So it would be selfish and not decent to urge you to go blindly on with me. I cannot tell you what to do with such an alternative. But I can tell you that I had rather a hundred times be in a shallow grave on the front in France than lose you now.

This is pure gloom, my dear. I am sorry to make you feel as I do. We certainly are not prospering in the precious plans that we have dreamed about for so long. I admire your faith that things must work out as we wish because we love each other.

The only ray of light I see is that your father may think better of his counsel. Somehow I believe that if he had been in the vicinity of Château-Thierry last summer where everybody was putting his insignificant little life into the game that he was trying to win, and lives were going out every minute freely, he would have realized that the manner of a man's worship is one of the less important things about him. That is to say that he is the least bit old-fashioned. If you think it will do any good I will pay him a visit! Surely he will not persist in his present attitude. I can't believe it possible. Does your mother agree with him?

Please don't get the flu.

With all my love,

Edmund

From Edmund to Dorothy

Camp Meade, Maryland
Thursday Nov 21, 1918

Dearest:

Only to say goodnight and that never have I realized more keenly what you mean to me and how much I depend on you. There has been a multitude of things to do and fortunately not much time was left to think about the major's attitude. The thought makes the world look cold and cheerless. Tomorrow there is an examination in Orientation, Dispersion and Conduct of fire for all officers in the brigade. Those who pass don't have to go to school anymore. I am très fatigué and will add to this tomorrow. Plus chère, God bless you and keep you safe, always.

Perhaps it is not permitted for a person to be as happy as I was in the realization of having you. True I used to complain of the status I occupied in the army, but that was only a surface disturbance. I was profoundly happy — and hopeful of everything and buoyant. It is easy to realize that looking backward. The possibility of losing you — I refuse to believe that it is more — is chilling and destroys my interest in things and in people and to keep from brooding I seek company and occupation. It is the first difficulty in my life that I could devise no way out of. The elements of the problem are so few, and you think your father unchangeable. Sometimes he makes me angry and sometimes I see that he is merely working for your happiness and looks at me only impersonally. I try to think of how I would regard suitors for my daughter and so justify his attitude, or at least understand it. Didn't you have any idea that this was coming, Dorothy?

I will enclose, if I can find it, something my father wrote about the general question. My mother has always impressed upon me that I should marry a Catholic girl. She used to say that she would find a wife for me if ever I should be able to care for one. The kind she would select was a subject for much family humor. But strongly though she might recommend a course to me, she would yield to my choice. And knowing you will be sufficient to make her praise God, that her son was so fortunate. The personal element would overweigh her abstract prejudice. But with your father, the abstract judgment is untempered by any qualification based on what I might be outside of being a Catholic. That is what I can't understand. Can you?

Sometimes I consider giving up my religion. It is unthinkable. Somehow it is so different from giving up anything pertaining to the world or this life. There is nothing that I possess or ever will possess that I would not cheerfully part with for the sake of one whom I am bound to. To abandon my religion would be false to my character, such as it is. It is not that I am so zealous a partisan of the church and her ways. Perhaps it is butt-headedness in part. To be a martyr has never seemed very difficult to me.

All of which, dearest child, is so egotistical that I hesitate to send this letter. I fear it may not be taken as I wish, and yet you always have understood me, and besides why shouldn't I tell you how I feel about the matter? It concerns us equally. At one end of my logic is the dilemma created by your sire. Opposite to it is every fibre of my being that says I love you above all things and that everything else will adapt itself if we love each other enough.

Goodbye until tomorrow.

Devotedly,
Edmund

From Dorothy to Edmund

Blackfriars
Agnes Scott College
Decatur, Georgia
Tuesday Night
Nov 26, 1918

Mon bien aimé,

Here is a letter from Marion which came today that I love. I know that you will enjoy reading it. It gave me the queerest feeling of pride to read it and all the splendid things he says about you. I am greatly relieved to find that he approves of me. I used to take Marion's silence as a bad sign.

I already knew all that he writes about you and a thousand things besides, and I am continually discovering new things. He seems to think he must plead your case. He does not know that is was decided fully two years ago as far as I was concerned and only depended on the charity of the Fates and yourself to be finally worked out.

And do not believe anything he says about my being a fine bit of machinery and likely to blow up pretty high if a monkey wrench is dropped into the works. I don't mind monkey wrenches provided you drop them and I shall follow his sound advice which I had decided on previously and not head for a lamp post. Also I have decided to dim my lights in order to exhibit to the world your "glow" which I know so well exists. It is that very quietness, Edmund dear, that I love so about you. I cannot see why you should care for me as I am now. I can read through every line of Marion's letter that I am not half good enough for you. I know it so well. Of course I'm not but I shall spend my life trying to be. And please if you ever feel inclined to "glow" in public cut off my bright lights which cannot help but be tiresome. I like "glows" far, far better. That is why I love you so.

You will get this Thursday which is Thanksgiving. Marion's letter, because it stirred memories of two years ago, brought over me with a rush all that we have to be thankful for. The greatness of what has happened to us fairly takes my breath away.[39] Having you safe and the possibility banished forever of losing you looms largest next to the priceless blessing of your devotion. It will be the most thankful Thanksgiving of my life

---

[39] Dorothy refers to the war having ended two weeks prior. Lt. Marion Rushton's letter was written from Paris a week before Armistice Day.

and this last thing which has threatened to come between us shall not mar it. It simply must work out. I know it will.

Goodnight beloved. I care for you always more and more,

Dorothy

P.S. Please send Marion's letter back when you finish with it as I want to write him.

From Marion to Dorothy

Battery E 112th H.F.A. Paris, France
Wednesday Nov. 5.18

Dear Dorothy:

Rachel's last letter brings the very welcome news that you are wearing Ed's ring and I am just as tickled as I can be. I wrote him a long time ago what I thought of you and, though one or two disciplinary actions (deserved I admit — but is justice kindness?) you have taken have nettled me quite a bit (par example, the present way you take of saying that I will be "interested for Shea's part" if not yours), the opinion still stands unchanged and will perhaps always. (Why can't you understand how I hate to write letters?)

You are a delightful mixture of the sane with the romantic unexpected, and you've energy enough in turning on the footlights to illumine the different sides of yourself. Old Shea will probably be kept busy year in and year out trying to find out who it is that he has gone and married, and what could be more charming than that, being assured that he will always find something good?

You will find in him absolutely solid worth, leavened with a demure dry good humor — a combination which appeals to me in such a way that I always say he is the best man I know — and I have seen a good many at the schools and in the Army. And I know, Dorothy, Soul of the Corporation, what I am talking about. I lived with that man near on three years, up in the morning, to bed at night: I've drunk beer with him (we confess to that crime) and I've buttoned the collar of his dress shirt while he tied my ties, and I've been rich with him and poor with him, and he stands the test. You will say with a flick of the Dorothea black eyes (Does the Soul dwell there?) "Oh, yes, he has the cardinal virtues, I'll grant that; most of the men I know have." But Dorothy, he has more; he has ability and an everlasting charm. He doesn't turn it on often. I can scarcely imagine an occasion when your bright lights will be dimmed enough for his glow to appear. But it's there, Soul of my Corporation, and it's up to you to make it glow ...

I do not regard these encomiums so belated though the battle is now won. Is it trite to say that marriage is the beginning of the love story? And, of the women I know, with you that is most likely to be true. I do not mean that you are fickle, but like any fine bit of machinery (a charming metaphor) you work best when best cared for, and you will blow up pretty high if anyone accidentally, or otherwise, drops a monkey wrench into the works. (Isn't it glorious to be brutally frank!) Now Shea isn't going around dropping wrenches, but if one should suddenly appear, can't you take my word for it (Corporation directors never lie to each other — they save that), throw out the clutch, and idle a while before heading for a lamp post? I repeat it, I lived with the man three years, and I know.

I have risked writing the last paragraph because I understand Shea is soon to return to France, and the engagement is liable to be a long one. There is nothing more trying in the social relationships of this earth. Added to that, Shea is not of our people, is not on the spot, and there are others who are—notably one who, Rachel half humorously says, argues that you love Shea "as a hero not as a husband." There is nothing more unsatisfactory than "living on letters" but a real affection will survive it. And I don't know how much of a hero Ed is but I do know he is a damned sight better husband than hero. Take it from me, cuss word and all.

I am writing to Ed today asking him if in the light of changed circumstances he would consent to a law partnership in Montgomery after the war. He refused it once before. I do not know whether it is what you want or what he wants, but if it does fit in with your plans, it will serve the double purpose of making me very happy, too. It will serve the purpose of saving you to us in Montgomery and of making a satisfactory addition.

Well, I have descanted long enough for one who is a side scene in the play. But as a parting word Dorothy Thigpen, I tell you that this is a very wise and a very happy thing that you have done. And I will expunge your Seal and revoke your charter if you listen to the blandishments of that anti-hero husband-candidate of yours.

Sincerely,
Marion

~~~

The second letters Dorothy's father and mother wrote to her reveal their continuing concerns over her decision to marry Edmund.

Chapter 25

From Charles to Dorothy

Fortress Monroe, Virginia
Nov 29, 1918

My dearest Dorothy,

Your letter came two days ago. After I wrote the letter I did,
I was sorry I had done so, but I was so upset at the moment
that I felt it was my duty to write it and say what I did. Your
happiness is mine and your future is yours, you can make it
what you will. I hate to think of you bringing up your children,
if there be any in your future life and that is your mission here,
in the Catholic Church. I have no use whatever for the Catholic
Church. It is narrow and bigoted and sacrifices principle to
further its own influence and ends. I have seen more of it than
you have. I spent three years in New Orleans, working under its
influence, when I was a student of medicine. It is full of deceit
and intrigue. I don't see how any intelligent person could be
completely subdued by its influence. It warps judgment and
makes everyone and everything not Catholic, one sided. But you
are to choose just as you please. I shall never say another word
to you on the subject. I only mean to protect you and ensure
your happiness on this earth, and I do not believe happiness
will result from a union of Catholicism and Protestantism. It
may apparently be at first, but there will surely come a time
when there will be a jar.

I know exactly how you feel, with reference to there being
no other person who you can admire and love. This comes
into the life of each of us. I have had the same experience in
my early life, but I see now, I was mistaken, and had I married
then, it would have proven a fatal mistake and my life would
have been a failure. As it is, I was past 30 years of age and your
mother 25 and past when we were married. We looked on the

sensible side of it and we have done the right thing. I have, I know, never regretted one moment of my married life. She had her fancies too, but she had sense enough to wait until she found one who she thought was worthy of her and who was able to provide for her. So, after all, it is more of a partnership, both members of which should be properly balanced, physically, mentally, morally, and financially, established upon a sound foundation. I have said now all I have to say about the subject, except finally to remind you that you don't have to get married to be happy or to have someone provide for you. That has already been done.

Charles has been in bed nine days today with Influenza. Just what I expected to happen if he left home. He is free from fever today and as soon as he is able to travel he is going home, and never again will I consent to your mother and Charles leaving home again when there is a flu epidemic over the land. It was against my judgment.

With much love,
Father

From Daisy to Dorothy

Hotel Chamberlin
Fortress Monroe, Va
Friday 29 November, 1918

Darling Dot,

Your letter to me and the one to Father came day before yesterday. I would have written you before today but was feeling wretchedly and pretty well worn out from the strain and worry. Charles is better today and is propped up in the bed writing a letter. He has no fever today, and I hope can get up tomorrow. He has had quite a severe little spell and it has been anything but pleasant.

About your letter to Father, he read it to me and I think it was a sweet lovely letter from a girl to her father and I understand your point of view perfectly. Also he read me his answer to you — you will think it is entirely too practical, I am sure, and looking at it with your eyes, it does sound practical and of course, it is not fair to look at your question from our experienced eyes. I know I had quantities of flattering fancies, but I never truly loved anyone but Father and I wonder how I ever thought I ever fancied the others. I realize too, that you have had previous fancies and that Edmund is really the love of your life. And if it were not for his religion, I should not even question the thing — leaving that entirely to you.

You do not know anything about his environment — and environment does count. You may have to spend the remainder of your days with people you detest and while he may be all sufficient — there will come days when things will jar — but all this I do not intend to go into, that is yours to settle, and I know you are sensible enough to weigh all these things.

But the religion I cannot get away from. It's not that I am personally prejudiced against the Roman Church. I have never had a single disagreeable personal experience. But I do know that there is nothing that can break up family union and happiness — unless of course you give up your faith — which I hope you will not — I have known too many cases — they make it a matter of persecution until they get you.

I feel it would separate you from us, but even so, I do not want to interfere with your freedom and your future happiness, and you must decide for yourself. Of course such a thing as our preventing you is out of the question and entirely out of date these days. I think we had better wait until Xmas to see about it. You could hardly expect Father and me to be very enthusiastic about your marrying a man we do not even know and whom Father has never seen.

There are many things to be decided and I do not suppose you will marry until you graduate, so there is no reason to rush into it.

Does Edmund expect to stay in the Army or go back to the practice of law?

I have only one aim and object in life and that is your happiness, but I cannot help being a little selfish and not wanting you to get married so soon. Be satisfied though with whatever is best for you — we will surely support it whether it is our pleasure or not — for we would not be happy — if we had done anything to hurt you — so cheer up and enjoy your happiness now and wait for final issues.

With a heartful of devoted love,
Mother

From Dorothy to Edmund

Blackfriars
Agnes Scott College
Decatur, Georgia
Tuesday Night
Dec. 3, 1918

Dearest —

Letters came from the Major and from Mother which made me ashamed to have had even fleeting moments of rebellion. I wept over them both. They tell me that they desire nothing but my happiness and that the question is for you and me to decide as we think best. And they demand quite reasonably to know you and to talk over the question with you when you come and see me before Christmas. Father said that he regretted the first letter he wrote on the subject, but that he could not retract any of his views on your religion. They both say that we can never be happy differing as we do, and that when they advise me it is for my happiness and yours. But they are both willing to consider the question and talk it over sanely which is a distinct improvement over the attitude of two weeks ago. I feel ever so much better about it and I am going to try to get it off my mind until you come. I am so tired of trying to reason about it. It has been fearfully hard when the people whom I love best in the world have been telling me entirely different things, you and they. I know only one thing and that is that I love you and trust you above all people. Beyond that I cannot see anything.

Let's not discuss it anymore in letters. I am absolutely confident that we shall arrive somewhere when you come and that we _can_ work it out. I shall read you these letters when I see you. You do understand their point of view, don't you? It is only because they care for me, too, that they are doing what they consider best for me. Because we disagree with them does not make their motives any the less sincere nor unselfish.

I am going beneath the stars in a few minutes. Out there this question does not seem to amount to a row of pins. I wish you were a trapper and I your wife in the wilderness.

Good-night and God bless you —

Devotedly,
Dorothy

From Dorothy to Edmund

Atlanta, Ga.
Dec. 8, 1918
Sunday night

Dearest:

This afternoon I had a message at college that the famille had arrived and would be at the Piedmont until tomorrow, having stopped over to see Dr. Hoke about Charles' foot. So I came in immediately and have been with them all the afternoon. And you can imagine how glad I was to see father. I had not seen him, you know, since July and I was almost as happy as when you came. I think he looks fairly well, but he looks so much older and he is so broken-hearted over Charles' foot which is far worse than it was before the operation … It makes the tears rush to my eyes to watch him as he looks at Charles. You know he simply worships him and he was so hopeful that this last operation would make him quite all right. He does nothing but brood over it and it just breaks my heart …

I have not even mentioned my own troubles to him because in the first place it would have been selfish and in the second — this is not the psychological moment. While father took Charles to Dr. Hoke this afternoon I mentioned it to Mother and she being of a philosophic and more or less cheerful nature told me to stop being gloomy and to wait until you came at Christmas. I know it will turn out as we wish …

Yesterday morning I got a summons to go to the Dean's office. It always scares me to death because usually it means that an offence has been committed or that a death in the family has occurred.

She wanted Lucy and me to take two wounded soldiers from Ft. McPherson to our tables for supper and entertain them afterwards. They were the most pathetic things. Especially the one who sat next to me: a Mr. Bullard from Detroit, a nephew of the General Bullard who was in command of a division I believe, during the early part of the war.

Mr. Bullard had been shot through the motor area of the brain and his left leg was paralyzed. Besides he had had shell-shock. His face haunts me. I have never seen such a beautiful and patient expression. He was so pathetic. I kept thinking all evening of you, dearest, and of how much we have to be thankful for. Suppose you had come back like that. I cannot bear even to think about it because you are so well and strong and whole. I think sometimes that I suffered during those months when you were there and when I did not know whether you were living or dead, but I know that it was as nothing compared with what I saw in that man's face last night. I have thought since then of what Lucy said about him — that all the suffering in the world was in his face — and it makes me so profoundly thankful for your dear life and strength that I am humble before the blessing.

Edmund darling I love you so. Do you know how much? I do not know myself because it is deep and strong and I cannot fully express it but I know that I cannot live without you. And I shall not. Tell me that this question upon which we disagree cannot and will not make any difference between us. Please tell me. Make me know it. I love you.

Dorothy

From Edmund to Dorothy

Washington, D.C.
December 14, 1918

Dearest:

Yesterday was the last at Camp Meade. There was nothing but the burning of records, packing of trunks and bedding rolls, drawing of final pay and goodbyes. I got away in the drizzle of late afternoon with all my baggage in a Ford jitney, and never left a place with fewer regrets. A cantonment is not a home, and the name is not one to conjure with. I was tired and went to bed early and slept hard. I didn't write because I thought the day — today — would bring results, which it did.

The Chief Counsel of the Federal Trade Commission in Washington D.C. is an old friend of my father, and knows the family quite well. He has been very thoughtful for my welfare and suggested that I come to look over the office before going west. So today I called on him. He explained the nature of the work, introduced me to the members of the Commission and the other lawyers of the office, of whom there are about forty and when he finally asked me what I thought about working for him I felt quite enthusiastic over the prospects. Of course I do not intend to stay there long — only until the country settles down a bit and until I can reconnoiter the golden west. I also am anxious to see Major Drain of the 146th who is a Spokane lawyer and a good one. I should like to go with him.

The beauty of the work here is that there will be considerable travelling and an opportunity to meet good lawyers who respect the firms and corporations prosecuted by the Commission. The work and association are congenial. It offers a present means of livelihood, which is not to be sneezed at in these uncertain times. The salary is $2820 a year. The C.C. said he turns away a dozen lawyers a week looking for a place in his department.

So what think you of my decision? I had you and our plans in mind every minute. It seemed to me that this opening will give me a chance to review my rusty learning and get back some facility in practice, and also cast about for a permanent location, without starving during the meantime. And the travel feature lures me with the prospect of seeing you occasionally during the next few months. Finally the boarding program can go on uninterrupted.[40] On the other side of the scales was only uncertainty. I hope you approve of my choice.

I am so anxious to see you that I can hardly keep from getting on the train. I am sending you a night letter to find out your wishes regarding my coming. The Major had better be ready for an offensive when our combined battalions approach.

With all my love,
Edmund

Buoyed by Dorothy's assurance that her parents wanted him to come, Edmund travelled to Montgomery the week before Christmas.

During his brief visit, he and Dorothy had dinner with Marion Rushton and his fiancée. And he enjoyed meeting Mrs. Nash Read and Dr. and Mrs. Baldwin. But he found no opportunity to forge a meaningful connection with Dorothy's mother and father, even though he stayed at the pillared house.

~~~

---

[40] Edmund plans to stay in Washington with his sister Louise and her husband, Dr. Paul Stone, until he can find an apartment.

225

After Edmund left Montgomery, he went to Ashland to spend the Christmas holidays with his family. In contrast to the silent treatment he received from Dorothy's parents, what greeted him at home was a barrage of angry criticism from his mother. Nora refused to sanction his decision to marry a Protestant. At least William bestowed his blessing, and Edmund felt confident that Dorothy's love for him was abiding. Somehow, he hoped they would find a way to soften the opposition to their marriage. But how they would go about this was far from clear when the year 1918 came to an end.

26

Dorothy Returns to Montgomery
Summer 1919

We must not wish for the disappearance of our troubles
but for the grace to transform them.
—Simone Weil, *Gravity and Grace*

After the Christmas holidays ended in early January 1919, Dorothy returned to Agnes Scott. Once she settled into her seat on the train, she closed her eyes, grateful to have a chance to reflect and sort through some jumbled memories.

What came back to her first was the tone of her father's voice, sounding worried and unhappy. More than once he told her that her life belonged to her, and yet he insisted that a marriage between a Catholic and a Protestant was bound to end in unhappiness.

And though her mother's phraseology was more indirect and her voice softer, her feelings against the Catholic Church were equally intense. Her parents' friends in Montgomery were staunch Protestants, mostly Presbyterians and Episcopalians. She herself had never had a Catholic friend growing up, and she could see that her feelings, like those of her parents, were bound to be one-sided and prejudiced.

Then she thought back to Edmund's visit just before Christmas, and to her hopes that some good conversations would take place between him and her father and mother. But there were none beyond the level of exchanging pleasantries. Her parents had not ignored him exactly — she didn't believe they would do that — and yet they had scarcely acknowledged his presence in their midst. He had made no comment to her about their cool reception, but it left her feeling disheartened.

Their chief objection, as they stated more than once, was Edmund's membership in the Catholic Church. They saw it as an impossible stumbling block, with the Church's imperious ways and its insistence in a mixed marriage that all children be baptized and raised as Catholic. It went without saying that they also lamented the unfortunate fact that Edmund was a Yankee, but no one could undo that.

Her mother had asked her if he might be willing to give up the Church. When Dorothy had raised the question in a letter, Edmund had said it would be impossible for him to give up what he considered to be an intrinsic part of who he was. He felt a profound kinship with his ancient Celtic forebears.

Dorothy didn't understand what he meant. What upset her parents was the arrogant present-day Church that asserted that everyone outside its ranks was headed for hell. And yet, she trusted Edmund's integrity, and knew she loved him and wanted to marry him. She was still mulling over unsolved obstacles when she drifted off to sleep as the train travelled on through northeast Alabama, heading toward the Georgia border.

~~~

Not long after Dorothy returned to college and registered for her second semester courses, she found a letter from Edmund in her Inman Hall cubby with distressing news.

Chapter 26

From Edmund to Dorothy

Fort Wayne, Ind.
January 18, 1919

Dorothy dearest I wish that you were with me. The world never seemed bleak and lonely before Isabel died. It would be a relief to talk to you about her, to tell you of her life, her death and of her pure and generous soul. I didn't realize how much I loved her. She went so suddenly — pneumonia. On the morning of her nineteenth birthday she died. The previous evening she said to my mother, "I am going to die tomorrow," and smiled as she said it. We laid her away in the cemetery at home. Her grave is on the very top of a hill that overlooks the bay and the distant ridges in the west. The snow is blowing there and she is sheltered by the birch trees, and pines and firs that she loved so well.

Good night beloved. God bless you.

Devotedly,

Edmund

In the winter of 1919 while the flu epidemic still raged in the United States and in other countries, Dorothy lived under new restrictions at Agnes Scott. Students were warned to stay away from movie theaters and large restaurants in Atlanta, or any place where people crowded together. Newspapers continued to report large numbers of flu-related deaths and it was well known that a virulent form of influenza could carry off a young healthy person within a few days. Dorothy was aware of the facts, and yet her understanding was abstract. When she learned from Edmund about Isabel's death she was shocked, and wrote to send her sympathy, but she could not yet fathom the depth of his grief.

~~~

The subject of denominational differences still troubled both Edmund and Dorothy. On February 6, Dorothy wrote to express some concerns:

From Dorothy to Edmund

Agnes Scott
Thursday Afternoon
Feb. 6, 1919

Dearest —

... The letter containing your convictions about the religious question came this morning and stirred me so profoundly that I have thought of nothing else since I read it. First of all, I wish to tell you that I understand perfectly the spirit in which you said what you did, and that I can never thank you enough for it nor for the things you said in it. You put the whole thing in such a beautiful way that I cannot tell you how it touched me.

I realize the pitiless logic of what you write so well. So well it all repeats itself over and over and over and appeals to me as a person who is capable of reasoning sanely and clearly at times. It is what I have been unconsciously saying in my own mind although I did not dare to utter it even to myself. It is all just as you have said. I felt the same way you did when you were in France.

It was your life that I was thinking about and because of the bigness and the breadth of the cause for which you were there, such a thing as a doctrinal difference faded into the background as an absurdity. And just as you do not care about my creed, neither do I care about yours, except as we said, that it might make a difference between us. Heaven knows I wish we were the same thing, no matter what, and I am not so narrow or so bigoted as to believe that you haven't just as much right to your faith as I have to mine. That is merely a repetition said in a poorer way of what you said in your letter and what we have finally evolved to from our various talks and discussions on the subject. And I know, and you know, too, that we were avoiding the main point in the whole question — that of the children.

Please do not think that I condemn your church because I do not. I see your right to it because you inherited it and because you were born into it. But can't you see that what I am, I am and that I was born into a church just as you were? I would willingly give it up if I could, to banish all the shadow which seems to darken the prospect of our marriage and simply because you ask it and because I trust you and love you as I trust and love no other human being. But I don't see how I am to do it. I can't see how I am to become a part of something and to have that something a part of me when I could not be sincere in the process. For it seems to be far more to me than merely the act of joining the Roman Catholic Church. It seems the radical change of my whole personality and it exists as such and I don't see how I am to change it.

Don't think that I hate the Catholic Church. I do not. I like some things about it and I do not like other things, as you know. But I am I, and it is it and I cannot help it. It is a horrible fact and Heaven knows that I wish I were it. I am not and personally I do not believe that I shall ever be. Sincerely though I promise to do what you ask me to — to attempt to be open minded about it. Since your letter, I am perfectly willing for you (but not for anybody else) to try to convince me, which you will remember I was not at Christmastime. It is hard to get rid of 21 years of prejudice if you wish to call it that, but because I love you I shall try. Please do not feel encouraged because I honestly do not believe I will ever change.

You are so good when you say that you love me enough to live without me if marriage is a mistake. I know you are thinking of my happiness. But I do not want happiness like that. I want only you and the happiness that I know you will give me if I marry you. And we can pray that God won't let this make a difference and He won't. For I love you too deeply and too strongly to live without you.

Goodbye and God bless you now and always.

Dorothy

~~~

In mid-February Dorothy learned from Rachel Rushton about the sudden death of Wyatt, Rachel and Marion's brother. Wyatt died of an infection on board a troopship while travelling home from France. When she saw Rachel break down in tears over her brother's death, Dorothy wept herself. Wyatt was a childhood friend. She had received a letter from him last November when he was in France.

After she accompanied Rachel back to Montgomery on the train and grieved with the Rushton family, Dorothy understood Edmund's own sorrow on a deeper level.

From Dorothy to Edmund

Sunday night
Feb 16, 1919

Edmund dearest —

I took the early train back this morning and arrived at Agnes Scott about noon and I am utterly weary tonight so I will send only a word. When Rachel got the news she wanted me to go home with her and of course I wanted to because it is such a miserable trip and I could not bear to think of her taking it alone. So I dressed and threw some necessities in a suitcase in fifteen minutes and we caught the 2 o'clock for Montgomery and arrived about 8:30 last night. I arose at 5:30 this morning and got here at noon.

I am enclosing an article about Wyatt. It was a fearful thing and I have never seen anyone so thoroughly broken up as Mr. Rushton. He left this morning for Newport News to meet the ship and came on the train with us. They do not know whether the body was buried at sea or not and the lack of details makes it so much more terrible.

It has dawned on me since I saw their grief and since I was with Rachel through it all how fearfully hard it must have been for you, beloved.[41] I thought I realized before but I didn't, and all the way to Montgomery yesterday I was thinking of you constantly.

I shall write more when I am not so tired and worn out.

Goodnight and know that I worship you.

Devotedly,
Dorothy

~~~

In one of his February letters, Edmund asked Dorothy what her father and mother truly thought of him. He was referring to his brief pre-Christmas visit. Dorothy responded on February 27, 1919, doing her best to tone down her parents' negative feelings.

---

[41] Dorothy refers to Isabel's death in January.

From Dorothy to Edmund

… You ask me, dear one, to tell you honestly what my mother and father think of you and my marrying you, and admonish me not to "tuck the letter away."

It is a difficult thing to tell you because they claim that they did not see enough of you to form anything but a superficial estimate. Mother has told me time and time again that I gave them no chance to really talk to you, and that they saw you only at the few meals you had at home. I suppose that is more or less true. I did not give them much chance. The superficial estimate from all I can gather is this: that you are well-mannered, quiet, reserved, dignified, and refined. They claim that they know nothing whatever about you, or your ancestry, and you cannot expect them to surrender their eldest (whom they consider an extraordinary being) to a stranger.

Of course, you and I see it in an entirely different light. I've never seen your family, but I've never had any doubts about their being all that they should be, simply because I know what kind of person you are, and I make my judgments concerning them accordingly.

Also, concerning your "environment": I have never lost a moment's sleep over that either. I simply know they are desirable and all that they should be. But you can see the viewpoint of my ancestors. They see that I am in love with you and they think perhaps I am a little rash, and of course, like all parents, they cannot comprehend that in the eyes of the world I am no longer a child, and that I can judge better than they in a matter of this kind …

You see, this thing came as a shock to them. They had no idea that I was considering marriage, and they can't realize that I am grown-up …

They don't regard you as a personality, or as an individual at all, merely as a type. They know absolutely nothing about you except what I have told them and naturally they consider my opinions prejudiced — which they are slightly.

Aside from two facts, I think they would look upon the whole proceeding favorably after a certain length of time, and after they had become reconciled to the fact that I cared for you more than for them.

The first is, of course, the religious question. The second is the fact that when I marry you I shall go to a "far country" to live. Of course I shall hate to leave. It will mean leaving many, many friends and associates which are very dear to me. But I don't want to live in Montgomery, though it will be hard to leave in a way.

And it matters not where we are so long as we are together. I know nothing whatever about the land to which you will take me. Nor do I care especially, since I trust your judgment absolutely in the matter. We have our lives to live as our parents had theirs before us, and they must realize that when a woman marries a man, and that when that woman be I, she leaves all others in the universe, and goes with him ...

When Dorothy told Edmund that her parents "did not regard him as a personality or as an individual at all, but rather as a type," she also threw light on their unconscious distress.

What Charles and Daisy saw in Edmund was a stereotype of a Roman Catholic Yankee, and while he was a guest in their house before Christmas, they did not show "a scintilla of interest in him," to use Edmund's phrase. They were too afraid their daughter would be unhappy if she married him to treat him in any other way.

~~~

On February 26, 1919, Dorothy wrote to Edmund to tell him she had been elected to Lambda Tau, the Agnes Scott honor society.

Her election was recognition of her ability to earn top grades in rigorous college courses as she had done in high school and in grade school. Receiving her Lambda Tau pin would later be a sweet reminder of the evening in July 1916 when Edmund put his Phi Beta Kappa key in her hand and invited her to become a member of the Corporation. In 1926, when Agnes Scott established its own Phi Beta Kappa chapter, Dorothy received her own Great Seal. She often wore her golden key on the wristband of her watch.

~~~

When Dorothy graduated from Agnes Scott and returned to Montgomery in May, Edmund was still living in Washington, D.C., while he worked at the Federal Trade Commission. He had begun to think about looking for a long-term job with a law firm, perhaps in the Northeast or Northwest.

~~~

During the summer of 1919, Edmund and Marion Rushton exchanged several letters. Marion told him he was planning to be married in September, and asked Edmund to be his best man, who accepted with pleasure.

The wedding ceremony would take place in the Methodist Episcopal church in Gloucester, Massachusetts, where Marion's fiancée — incredibly, also named Marion — lived. Marion Hedin was a young woman Marion had met when he and Edmund shared an apartment in Cambridge during their Harvard Law School days.

In late September Edmund travelled to Gloucester for the festivities, and during the weekend Marion found time to sit down and tell Edmund how opposed Dr. Thigpen continued to be over Dorothy's plans to marry Edmund. As a result of Marion's sobering words,

Edmund became more aware than he had been of the pressures Dorothy was living with. Marion's report also made him realize that Dorothy's parents considered him to be an ineligible suitor for their beloved daughter's hand.

After he returned to Washington, Edmund wrote to Dorothy, telling her of his anguish in the light of Marion's disclosure.

From Edmund to Dorothy

Washington D.C.
October 4, 1919

Beloved:

I am not cheerful tonight. Perhaps I should hold my peace instead of telling you what troubles me—and yet I must tell you because it touches both of us equally. I have been thinking about your father's attitude towards our plans.

Marion told me quite candidly how he feels and it was hardly news, but only confirmation of what I gathered from your few allusions to the matter. How he got to his present position is beyond my power of comprehension, but that is neither here nor there in the face of the fact that he is possessed by a blind and strong prejudice because I am a Catholic and because I am a northerner. There may be other objections and probably there are, but at any rate these two are the principal ones. And in speaking of your father, your mother is included, for though she holds her counsel it is not hard to sense that she supports the administration. She is an astute diplomat.

Now the dilemma. You are devoted to them, naturally and rightly. They are half of your life and normally would continue to be so after your marriage. You are bound to them by the strongest ties of affection and filial duty. Nothing has ever marred this relationship and aside from one thing only, it is the richest and most significant possession that you have. And by marrying me what becomes of the other half of your life?

That is the question that haunts me. It is I that has led you and I am absolutely responsible for the path that you take. Though having you for my wife is the only happiness that I want, yet if eventualities rendered you unhappy I should exist in misery and consider my life a tragic blunder. And in this connection I mean unhappiness resulting from the attitude of your family. It is such a hard question for you to decide and I can't give you any help. But I want you to know, Dorothy, that if you feel that the parental opposition is more than you can bear, your promise to me will be given back to you, truly, as it was given a year ago, and understandingly. You know that I mean exactly what I said. I trust your judgment and in deciding for yourself you decide for me. Take your own time in deciding.

> In the meantime, I love you wholly,
> *Edmund*

~~~

Edmund's letter arrived in Montgomery a few days later, and when Dorothy found it on the hall table late one afternoon when she returned from her job at the State Capitol, she carried it up to her room. After taking off her hat and gloves she sat down on the pink chaise, eager to find out about Marion's wedding. Instead, from the opening sentences she learned that Marion had told Edmund in frank terms how deeply opposed her parents still were to her plans to marry him.

She had tried to soften the reality of her father's harsh attitude. But Marion had responded honestly to the questions Edmund had most likely asked him. How like Edmund, she thought, to be so concerned in his letter about the burdens she was carrying. There was no mention of his bruised feelings. Instead, he offered her a graceful chance to return the engagement ring if she found the pressures she was living with were more than she could bear.

He was right about pressures, she thought. She lived with them every day because her parents felt that she was making a terrible mistake to marry someone who came from a different world and belonged to a different religion.

But how would they ever come to understand or appreciate Edmund's inner self when they were too afraid to get to know him? She thought of Dr. Gaines and the wisdom he imparted during his chapel talks, and she realized what he was referring to when he told her that she would recognize her true calling in life, her real vocation, when she experienced a profound sense of meaning and purpose. She did experience an inner conviction and an inner peace she had never felt before when she fell in love with Edmund and decided to marry him, for he incarnated the ideals she herself wanted to live up to. Of course, she realized that there were still obstacles to face regarding the doctrinal differences in their churches, and they were difficult ones, she admitted. But she also had faith that together they would find a way to resolve them.

From Dorothy to Edmund

Montgomery
October 8, 1919

Dearest,

… Thank you, beloved, for your letter and more than that, for the understanding and the love that prompted the writing of it. It was quite like you to put things as you did. Of course, I wept when I read it, simply because you are the most understanding soul in the world and the greatest.

I have made my decision, and I made it not yesterday when I read your letter, nor the day before, but I have known it ever since all this question came up and since I fully realized what you mean to me. It is this, quite simply: that I love you enough for any and everything, and that I shall marry you.

Perhaps Marion colored the parental attitude too deeply — sais pas. But I know this, and I think I have told you before — that they leave me the choice, and that they will abide by it without comment or murmuring. It is going to be hard — not because they will be in any way cut off from me ... but because I am going to hurt them, and I can only pray when I do it, that time and circumstances will heal the wound ... The hard part, and it is fearfully hard, is that they are not going to understand, and it is going to hurt me and them ...

Dorothy

From Dorothy to Edmund

Montgomery
Oct. 12, 1919, Sunday Night

Beloved —

... Mother came back last night from the Confederate reunion in Atlanta and pronounced the gathering a thorough success wherein were mixed in happy confusion veterans in ancient gray uniforms, balls, parties, Confederate flags and strains of Dixie. How the Angelic Child would have gloried in it![42] She is homesick, I think, but she bears up quite bravely and is a credit to the family in the way she refrains from dwelling on her trials and difficulties. And the Lapin is also doing well. He is passing

---

[42] The Angelic Child was in her freshman year at Sweet Briar College.

in everything in the class for which I coached him this summer and he seems to be holding his own. He grumbles about the food and the number of Yankees with whom he is forced to associate (the aversion is probably inherited), but otherwise is cheerful.[43] The effect which absence from home has on him is quite remarkable. He is actually becoming philosophical! He wrote the other day that he had just about arrived at the conclusion that the best way to get along in the world was to treat everybody right as you would expect to be treated. The philosophical truth of the faith part of his statement might be questioned — or rather the moral truth, but I said nothing about it to him being loathe to discourage philosophical thinking in the young.

… Tonight we held a discussion on religion. Their principal objection lies in my being married by a priest and the promise which the proceeding involves. They were quite bitter about it and I refused to argue the question knowing that the sacrifice is my own and believing firmly that if the heirs turn out to be as good as you, notwithstanding the fact that they are Catholics, I shall find at the closing of my life that it has not been lived in vain. I have progressed or not — as one chooses to regard it — a good deal since a year ago and I have come to believe with Emerson that "the only picture book of a man's Creed is his action." And your picture book is so much truer to the great spiritual truths that I do not believe it wrong to have my children model their lives after yours and your creed.

Goodnight my darling — may this time next year find our two lives united.

Devotedly,
Dorothy

---

[43] Charles was a student at the Gilman School in Baltimore during 1919–20.

On the morning of November 11, 1919, one year after the official end of World War I, Dorothy stood on the sidewalk along Dexter Avenue in downtown Montgomery and watched while groups of Alabama soldiers filled the streets as they marched in formation up the hill toward the state capitol. As they passed by, the tramp of their boots in unison and the sound of drums and martial music brought back vivid memories of Edmund's eight months in France. His letters sometimes took three weeks to arrive, and opening an envelope with his familiar handwriting provided another precious confirmation that he was alive and that he loved her dearly.

Then she recalled the telegram he sent a little more than a year ago, with details about his arrival in Atlanta in late September. She had gone to Union Station early and had been there when the train came to a stop. But which car, she had wondered, not sure where to look — and then suddenly, there he was, standing before her, smiling.

From Dorothy to Edmund

November 11, 1919

My dearest,

... In the parade were remnants of the 167th Infantry, and the 82nd Division and the Dixie Division besides all the organizations of which the town boasts. It made my heart tighten to see those men march by and to review my emotions on the war in general. When they passed by with their "comme cà" caps sitting at such a gay and cheerful angle, I had only to close my eyes to see you as I saw you that first night in that dark old dingy station in Atlanta when I looked into your eyes and heard you say: "Well, Dorothy Thigpen!" and when I knew that the miracle was an everlasting truth. I shall never, never forget that instant, beloved, nor all that it meant, and I have lived it over a hundred times and I shall continue to do so all my life ...

Dorothy

In mid-November Edmund travelled to Milwaukee to interview with two law firms: Lines, Spooner, and Quarles; and Flanders, Fawsett, and Smart. He wrote to Dorothy from the Pfister Hotel and told her he was particularly interested in the second firm, because Mr. Smart indicated that he planned to take on another young lawyer in the near future.

A week after the interview when Edmund received an offer to join Flanders, Fawsett, and Smart, he sent Dorothy a telegram to tell her the news. The enthusiasm of her response lights up the letter she wrote him on Thanksgiving Day afternoon.

From Dorothy to Edmund

Thanksgiving 1919, November 27

My dearest,

When I came home from church this morning where I went to thank the good Lord for you and for some of my other blessings, I found your telegram about the Flanders firm, and to say I was thrilled and excited and happy would be inadequate. I felt I wanted to get out on the roof and scream to all the passersby that my future husband, because of his abilities, had been accepted by an extraordinary firm which offered a rare opportunity!

Instead, I dashed into the kitchen to impart the news to the only people on the premises — Mother and Patsy who were making a cake together. I went flying in and I caught the long-suffering Patsy by both hands and swung her around in a mad dance and whirl until she could only gasp "For de Lord's sake, chile, what ails you?" Mother retreated to the other end of the kitchen with the bowl of cake batter ...

I am proud and happy that fortune is smiling upon us so benignly.

And that blessed Fawsett! I feel like reducing myself to sackcloth and ashes because I called him a miser and a brute. He is an angel …

This is Thanksgiving afternoon and as the sun makes warm, slanting shadows across the lawn, my heart is filled because of all that God has given me — There are so many things that I can never enumerate, like health, and stars and winds and sunsets. And there are people like Lucy and Margaret Rowe and Virginia and my family, my home, and my college. But most of all it is you and your love for which I am so profoundly thankful for that I can never express myself. Mr. Fawsett made the day joyous by his excellent judgment, but all that sort of thing fades into insignificance beside the great spiritual miracle of your love for me. To know in my heart that we belong to each other unendingly makes me want to go down on my knees and never cease thanking God because He has let me see that love is the very substance of reality.

Goodbye, my beloved and know that I love you with the devotion of my life.

With all my heart,
Dorothy

A Last New Year's in Montgomery

God … has let me see that love is the very substance of reality.

—Dorothy Thigpen, letter, 1919

New Year's fell on Wednesday in 1920, and in the afternoon, after Dorothy shared a holiday dinner with her family, she went upstairs and stretched out on the pink chaise and closed her eyes. She needed some time by herself.

A thought had caught her by surprise while she was enjoying the last bite of Patsy's lattice-crust apple pie, but she said nothing. How could she say it when she was looking around the table at her father and mother, the Angelic Child, and Charles? This was the last New Year's she would spend with her family in Montgomery.

While she was lying there in her bedroom with her eyes closed, she also realized that what she was feeling was not only sorrow over leaving family and home. More than once recently she had thought back to the summer of 1916, to the afternoon she and Susie had gone to visit Leota in her gypsy wagon. Leota had predicted that she was going to marry a young man her parents would not approve of. At the time she thought that, of course, Leota was referring to Tom, and had dismissed the prediction.

Now her four years away at college had ended and the experience of living at home again during the last six months had given her a chance to understand what parental disapproval felt like. She had shocked and deeply disappointed her father and mother by deciding to marry Edmund. Leota was right after all.

Yet the experience of falling in love with Edmund had changed the way she perceived everything. In this new and miraculous light of love she could see that his integrity was real. At the same time, she understood that the outer labels of Yankee and Catholic were still stumbling blocks for her parents, obstacles that prevented them from appreciating his rare inner qualities. It was inescapable, the regret she felt for causing her mother and father to feel worried and unhappy. Yet she knew in her heart that in deciding to marry Edmund, she was following her true vocation.

~~~

On a cold morning in early February, after Edmund arrived at the First Wisconsin National Bank building and shook the snow from his boots, he took the elevator to the ninth floor. Then he walked down the hall until he reached his destination. That evening he shared some good news with Dorothy:

From Edmund to Dorothy

… Today a momentous painting occurred: the inscription that formerly appeared on the outer office door, corresponding with that on the letterhead, was erased and in its place:

FAWSETT & SMART
Chas. F. Fawsett
Edward M. Smart

Charles E. Monroe
Edmund B. Shea
Harry C. Bradley

Frederick C. Winkler

... I told you that Monroe is about sixty years old. And it appears that I rank with Bradley, though he is ten years my senior and was formerly married. If only I can produce sufficient speed, the doorplate indicates the path of progress.[44]

~~~

In early 1920, while Edmund braved the coldest part of Milwaukee's winter, Dorothy left her job at the State Capitol and began working as her father's secretary.

The old one-story building on South Court Street that stood near downtown Montgomery bore little resemblance to a modern medical office. The large room where Dr. Charlie saw patients had a high ceiling, spacious proportions, and a bay window. Perhaps it had been a living room in an earlier, nineteenth-century era. A new patient arriving for a first appointment soon felt confident that the man he had just met was a rarely gifted physician.

A large roll-top desk dominated one corner, and nearby stood a table holding an open box filled with rows of glasses' lenses. In addition to testing his patients' eyes for glasses prescriptions, Dr. Charlie also treated a wide variety of other problems afflicting eyes, ears, noses, or throats. On Thursdays he spent a long morning in the operating room at St. Margaret's Hospital.

Dorothy's office was directly across the hall from her father's. She answered the black candlestick telephone, made appointments, and settled accounts with patients, usually in a cash transaction.

Patients waiting to see Dr. Charlie sat on chairs lined up against one wall of the long hall. When the one sitting at the top of the line

---

[44] The doorplate did in fact record a number of milestones. While Edmund kept the same corner office for over fifty years, the names on the frosted glass changed a number of times. When he became senior partner in the 1940s, the firm took the name Shea and Hoyt.

was called to go into his office, the others moved up accordingly, by one seat.

Dr. Charlie treated both white and black patients, unusual for a doctor at this time in Alabama. When he had said goodbye to the last one, he and Dorothy climbed into his car and drove up the hill to South Perry Street and home, where Dorothy's mother was waiting. Soon after their arrival, Patsy would appear, ready to begin serving the main meal in the dining room.

Working in close proximity to her father gave Dorothy a chance to appreciate him in his role as a physician. She saw for herself the way he devoted his time and skill to caring for each person who came seeking his help.

~~~

For most of 1920, Edmund lived at the University Club near downtown Milwaukee. One evening in mid-July, after taking a walk near the lake, he told Dorothy he returned to the familiar precincts of the club and "took a comfortable place in the enveloping cushions in the lounge, where the other bachelors, like great well-fed tabby cats, stretch themselves after dinner and doze and sigh as they doze for sheer creature comfort."

Then he noticed a magazine lying on a nearby table and soon entered into the world of a story

> ... about a boy who went to the front, and I remembered that two years ago last night, *le quatorze juillet*, began the Peace Offensive of the Boches ... when the fortunes of the Allies ebbed and flowed in the tide along the Marne, and I can always project myself into the vivid state of mind of those days, and it has a purifying effect ... Well, in the story, the boy comes back blind — gas will do it. And I remembered in a flash how I calculated the possibility of doing likewise, and of giving you

up, on that account. Needless to say, my sense of proportion came into its own, and I felt most humbly thankful for you, my own dear, gentle partner, and for the gift of health that makes our enterprise possible ...

~~~

Later in July Edmund and Dorothy made arrangements to meet in St. Louis for a brief visit. Dorothy stayed with Emma Jones, an Agnes Scott classmate, while they attended meetings of the Southern Association of College Women. When Edmund arrived for the weekend, he and Dorothy talked over various details concerning the wedding and also discussed the requirements of the Catholic Church regarding a mixed marriage.

In order for Edmund to remain in good standing in the Church after participating in a ceremony with a Protestant clergyman, he needed to provide the chancery in Milwaukee with written proof that a Catholic priest had witnessed the wedding vows and that Dorothy had promised that their children would be baptized and raised in the Catholic Church. Dorothy already knew about the demands and had made her peace with them before going to St. Louis, even if her parents still thought them objectionable.

~~~

Upon his return to Milwaukee from St. Louis, Edmund found his first letter from Dorothy's mother, Daisy. Going into considerable detail, Daisy expressed reluctance to release her daughter into what she perceived as a precarious future. She also demurred over setting an actual date for the wedding. Edmund answered her letter with politeness and firmness.

From Edmund to Daisy

August 5th, 1920

Dear Mrs. Thigpen,

... I have often thought of your feelings in this question and I know it is dreadfully hard for you to let Dorothy go — though being a mere man and not a parent I can't know how hard it is. Your zeal for her future happiness and well-being I respect deeply and sincerely. So I shall try to tell you, as her mother, what I think of the general situation, upon which you have touched at so many points.

It is risky, you say. In a degree, yes, but after studying the problem throughout the last two years I firmly believe that no two people ever began life with a fairer chance than we have of succeeding in their mission on earth. The winds of fortune will not all be favorable. And we cannot be certain of winning the prize which so few married people attain. Life is built not on certainties, but on probabilities varying in degree. Your own domestic life has been regularly blessed, and looking backward, it may seem to have been fore-ordained so. Yet you know that the things you value most dearly may be snatched away tomorrow. As you and as everyone must take the risks of the future, so must we.

But my point is this: if you will deliberately take all that Dorothy and I have in common on which to build this enterprise — and she will enumerate the assets — worldly and otherwise, on which we are banking, and if you will weigh what we have against what other Montgomery girls of our generation have had in entering marriage, I believe you will be reassured. Please don't overlook the fact that we have a great deal besides the important circumstance that we love each other devotedly ...

… Honestly, you make me smile when you caution us to think over this step carefully — when for two years since I came back from France, we have constantly and studiously pondered, weighed, considered, analyzed, deliberated, debated, dissected, and reconstructed this entire question from all angles, and in every respect. And always reached the same conclusion, namely, that together we can live our lives completely and happily as the Creator intended. Had we been together constantly, one unfamiliar with the facts might suspect an infatuation, but the fact that we have constantly grown closer together in spite of our being far apart, proves a very solid and fundamental agreement. Is it not so?...

So we came to the question of when. We want to be married soon, the sooner the better. You see, we have waited two years, and they have been interminable. We have planned and built hopes, and now the goal of our desire is within reach … You know how anxiously we await the day. I am sorry you are tired, and that Elisabeth may go to New York, and that Montgomery has such a beastly climate, but please don't make us wait for those reasons.

There is another thing. Winter sets in here in November, and in January and February reaches its height. I should fear the shock of transplanting Dorothy at that season … Our climate cannot be explained away. So please let it be October.

Yours sincerely,

Edmund

~~~

It was not to be October, but the wedding would take place in early November. In September Dorothy began shopping for heavy clothing to prepare herself for the rigor of Milwaukee's climate. But she was in the dark about what sort of undergarments young women wore in Wisconsin and wrote to Edmund to ask.

From Edmund to Dorothy

September 20th

... I have your inquiry about underwear. It is the first I have ever received, and being consulted on so delicate an issue has caused me to deliberate gravely before reaching a decision ... Really, I can't tell you much about u.w. The only kind I see in store windows is the flimsy pink silk kind and I am quite at a loss to understand the various designs ...

Later in September after Dorothy heard that Edmund had been granted a three-week vacation, she shared another piece of exciting news ...

From Dorothy to Edmund

September 28, 1920

Most dear,

... it was very decent and generous of the great Fawsett to give us three weeks. Do you think he would object if after I get to Milwaukee I thank him for being so kind?

Today we got a wedding present! It was from Dr. and Mrs. Pollard, Mrs. Nash Read's sister, who is going away and who sent her offering early. The offering consists of four very heavy, beautiful old-fashioned brass candlesticks. Even if I were choosing something for the castle after my own taste, I could not improve on these. You remember I told you I wanted a room with brass things standing around? Well, these are the things, and I can hardly wait to get them stationed in the castle ...

Chapter 27

Edmund's letter of October 3 communicates joy, and it's no wonder. He had been searching for a place for them to live for nearly a year.

From Edmund to Dorothy

Milwaukee
October 3, 1920

Dearest Child,

Well, I think that the question of where we are to live is settled, praise God! It is a petite unfurnished apartment in the Astor, on the corner of Astor Street and Juneau. The Astor is a tremendous new building not yet completed. It is without doubt the best thing of its kind in Milwaukee. The apartments on one side overlook the blue lake, about three blocks away, but they are too expensive for you and me. These expensive units, as they are called, consisting of two rooms, kitchen and bath, will be leased for the modest sum of one hundred seventy-five dollars per month, each.

On the west side there is on each floor one unit consisting of one room, kitchen and bath, which we can get for $100 a month, and I shall grab one of them as soon as the leases are ready. The view of the setting sun will be grand, and by walking a few steps we can see the lake. It will be virtually at our door. I forgot to say that these rooms have Murphy beds that fold up and swing into a dressing room, so called, and the beds are not twin affairs but the kind our forefathers knew, as to width …

We can walk to town and need not bother with street cars which are stuffy and crowded in winter. And it is near the Town Club where we skate and not far from the river where I shall have to swim next summer. We play tennis also at the Town Club. So no wonder I am blithe. I think of you passing through the lobby in your squirrel coat, your cheeks flushed by the cold wind, your dear eyes shining like stars, and everybody in the place will pause to look and say: "By Jove, what a stunning girl. Is that Shea's wife? ...

Edmund

~~~

Three weeks before the wedding, Edmund's sister Edith wrote to express her concerns. Five years younger than Edmund, Edith had always felt a close bond with her brother. Dorothy knew this, and invited Edith to be a bridesmaid. In the fall of 1920, Edith was living at home and was keenly aware of her mother's distress. Recent years had brought some painful blows. Several years before, Nora's oldest child Will had secretly married a Protestant. When their son was born, they refused to baptize him. Nora feared Edmund's children might suffer the same terrible fate. In addition, she still felt desolate over Isabel's untimely death less than two years earlier.

From Edith to Edmund

Saturday, October 17, 1920

Dearest Brother,

I have a thousand things to say to you so I will begin without further ceremony. I <u>am</u> glad from the depths of my soul that you are going to marry Dorothy so soon. I am fiercely loyal to you, and I have been always, and Mother's opposition has crystalized that feeling. Mother is much changed since a year ago, and she is so hostile to you absent, that I fear your Antigo visit will end in disaster.

There is a possibility that you may have a soothing effect, but it is much more probable that she will cut loose in spite of your sweet reasonableness. She calls down the most unmotherly maledictions with quavering reverence, and <u>rants</u> about her disobedient children, her hard lot in this world, and the bitterness of life in general. Living with her is the hardest thing I've ever done, because she doesn't shed one ray of happiness and finds fault because I want to marry Ralph ...

I didn't mean to regale you with everything in the lexicon of woe, but I slipped into it. What I do mean to say is that no good can possibly result from your seeing mother until after your marriage. Edmund, <u>please</u> don't because you won't part in peace. Catherine feels as I do about it so don't take my words lightly.

I'm sure father would go down for the nuptials if you wrote asking him. He was on the point of writing Mrs. Thigpen of his intention, but mother intervened. She said it was sanctioning something that she never could sanction.

Is it to be an evening event? I hope so, because our father wants to wear his dress clothes. Tell Papa you want him to come. You understand of course that mother's going is out of the question ...

I'm glad we are to see you at Christmas. You will hear from me again soon ... When you read this, put it out of your mind, but don't go to Antigo.

Love unending,
Edith

<div style="text-align:center">~~~</div>

Two weeks before the wedding, William Shea's first letter to Dorothy's mother reached Montgomery.

From Dorothy to Edmund

Oct. 21, 1920

Edmund dearest,

I have been walking on air all afternoon and tonight since a letter came from your father to my mother. Really, it was such a good letter. He thanked her for asking him to come to the wedding and he has decided that I am "a loveable girl" and his "most estimable daughter" and he hopes you will be worthy of me! Imagine! He also appreciates the position of my father and mother in having me go off to a strange country. Altogether it was a warm human friendly sort of thing that made me love him immediately ...

~~~

As the third of November drew near, the question of where to spend their honeymoon came up for discussion in Edmund and Dorothy's letters.

Through Jean Craik Read, one of the few tolerant souls in Montgomery who supported Dorothy's and Edmund's decision, Dorothy learned of the Pisgah Inn, a rustic place in a recently opened National Forest area near Asheville, North Carolina. For two people who wanted to begin their lives together in a secluded setting of natural beauty, the Inn sounded like the answer to their prayers. Edmund booked a reservation for a two-week stay beginning November 5.

On October 27, Dorothy realized she was writing her last letter to Edmund before the wedding:

... We have used this form of communication to good advantage ... it makes me very confident that our devotion is built on things of the mind and the spirit ...

~~~

Dorothy and Edmund's desire to have a small wedding was an attempt to downplay the hostile feelings that divided Protestants and Catholics in general, and split apart the Thigpen and Shea families in particular. Two years after learning of Dorothy and Edmund's engagement, loyalty to sectarian creeds still stirred up turmoil in the hearts of three out of four parents.

Yet, despite Charles and Daisy's misgivings, they presented a united front and granted their daughter virtual freedom to design the ceremony. A mixed marriage was not permitted in a Catholic Church in 1920, and choosing Daisy's Episcopal Church would have emphasized the Protestant element. Thus, the parlor in the pillared house seemed to provide a workable solution in a neutral setting. Still, Edmund's mother would not allow Edmund's sister Edith to be a bridesmaid in a non-Catholic ceremony.

When Marion Rushton read Edmund's letter asking him to serve as best man, he closed his eyes and smiled, remembering the way everything looked that rainy summer evening in the ballroom of the Country Club. It was four years ago, and he was just about to say: "Dorothy, I want you to meet my good friend Edmund Shea ..."

~~~

The day before the wedding Daisy and Jean Craik Reed worked together in the parlor. Soon the wall above the fireplace resembled a reredos behind an altar, and with the help of a pair of large brass candelabra and several pairs of silver candlesticks, all borrowed from the Church of the Ascension, the high-ceilinged room in the house on South Perry Street took on the convincing look of a small chapel.

Well before seven o'clock on Wednesday evening, November 3, 1920, a small group of wedding guests took their seats in the large entry room just outside the doorway leading to the candlelit parlor. Bridesmaids Elisabeth Thigpen, Lucy Durr, and Katherine

Seay carried pink roses. The three groomsmen were all Harvard Law School friends of Edmund and Marion's.

When Dorothy began to walk down the stairway, the musicians played the opening bars of the wedding march. Dr. Charlie stood at the foot of the stairs, waiting for his daughter to take his arm. Then they walked together through the entry room and into the parlor.

Edmund and Dorothy stood next to one another in front of the altar, facing the Reverend Peerce MacDonald, Rector of Daisy's church. Reverend MacDonald was a tall, robust-looking man with a deep voice that lent solemnity to every word he spoke.

Charles and Daisy sat in the front row with young Charles, who was close to tears. Daisy's eyes were trained on her daughter's face, ready to pick up the slightest hint of hesitation. But the way Edmund and Dorothy looked at one another while they were exchanging their solemn promises led her to comment afterward that she believed she had seen something holy.

~~~

While the last guests lingered in the dining room, where vestiges of a large homemade fruitcake remained on a silver platter, Dorothy slipped out and made her way up the back stairway. When she reached the end of the hall and walked into her bedroom, Sallie Larkin was still there. Sallie, Dorothy's beloved black nurse from childhood, had helped her get ready, had fastened the ivory satin buttons on the back of the wedding dress. Now it was time to undo them, one by one. When Sallie finished, Dorothy stepped out of the dress. And while Sallie was hanging it up in the armoire, Dorothy began to put on her going away clothes. First, a high-necked ivory satin waist. Then an ankle-length navy wool skirt and a matching long-fitted jacket with bone buttons. When she was ready, she stood in front of the mirror and adjusted a wide-brimmed navy felt hat garnished with grey feathers. After taking a last glance, Dorothy turned around and smiled. Sallie almost managed to say what she wanted to without crying: "O, Little Miss, I declare you do look beautiful ..."

Then Dorothy threw her arms around her beloved friend from early childhood and kissed her goodbye. She started walking along the hall, and halfway down the long staircase, with her hand holding the banister, she saw what was happening: she was leaving.

~~~

After their honeymoon in the Pisgah National Forest, Edmund and Dorothy travelled to Milwaukee. What thoughts ran through Dorothy's mind when Edmund turned the key in the lock and opened the door, and she glimpsed the tiny interior of their living quarters in the Astor Hotel for the first time? She had said goodbye to her beloved family and to friends and the whole world of Montgomery and had travelled nearly a thousand miles north to live in a city where she was a total stranger.

No one knows. But one can imagine that Dorothy Thigpen Shea knew she was where she most wanted to be—standing next to the man she loved, the one who had just become her husband. The threshold moment she and Edmund experienced while they stood together in the doorway evokes a poem written by John Donne in 1633. In "The Good Morrow," Donne describes how the unity that binds lovers together transforms whatever their eyes take in:

> *And now good-morrow to our waking souls,*
> *Which watch not one another out of fear;*
> *For love all love of other sights controls,*
> *And makes one little room an everywhere.*

And Then What Happened?

In your house I am a passing guest, a pilgrim,
like all my fathers ...
—Psalm 39

One day in November 1921, a little more than a year after the wedding, Edmund and Dorothy returned from Columbia Hospital to their apartment in the Astor Hotel. Edmund opened the door for Dorothy who was carrying their firstborn child, Charles Thigpen Shea. Daisy soon arrived to help with the baby, and after she left Sallie Larkin came and stayed for a spell.

Three months after his grandson's birth, Dr. Charlie's letter reveals his tender-hearted side:

From Charles to Dorothy

My dearest Dorothy:
We are sending, by express, a box containing one country cured ham, from Tom Brown at the plantation, two bottles of pure cane syrup, which I think is very fine on cakes, such as they make at the Astor. Rosa makes them just as good, and I believe Sallie can, also, if she will get some of Aunt Jemima Pancake flour, and follow the directions. I thought you and Edmund

might like the syrup, if not, you can give a bottle of it to one of your friends who likes it. All of these grew on the plantation, where you and Elisabeth and Charles used to accompany me, and which you enjoyed so much. Have you ever forgotten the day we all piled in the little Packard Run-About, and went down there? That was in the happy past, where I revel, mostly. Then there is a pound of fresh butter, from the cow we raised from a little calf. I doubt if you have any in Milwaukee, any better. And some birds, also from the plantation. These will be the last, until next season, as the shooting season closes this month. I have enjoyed the sport very much, and it has kept me well and strong. The weather is getting warm, and it will not be long before you and "Little Lord Shea" can come to pay us a long visit, and we shall be happy to see you.

Much love,
Father

Three years later, in January 1925, Elizabeth Thigpen Shea arrived to keep her brother company. By then Edmund and Dorothy had moved to a nearby rented row house on Ogden Avenue, and among the seven other young families who lived there they found several congenial lifelong friends.

In the fall of 1927, the need for a larger place to live became pressing again, for Dorothy was expecting another baby and the row house had only two bedrooms. Dorothy began house hunting in earnest and in late October, she telephoned her father and mother to tell them she had found the place she and Edmund had been dreaming of ever since they began discussing the "castle" they hoped to live in after their marriage. When she opened the front door and stepped into the living room, she told them, it was love at first sight.

Built in 1898, the same year as the pillared house in Montgomery, the large summer house in Fox Point stood on a bluff overlooking Lake Michigan. Long porches ran along the east and south sides and offered magnificent views of the lake. There were seven bedrooms, with two more in the maids' quarters over the garage. The front door opened into a spacious living room with dark wainscoting and a wood-beamed ceiling. A fireplace enhanced the living room and dining room as well as two of the upstairs bedrooms. There were three acres of land, and white birch trees stood on the south and west sides of the house.

By the end of 1927, thanks to Dr. Charlie's generous willingness to help, Edmund and Dorothy became the owners of a house that made their fondest dreams come true.

In March 1928 Dorothy gave birth to another daughter, Sheila Madden Shea (myself). Later that year, after Edmund and Dorothy had moved back to the Ogden house for the winter, they began to explore central heating options. A furnace would make the house habitable year round.

The next year, 1929, a new coat of white paint covered the exterior brown clapboards. And in early March of 1932, the arrival of a tremendous blizzard coincided with the birth of Dorothy and Edmund's fourth child, Dorothy Bissell Shea (Wendy). By then, our family felt thoroughly at home in the house we would always know as White Woods.

~~~

In the mid-thirties, Fox Point was a small rural outpost consisting of a few hundred souls. The village stood eight miles north of Milwaukee, and its peaceful setting made it a veritable paradise for children. Charlie, Betsy, and I roamed around the ravines and played in the large unmowed field behind the house. There were cottontail rabbits, ring-necked pheasants, skunks, and an occasional fox. Songbirds twittered in abundance: brown thrashers, yellow warblers, goldfinches, as well as robins, catbirds, and meadowlarks that made nests and raised their young.

When we moved into the new house year-round in the spring of 1931, to add happiness to the lives of his young grandchildren, Dr. Charlie sent a springer spaniel, Skipper, and an Airedale, Bunkie. Both became beloved companions, but to our great sorrow, both dogs were poisoned some years later. Several other Fox Point dogs suffered the same fate. Strychnine was found in the stomachs of the victims.

I can still remember the shock. Betsy and I were sitting in the backseat of our mother's Ford the afternoon we reached the field and saw the bodies of several dogs lying stiff and cold, including our pets. The next day my father dug a grave near the end of the driveway, and my mother read some prayers from the Book of Common Prayer.

Dr. Charlie had other dogs in reserve, and before long we welcomed Rex, an energetic black and white English setter. But Rex preferred to roam the countryside, and showed little interest in joining the family. After Rex made a return trip in the baggage car of the train to Montgomery, Dr. Charlie sent a young red cocker spaniel we named Tony, a well-behaved homebody who lived happily with us for many years.

Dr. Charlie found other ways to stay in touch. He sent boxes of pecans he gathered from the tree behind the pillared house, and a turkey usually arrived before Thanksgiving and Christmas. He sent wool blankets to keep us warm in cold weather, and also became the chief Montgomery correspondent when Daisy developed a hand tremor in the early 1930s.

~~~

During most of my early school years my siblings and I rode to Milwaukee with my father and hopped out at the large redbrick Normal School. By the fall of 1939 when Charlie went off to Williams College, Betsy, Wendy, and I were all students at Milwaukee-Downer Seminary, a private girls' school. Though MDS had no official affiliation with the Episcopal Church, we walked into chapel each morning singing hymns from a blue hymnal, still used in the Episcopal Church today. Classes were small, taught by dedicated women who made the realm of medieval England come alive. I memorized Latin case forms, conjugated French verbs, and learned to love the poetry of Wordsworth and John Keats. I still look back on those years with gratitude.

On Sunday mornings my mother got up early and went to an early service at her tiny Episcopal Church in Whitefish Bay. Later in the morning, my siblings and I climbed into my father's boxy green Franklin sedan and drove to St. Monica's Catholic Church, just two blocks from my mother's Christ Church. He loved the men's choir and we usually went to High Mass at ten thirty.

The fact that our parents went to different churches was part of the way things were in our peaceful lives. I never recall hearing a dispute between my father and mother about church doctrines. Nor did they ever refer to the parental misgivings Nora Shea and Charles and Daisy Thigpen felt before their wedding in 1920. That revelation only came to light when I read the letters many years later.

~~~

When late March arrived each year in the 1930s, my mother's black steamer trunk was carried up from the basement to the master bedroom, a signal that we would soon depart for our annual visit with Daisy and Doctor Charlie. After my brother Charlie went away to school at Exeter in 1936, my mother packed for her three daughters and herself, filling most of the drawers on one side of the upright trunk with three sets of little socks, shorts, shirts, sweaters, and jodhpurs. Her suits and dresses and our coats hung on hangers inside the other side of the trunk.

After an overnight ride, when we finally stepped off the train into the warm air of Montgomery, Daisy and the Angelic Child were there to greet us. On the way to the house we stopped at Dr. Charlie's office, each of us taking a seat in the long hall with waiting patients. When we reached the front of the line, the door opened and there was our tall, spare Southern grandfather in a short white coat, wearing a head mirror. After visiting with him for a few minutes, we continued up the hill until we reached the pillared house.

Once upstairs in my mother's bedroom, we unpacked our clothes and pulled off our disliked heavy stockings, designed for Milwaukee's cold weather, and put on shorts. It was time to go outside and investigate the dog yard behind the house and find out if there were any puppies among Dr. Charlie's hunting dogs.

After his return from the office in the afternoon, we gathered in the dining room to enjoy Rosa's fried chicken and other Southern treats: okra, black-eyed peas, butter beans, artichoke relish, and beaten biscuits. On Sundays Otis, my grandfather's handyman and chauffeur, often made strawberry ice cream, cranked with rock salt in a metal container until it was chilled to perfection.

~~~

Years continued to pass, and by the time the winter of 1943 arrived, the United States had been at war with Germany and Japan for two years. Charlie had graduated from Exeter and Williams College and was in the army, in a field artillery unit at Fort Sill, Oklahoma. Betsy was a senior at Milwaukee-Downer Seminary, where I was a freshman and Wendy was in fifth grade.

One day in early December, after Betsy and I walked home from the school bus stop on Lake Drive, I felt chilled and under the weather. The next day I had a fever, felt worse, and stayed in bed. When my cough worsened, Dr. Schwartz and Dr. Patek both made house calls and looked concerned when they spoke with my mother. It was time to move me to a hospital, they said. I had lobar pneumonia in both lungs.

The next morning was Saturday. Betsy was standing in my room with my mother when the ambulance arrived and handed me my favorite stuffed animal, a sweet comfort. Then the men lifted me onto a stretcher and carried me downstairs and out the front door. After we drove through downtown Milwaukee, we arrived at Milwaukee Hospital, staffed by Lutheran nuns who wore little white bonnets and floor-length black dresses.

High fever put me in a haze and I learned later that I was on the critical list for several days. That explained why my mother slept on a cot in my room. My coughing continued and after I felt a terrible pain, an X-ray showed a broken rib. Nurses came, and then a doctor encased my chest in yards of adhesive tape in the hope that this might ease the pain each time I coughed.

Finally, one morning the doctor and nurses came and cut the adhesive tape on both sides of my chest and gave two mighty pulls — first to remove the tape on the front and then on the back.

In the 1940s, it was not unusual for a patient to stay in bed for a long time without getting up. But not getting up for four weeks resulted in great weakness. When I finally did stand for the first time, a nurse was there on each side to hold me up.

I returned to White Woods in mid-January and moped around the house, feeling demolished when doctors forbade my returning to school. There was no alternative, they said. I would have to repeat my freshman year, which meant losing my class, my classmates. To my fourteen-year-old self, the world seemed to be coming to an end.

In February my mother and father, in conversation with Daisy and Doctor Charlie and the Angelic Child, decided to send me to Montgomery for the rest of the winter.

With the help of a kind taxi driver, I managed to change trains in Chicago and arrived in Montgomery the next day. My cousin Wiley Hill, the Angelic Child's son, was away in the Navy but another cousin was there, young Charles's daughter Elisabeth (Lizard), eight years old, a sweet child with blonde hair and blue eyes.

I felt grateful to be alive, and I decided I would go to medical school and become a doctor so I could help others with ailments to get well. I wanted to explain this to Dr. Charlie, even if he sometimes had a gruff outer bearing, for I also knew that he carried dog biscuits in one coat pocket for his dogs and sugar lumps in the other pocket for the horses at his country place outside Montgomery. When I told him of my medical aspirations, adding that I hoped to come watch him operate at St. Margaret's hospital, he hesitated for a moment and then said, well, yes, but on one condition: "Don't *faint* in the operating room!"

~~~

When Thursday arrived, I drove with him to St. Margaret's. We walked in the front door and made our way to the operating rooms where he introduced me to his nurse, Miss Bromley, a tall woman with glasses, dressed in white gown and cap. She took me under her wing and gave me a long gown just like hers, and a cap, all rather wrinkled. Then we walked across the hall where Dr. Charlie was already standing next to the operating table, similarly garbed.

I stood next to him. The patient on the table was a large black woman. She had suffered great pain in one eye that was afflicted with glaucoma. She was blind in that eye, and Dr. Charlie had told her that by removing it, her pain would be relieved. She favored this, since the eye was "no count" and caused her constant discomfort. She was there that morning for the removal.

Several minutes later, I found it hard to believe what I was looking at, but there it was — a large, entirely whole, round eyeball, still connected to its limp-looking muscles. It was lying in a little chrome dish.

The next operation left me with more indelible memories. This time the patient was a middle-aged man in an upbeat mood. He said this was the moment he'd been waiting for, and I soon understood why.

He was a private detective and shared the story of what happened on that fateful afternoon he would never forget. He was chasing a robber through the streets of downtown Montgomery. The robber ducked into a doorway in an alley, and when the detective reached it, the robber was waiting: he threw lye in the detective's face, blinding him in both eyes. I can still hear his voice:

"And Doctuh Charlie, I tell you the last thing I saw was that angry man's face just before it happened. His angry face ..."

When the detective came for his first appointment, my grandfather told him some time must pass to allow the scars to heal. Then he would cut a new window in each cornea. The hope was that this would restore his sight. But one couldn't be certain ahead of time.

That morning while I watched, Dr. Charlie made a small cut in each cornea. When the surgery was done, he placed a gauze pad on each eye and then wrapped the man's head with what looked like yards of gauze. Then he was wheeled out of the operating room and taken upstairs to a hospital room.

I was with my grandfather the morning he went to see the detective. When we reached the hospital room on the second floor of St. Margaret's, the man was sitting in a chair next to the bed. My grandfather greeted him and said he had come to remove the bandages and see how things were coming along.

I stood beside my grandfather while he unwrapped the yards of gauze. Then he lifted off each pad. Silence for a few seconds. Then I heard the man speak:

"Oh, Doctuh Charlie! Doctuh Charlie, I can see, oh, I can see."

Then he burst into tears.

~~~

Heavy snow fell three years later in the winter of 1947. By February high drifts rose up on both sides of the long driveway that led from Merrie Lane to the turnaround in front of the house.

It's Sunday afternoon and we have just finished dinner. My father had carved a roast lamb Martha brought to the dining room table on a silver platter. Browned onions and new potatoes surrounded the meat. Martha also passed green beans and carrots around the table in oval silver dishes. Wendy and I are still at the table with our parents.

Now the four of us move to the living room. Snow is falling outside and big flakes of it swirl past the diamond panes of the French doors on the south side of the room. Edmund turns on the radio and tunes into the Philharmonic. Brahms's Second Symphony is playing. He crinkles up some pages of the *Milwaukee Journal* and puts them under the fireplace grate and lights a match. Soon the fire catches under the birch logs and begins to warm the room.

Edmund is sitting next to the fireplace in a yellow wing chair and wears a blue cardigan sweater. The golden key is visible, hanging from a watch chain on the front of his vest.

He holds a yellow legal pad on his lap, as well as a book with a green cover, a volume of Shakespeare's tragedies. Edmund and Dorothy belong to a reading group with four other couples. They meet every few months and before dinner, group members read scenes aloud from a Shakespeare play chosen for that evening. The host couple makes the selection of scenes and after dessert, concluding scenes are read and then a summing up of the play ends the evening. Dorothy and Edmund will host the next meeting, and Edmund is choosing scenes and assigning parts for each reader.

Edmund is fifty-five years old and he and Ralph Hoyt are now senior partners in the law firm Shea and Hoyt, originally Flanders, Fawsett, and Smart. He enjoys playing an active role in city affairs and has already served as president of the town club. He is now close to the end of his second term as president of Fox Point, a village that now has about two thousand residents. He also serves as chief counsel for the *Milwaukee Journal*, one of the city's two daily newspapers.

Dorothy is sitting in a chintz wing chair on the other side of the fireplace. She's reading *The King's General*, a historical novel by Daphne de Maurier. Her hair is still dark and she wears a high-necked blue wool dress with *DTS* embroidered on the front. A light blue wool sweater covers her shoulders. She, too, has been active in the community, and is now the current president of the Visiting Nurse Association, an organization that sends nurses all over Milwaukee to provide homecare for families, often in poor neighborhoods. She is a communicant of Christ Church in Whitefish Bay, and is a past president of the Woman's Club of Wisconsin. She is also a passionate gardener and indefatigable letter writer who keeps in close touch with Charlie and Betsy and Dr. Charlie and Daisy, and the Angelic Child.

Daisy's Parkinson's has gradually worsened since her diagnosis in 1936. She is now housebound, with a nurse to attend to her needs. The Angelic Child lives close by and keeps in daily touch. Dr. Charlie is eighty-two and still works full-time. He stopped operating two years ago.

My brother Charlie has been married to Lorna McLeod since 1942, and is now a student at Harvard Law School. He was a forward observer in Patton's Third Army during the war and took part in the Battle of the Bulge in the bitter cold winter of 1945, in the Ardennes Forest in Belgium.

Charlie returned to White Woods one afternoon in May 1946. My father was sitting on the east terrace, talking with Fox Point's chief of police about village matters, when a taxi arrived in the driveway and Charlie stepped out. We knew he would be coming home soon, but his actual arrival was a total surprise.

Later that afternoon while we were sitting in the living room next to the fireplace, I was shocked to see Charlie's hand was shaking when he lifted his glass to sip his old-fashioned. He wrote many detailed letters about his experiences in Patton's army, but burned all of them.

Betsy is in her senior year at Northwestern. Next year she and Bob Hottensen will announce their engagement. Bob lives in Milwaukee and is part of the management at Globe-Union, a company that makes automobile batteries.

Wendy is a freshman at Milwaukee-Downer Seminary. Her congenial friends and classmates Kitty and Mary and Trudy are frequent visitors at White Woods.

I am a senior at Milwaukee University School. At eighteen, I am still searching for my sense of self and feel rebellious toward my mother. When she recently made a mild suggestion that Wellesley might be a possible college to apply to, I announced that I planned to apply to Stanford University, a school as far away from Wellesley as I could imagine. There was no way for me to know what homesickness felt like until I got my wish.

~~~

Two photographs show Edmund and Dorothy as they looked in 1947. Dorothy is fifty years old and still enjoys wearing a hat whenever possible.

Edmund has the look of a man who stays calm in the midst of a crisis. He is the most even-tempered person I have ever met. It was thirty years ago that he sailed for France on the SS *Lapland* with the American Expeditionary Forces, the year he and Dorothy exchanged photographs for the first time.

~~~

In the summer of 1948, after Betsy and Bob Hottensen's wedding, they settled down in a little house in Fox Point. A year later when their daughter Dorothy Shea Hottensen was born, Edmund and Dorothy welcomed their first grand heir. By 1957 Betsy and Bob had four children: Dory, Bobby, Alexander (Sandy), and Judy, all of whom had the good fortune to grow up in a house near White Woods.

Sadly, in 1970 Bob Hottensen died of cancer, leaving Betsy a widow at forty-five. More sorrow followed soon thereafter when

Bob's brother Bill and his Uncle Robert also died. A year and a half later Betsy married Hugh Slugg, a close friend of Bob's.

~~~

In the summer of 1951, my marriage to Lawrence Harvey took place at St. Monica's Church in Whitefish Bay. Larry and I met the summer before in France during an Experiment in International Living program. Larry was the leader of our group of ten American college students and ten French counterparts in Belfort, a town near Grenoble. Each of the American students lived in a French family, and I was soon drawn into Larry's enthusiasm for every-thing French—the language and country, the food and wine, the people, their folk songs. Behind all the contagious enthusiasm was a person of integrity and goodness I fell in love with. Larry and I stayed in touch by letter during the next nine months and enjoyed visits with one another's families at Christmas. He was at Harvard then, working on his Ph.D. in Romance languages.

During the weeks preceding our June wedding, my mother consulted the nun in charge of music at St. Monica's. My mother wondered if the wedding march could be played. She was sorry, the nun said, but that wouldn't be possible because Wagner was a Protestant. "Well, sister, couldn't you just weave a little of it into the music you do play?" And she did.

By 1957 our family was well settled in Hanover, New Hampshire, in a new house. By then Larry was Assistant Professor of French and Italian at Dartmouth College and we had four children—John, twin daughters Kate and Elizabeth, and Ned. Sorrow descended on our family too in 1980 when Larry was diagnosed with Alzheimer 's disease. He was fifty-five years old and died eight years later.

~~~

In June 1955, Edmund and Dorothy's youngest daughter Wendy married Bill Randall at St. Robert's Church in Milwaukee. They met while Wendy was at Smith and Bill was a student at Dartmouth. After Bill's graduation from Michigan Law School the following year, they settled down in Whitefish Bay and raised four children: Cynthia, Rebecca, Clifford (Kip), and Kevin.

The next summer, of 1956, marked more than one significant anniversary for Edmund and Dorothy: forty years had passed since their first meeting on a rainy July evening in 1916 at the Montgomery Country Club. In addition, realizing that all four of their children were out of the nest and married, they decided the time had come to celebrate and to plan a trip to Europe, one that would include visits to several Gothic cathedrals in England: Winchester, Wells, York, and Canterbury.

Following their return from Europe, Bill took a picture of the single-hearted knight and the lady from a faraway land in the living room of their castle.

They had been in the house for twenty-eight years, and the living room gleamed with many pairs of "beautiful old-fashioned brass candlesticks," companions that joined the very first wedding gift they received in 1920.

Dorothy's slant-top desk (in the corner, behind them), flowered chintz at the windows, French doors, and floor-to-ceiling bookcases on both sides of the east windows all contributed to the warmth and beauty that filled the room.

~~~

It was mid-February 1963 when the telephone rang in our house in Hanover. Larry, in his seventh year at Dartmouth, was an energetic full professor of French and Italian language and literature, and our children were all in the Hanover school—John in sixth grade, Elizabeth and Kate in fourth, and Ned in first.

My mother was calling to say she'd seen Dr. Madison again. I knew she had been feeling under par for the last month. The week before, Dr. Madison ordered a barium enema, and she was calling to report that the test results showed what appeared to be a smooth muscle tumor in the large intestine. It was small, about the size of a mushroom, and Dr. Madison did not seem concerned, she said. She felt at ease about her scheduled surgery the next day, and we both felt confident at the end of our telephone conversation.

But the next evening after supper, Wendy called to deliver news that was dire. The surgeon reported to Edmund that cancer of the colon had spread to the liver and that Dorothy's condition was inoperable. He estimated she would live about six months.

Several days later, my father telephoned and described a conversation that took place in my mother's hospital room earlier that afternoon. The pathology report had come back, and Dr. Madison, a family friend as well as the internist, was entrusted to deliver the details.

My father was in the room when Dr. Madison arrived. After greeting Dorothy and Edmund, he pulled up a chair, kissed her on the cheek, and sat down next to her bed.

"Well, Dorothy ..." He paused to clear his throat.

"I know."

"How did you know?"

"I could tell by your eyes."

Silence.

Then she continued, my father reported, adding that she had never wanted to reckon her life chronologically.

"I'd much rather measure it by intensity. And when I measure that way ... I have had the happiest life imaginable ..."

That was the cue she gave to her stricken husband and internist. Edmund passed on her words to each family member.

In 1963 the word "cancer" was not yet in ordinary usage. Dorothy never did say it herself, though she was perfectly able to refer to the reality of her incurable condition. When I went to Milwaukee in June, she could barely walk as far as the garden. Yet she found solace in its summer beauty while stretched out on the metal chaise. One day while she was sitting there she handed me a poem she had written.

Roots

When I am quiet and under the bough
Unconscious of bending branches and trees,
Shall I be quickened with new amaze
At the hidden wisdom of roots and their ways?

Shall I know maples by roots that drill
With slow persistence that never fails
To depths where the granite's somber face
Darkens the earth's most secret place?

Will I know then by a mystic sign
From slender birches that lean in the wind
Whose snowy whiteness melts in the ground
Which are their roots that bind me round?

And by some miracle of flowers
Will Hawthornes blossom underground,
Breathing the spring's ecstatic breath
To make me know this is not death?

Seven months after she was diagnosed, and on a mild autumn morning, September 19, 1963, Dorothy Thigpen Shea died at Columbia Hospital in the same place where she brought four children into the world. She had just turned sixty-six.

~~~

Years before her death, in consultation with her in-house legal advisor, my mother put her affairs in order. Among the various matters she and Edmund talked about was their desire to be buried next to one another. My father followed up on their conversation, and made an appointment at the Chancery at St. John's Cathedral in Milwaukee. After speaking with the Archbishop, he received permission for my mother's body to be buried in the plot next to his. Holy Cross was a large Catholic cemetery on the west side of Milwaukee.

~~~

On the morning of Dorothy's funeral, members of the Shea and Thigpen families filled the front pews at Christ Episcopal Church. It was the first time our family had ever come together there.

Later, when the group of mourners was gathered at the graveside, Father Bolle, my mother's rector, stood silent, head bowed, holding his Book of Common Prayer. My father's pastor, Father Makin, read the prayers of committal. In 1963, only a Catholic priest could officiate at Holy Cross Cemetery.

~~~

In late May 1969, after Edmund's sudden death, I flew to Milwaukee from Italy where our family was spending the year during Larry's Fulbright.

I remember sitting at St. Eugene's Church, listening to Father Makin speak about his friend—a good man, a good Christian gentleman—but I felt numb then as I did later that morning when our family members gathered at Holy Cross Cemetery for the burial rites. Then we drove away, leaving Edmund and Dorothy lying in their graves, side by side.

Epilogue

The heart has its reasons that reason will never understand.
— Blaise Pascal

Now, nearly a hundred years after their wedding in 1920, I realize that Dorothy and Edmund were intent from the very beginning on building a close and harmonious life together, one that would transcend the hostile relationship that kept the Vatican I Catholic Church and Protestant churches wide apart, with swords drawn. How wise they were never to quarrel about doctrinal differences.

My discovery of two letters written by my distressed Southern grandparents in late 1918 when they learned of Dorothy's engagement also helped me to sympathize with their fears as parents. Their chief objection to Edmund was that he was a Roman Catholic Yankee, but they were also understandably worried because Dorothy had spent practically no time with him. She and Edmund had been together only a few brief times in 1916 and they had been separated completely for the last two years. In the eyes of her parents, Dorothy's decision looked like folly.

Yet, in the midst of her highly unconventional courtship, at the tender age of twenty-one, Dorothy discerned Edmund's true qualities. In an eloquent letter to him written in late December 1918, she described a conversation with her strong-minded father:

December 22, 1918

...He sent the rest of the family up to bed while he conferred with me. He asked me why I cared for you. I sketched your character and brought up your good points ... I told him what Marion thought of you and of the Great Seal and of your rating in the army as an officer, and of your brain and your character.

And then we discussed religion. He does not see how you can be intelligent and believe in the faith you do. I told him that I believe that a man named White who happened to be the Chief Justice of the Supreme Court was rather intelligent and was also a Catholic. He said that his intelligence did not compare with one Mr. Marshall's who was a Protestant! The argument grew lively but remained unheated because I told him that I was trying desperately to forget the externalities of form and to remember what someone said, that "a religion is good that makes a man good." And I told him that you were the finest person I know or had ever known.

Dorothy wasn't defying her father. She was working her way through the minefield of his opposition, attempting to help him understand that she believed the man she loved and had promised to marry was a man of goodness.

~~~

While Dorothy embraced new challenges as a loving wife and mother in an unfamiliar world, she also stayed in close touch with her family in Montgomery. The letters she exchanged once or twice a week with Doctor Charlie and her sister Elisabeth kept her informed about Daisy as her symptoms of Parkinson's increased. By 1940, Ruth, a black registered nurse, was living in the pillared house, attending to Daisy's needs. Daisy died in 1947.

From Doctor Charlie's exasperated letters of the 1920s, Dorothy got glimpses of young Charles's sorrowful destiny. When he was in his early twenties, there were signs of a dependence on alcohol. Shortly after he married a young woman named Lovelace, the marriage fell apart and ended in divorce, a rare and unacceptable event in the 1930s South. These unhappy circumstances could not be openly discussed by family and friends around him. Dorothy watched the distressing trajectory of her younger brother's life from a geographical distance, aware that she could do nothing to alter it.

Though the subject never came up openly in their frequent letters, Dorothy was well aware that the close bond she and Edmund shared was not a gift that Elisabeth found in her marriage with Wiley Hill. Part of a distinguished Montgomery family of doctors and lawyers, Wiley suffered from bouts of recurring depression, a malady that darkened the lives of his two sisters as well. All three committed suicide.

Did Dorothy's bold decision to marry Edmund influence Elisabeth's choice to break her earlier engagement to the young man she loved in Virginia? Did Elisabeth feel called to be the dutiful daughter who stayed at home? These questions join countless others about how life decisions get made and how individual destinies are shaped.

While Dorothy maintained constant communication with her family in the South, Edmund sustained a close and lifelong bond with his father, William, and preserved a cordial relationship with his sisters and brother Will. But sadly, Edmund's mother Nora was never able to accept her daughter-in-law because Dorothy was not a Catholic. I remember the scene clearly when the news of Nora's death came. It was 1936, and I was eight years old. We were sitting on the screen porch at White Woods, and Edmund burst into tears. It was the only time I saw my father cry.

~~~

Dorothy's decision to marry Edmund in 1920 changed her into a daring border crosser. She left her safe haven in the Deep South and moved far beyond the Mason-Dixon line to Milwaukee, a city almost a thousand miles north of Montgomery. Winters there were long and cold and snow covered the ground for months.

Yet the beauty of the snow inspired in Dorothy mystical insights. Years before she met Edmund, she had expressed wonderment over her first glimpse of it in December 1911. She was fourteen then, when she began a new memory book and wrote her astonishingly prescient dedication:

> Oh, "little grandchildren that are to be," what do you think? It snowed tonight!!!! Isn't that wonderful? If you are Yankee "little grandchildren that are to be," you will laugh, but to us it was simply wonderful![45]

After actually living through twenty long Milwaukee winters, Dorothy's wonderment over the phenomenon of a fresh snowfall was still keen. In 1940 she dedicated a poem to her close friend and Fox Point neighbor, Helen van Dyke:

December Snowstorm

To H.B. VD.
From D.T.S.
Christmas — 1940

I.
No other blossoms which this tree will bear,
Are spun of particles as clear
As these white petals flowering on the bark
Like clouds of stars which blossom in the dark.

---

[45] As it turned out, Dorothy and Edmund experienced the joy of welcoming thirteen grandchildren into the world, every one of them a Yankee.

II.

Strange irony of snow, bright alchemy
Whose magic makes this white fecundity.
Your bold enchantment prophesies the power
Of vital breath within the living flower.

The poem opens with a description of the ephemeral beauty of snowflakes as they come to glisten on the dark bark of a tree. They resemble six-petalled white flowers and also evoke clouds of stars "which blossom in the dark."

In the second stanza Dorothy alludes to the essential relationship that exists between snowflakes in melted form — water — and living creatures and plants that flourish on the planet Earth: all living things depend on water to survive. And just as humans and animals depend on oxygen given off by plants, flowers, and trees to stay alive, so all the individual species in the tree and plant kingdom need carbon dioxide breathed out by humans and animals to go on living.

One meaning of *ruah* in Hebrew is "breath." And the phrase "prophesies the power / Of vital breath within the living flower" may point to a moment in time when the Source, the Creator, breathed "vital breath" into the clay of Adam, at the time the whole visible world came into being.

Dorothy noticed and appreciated beauty in the natural world around her. And sometimes her intuitions about the seen and unseen realms found their way into poetic form.

In contrast to Edmund who fell in love at first sight, Dorothy's love evolved gradually, as she learned to perceive Edmund's essential qualities through his letters. Because social conventions of the day prevented him for a long time from making an open declaration, he "told it slant" in a story, and alluded to a knight and a lady who lived in a distant land. All he could do in the first year of their correspondence was hope that Dorothy would enter into the story imaginatively and recognize the true identity of both characters.

By the summer of 1918, when Edmund was in France preparing to go to the front, Dorothy had figured out, and was able to tell him openly, that she loved him. The inner qualities she admired in Edmund resembled the ideals she wanted to embody herself: both of them felt connected to an inner Holy, a presence that drew out of each of them a desire to do their best and become a faithful follower of the Way, the Truth, and the Life.

Dorothy's ongoing recognition and appreciation of the enduring qualities she perceived in her good and faithful knight lived on long after the war ended. Her appreciation for his purity of intention shines through in an insight she recorded on a scrap of paper in the mid-1940s. By then she and Edmund had been married for nearly twenty-five years.

> *Some people are different.*
> *There are a few, a faithful few,*
> *Who burn like those altar*
> *Lights that never go out, that*
> *Are always lit by care and*
> *Devotion. A lamp always lit,*
> *Steady because it is tended.*
> *It is devotion that tends them.*

A sanctuary lamp, found in Catholic, Orthodox, Episcopal, and Lutheran churches, burns near the altar day and night where it serves as an illuminating metaphor of goodness itself, a symbol for Christ's unselfish and inextinguishable love. The light "costs not less than everything," for once the wick is ignited, it is able to go on burning because of the warmed beeswax that surrounds it. The wax melts, melts away, giving of its substance so that radiant light can shine.

The lighted lamp serves as a metaphor for the pilgrim who makes his way along the path of life, day by day. The pilgrim desires to follow the path and to stay on it. And the pilgrim understands that reaching the final goal is not what matters most. What matters is doing one's best to stay on the path and remain faithful to the task in the face of any and all obstacles.

In their almost forty-three years of married life, Dorothy and Edmund walked on the path together as faithful seekers of the Light, strengthening one another with devoted love, a gift they shared generously with their children and grandchildren, with their own families and their many friends.

All the while they cherished a memory that went back to the summer of 1918, to a time when they first became aware of the miraculous psychic closeness they felt and could never logically explain — a bond so deep and strong that it mingled their souls while an ocean stood between them.

Postscript

"Where there is great love there are always miracles."
— Bishop Latour, in Willa Cather's *Death Comes for the Archbishop*

For: Dorothy (Dory), Bobby, Sandy, and Judy Hottensen; Sandy Shea; John Harvey, Akeyla Silver, Elizabeth Harvey, and Edmund Harvey; Cynthia, Rebecca, Kip, and Kevin Randall.

Dear Little Grandchildren,

In the fall of 1963, in the months following Dorothy's funeral, the finality of her earthly disappearance began to sink in, and the knight realized the time for telling her stories was over. The lady was dead.

He took her gold key and the diamond engagement ring and put them in the white box, sealed it inside an envelope, and put the envelope in his dresser drawer. Someday, he must have imagined, someone would find the envelope, open the box, and wonder why the key and the ring were there together.

After Edmund's death in 1969, when Betsy and Wendy had begun the sorrowful process of dismantling the rooms at White Woods, Betsy discovered the envelope and its contents. She took it home and put it in her jewelry box for safekeeping.

Forty-three years later, in June 2012, Wendy and Bill came to spend the weekend with me in Hanover during Bill's sixtieth Dartmouth reunion. Aware that I was still hard at work on a draft of *Mingled Souls*, Betsy entrusted the envelope to Wendy to pass on to me.

After Wendy and Bill's departure, I found myself thinking about the key and the ring, wondering why my father put them together. I placed the opened box on the dining room table where I could glance at them while I worked. The table's surface was almost entirely covered by file folders and materials connected with the book.

One evening several weeks later, a detail in Dorothy's diary entry for July 1, 1916, called itself to my attention. That was the evening she met Mr. Shea for the first time, when they had sat in the front seat of a Ford touring car parked outside the Montgomery Country Club and conversed. In her diary entry, she wrote: "When I left, I was wearing his Phi Beta Kappa key around my neck on his watch chain."

Their conversation that evening took a philosophic turn. He explained to her that the three Greek initials engraved on the key stood for the Greek words meaning "wisdom is the path of life" or "the way of wisdom." One who desires to walk on the path of wisdom learns to perceive each situation well, and with care, before making a decision. Developing a habit of choosing wisely helps one to find meaning and purpose in life.

On that first evening, Dorothy had told Edmund her elementary-school motto, *non quantum sed quam bene*: "not how much but how well," a wisdom insight that bears a close resemblance to the key's inscription: both ways of living focus the seeker's attention on following the good, the ultimate virtue.

And so the golden key played an important role in the first meeting Edmund and Dorothy had in 1916, for after they talked about the ideals they shared and wanted to live up to, it passed from his hand to hers.

~~~

In the fall and winter months of 2012–13, I worked my way through the letters exchanged during the spring and summer of 1918, a time when Dorothy and Lieutenant Shea were beginning to make their first open declaration of love.

The war had "speeded up the blood," to use Edmund's phrase. By the summer of 1918 they both realized that he was in harm's way and that he might be killed or wounded. Yet in the face of tremendous uncertainty they were each willing to pledge their love and devotion to one another.

In July, Edmund's field artillery unit fought in the Second Battle of the Marne. Six weeks later he received unexpected orders to return to the United States for a three-month assignment.

On September 3, while en route to Brest to board a troopship, he stopped in Paris for twenty-four hours. In a one-sentence entry in his army journal, he noted that he "bought a ring for Dorothy at Tiffany's." His brief comment was enough for me to conjure up a detailed scene where a Tiffany's saleswoman showed Edmund an assortment of rings and commented on the beauty of the one he chose. Then, so many years later, I reread the inscription inside the lid of the little white ring box — "I will love you more than I did yesterday but less than I will tomorrow" — and I had another glimpse of Edmund putting the box in the pocket of his army jacket as he was leaving Tiffany's. He loved Dorothy and felt confident of her love for him. What he had already begun to envision was the moment when he would ask her to marry him and give her the ring. No wonder he wanted to keep the key and the ring together in the white box after her death.

~~~

In the winter of 2013, subzero temperatures descended on Hanover. On one such evening, I was sitting at my usual place at the dining room table. I had a hot water bottle on my lap and a shawl around my shoulders. The little box was within arm's reach, for I remember reading years ago about the medieval philosopher Duns Scotus and his philosophic theory of *haecceitas*. According to the theory, if you keep looking at something closely, deeply, patiently, and attentively, sometimes what you're looking at looks back at you, and a connection and understanding take place.

On this particular evening I glimpsed another resemblance between the key and the ring.

The key's Greek words, "wisdom is the path of life," teach one to perceive each situation well and then choose wisely. This is the "way of wisdom."

When I held the ring in my hand, I thought of it as a symbol of unity between two persons about to become engaged. They are ready to promise to love one another fully, deeply, unselfishly, wisely. The round shape of the ring is like an unbroken, timeless circle, like the "wisdom of love."

The two "ways" work well together: the "love of wisdom" and the "wisdom of love." And for Edmund, the key and the ring also held profound personal meaning: they recalled for him two unforgettable conversations with Dorothy — the first in 1916 when he gave her his golden key and the second after his return from France, when he gave her the engagement ring.

By then they were ready to promise to love one another "with the wisdom of love" and to join together and live as devoted seekers of goodness.

~~~

O little children what will you think when
You open the box and your heart is touched
By what you find — the story is true and
The gift is real — they leave it to you.

Sheila Harvey Tanzer
2016